for love or honey

STACI HART

STACI HART

Cover by Quirky Bird
Interior Design by Devin McCain | Studio 5 Twenty-Five

Pinterest: https://bit.ly/3tqV2jf
Playlist: https://spoti.fi/3lcTllw

To knowing when to stand your ground
and when to get out of your own way.

To knowing when to hold tight
and when to let go.

To knowing when to be loud
and when to listen.

To knowing love when it finds you.

farm fresh

JO

The mood was pretty light, considering we were in the middle of a protest.

My sisters followed in the train behind me, the lot of us smiling a little as we marched in a circle in front of the news crews outside our tiny city hall, chanting, Frack Off!

It wasn't that we weren't serious—Flexion Oil's move to buy up mineral rights for fracking in our town was nothing to laugh about—but given that a whole bunch of us had shown up with puns on our signs replacing the eff in many slang terms with the word frack, it was just plain funny. Especially ninety-year-old Bettie with What the frack? on her T-shirt and Pastor Coleburn wielding a sign reading Frack You!

We'd pulled out all the stops once we learned the San Antonio news outlets were going to cover the press conference Flexion had called, printing up all kinds of merchandise for the occasion, which many of our townies had donned with spirit. There were, of course, plenty of people there to glare, happier to label us a bunch of hippies than consider what it would do to places like my family's bee farm. Some of the people in our conga line didn't have a say in the matter when Flexion found a cache of natural gas in our little town of Lindenbach, Texas, population eleven hundred and five—their mineral rights were owned by the state. But a whole bunch of us had land in our families for long enough that Flexion would have to convince us to sell.

And we weren't budging.

My mother, sisters, and I had been schmoozed by representatives of Flexion to no avail, even as their offer rose to heights that would give anyone pause. But selling out wasn't an option—Flexion could make all the offers they wanted. No way would we sign our legacy over to the devil.

Great-great-great-grandpa Blum would have rolled over in his grave the second we put pen to paper.

We'd switched gears to, Fracking smells, we won't sell! when a murmur rolled through the rest of the crowd. Movement around the door to city hall caught my attention, and when it opened, I stopped so suddenly, my sister Poppy slammed into the back of me with an oof that left me wondering distantly if she'd smashed the eggs in my backpack.

Because the actual devil himself walked through that door and down the stairs toward the podium.

His hair was the color of a starless night, his jaw chiseled from stone and lips somehow both lush and sharp at the same time. Maybe it was the line they made that felt like a coercion, a temptation. Maybe it was his switchblade eyebrows framing eyes I expected to be as dark and soulless as the rest of him. But they weren't. They were a blue so intense, I felt their chill in the warm September sun.

He was the embodiment of power, somehow consuming all air, all attention, all thought, until he was the only person left standing. He clearly knew the art of intimidation, but every sharp edge of him was softened by a lusty sort of charm, the kind that let everyone know that he got what he wanted. Anything he wanted.

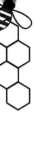

Everything he wanted.

Poppy nudged me forward, and I hurried to close the gap between me and Bettie, who couldn't see over my shoulder on her tiptoes. She'd noticed him too—I caught her gaping over the top of gigantic hot-pink sunglasses, though she was practiced enough that she didn't miss a step, ogling in stride like a goddamn lady, learned over the nine decades or so she'd been a perv.

I noted his size as he stepped to the microphone—he dwarfed the podium and those who had walked out with him, including Mayor Mitchell, that grade A son of a bitch. Mitchell probably got a cash kickback on everybody he convinced to sell to Flexion, though he was nothing but a lowly demon. Stone was the real deal.

When the devil rested his gargantuan hands on either side of the podium, everyone went still and quiet. I marveled over his sheer, overwhelming charisma, understanding completely why Flexion had sent him to close the deal on Lindenbach.

If he could get past my sisters and me.

He began to speak, the deep, easy lilt in his voice hypnotic. When I glanced around me, everyone's pupils could have been pinwheels—they even leaned toward him just a little.

The man was a black hole.

And it seemed like I was the only one who'd snapped myself out of it.

I elbowed Poppy. She blinked herself awake and elbowed Daisy. Our eyes narrowed at him in unison.

All I heard was blah, blah, blah and hiss, hiss, hiss with a little nom, nom, nom from undeniably skillful lips that made me salivate just enough to piss me off. Poppy pressed an egg into my hand with a wicked smile on her face as tall, dark, and slithery went on about how committed Flexion was to the environment in what was probably a ten-thousand-dollar

for love or honey

Italian suit.

I hesitated for a second—I was still a woman with manners and a mother to make proud—but when he started talking about Flexion's clean diesel, all ability to maintain executive functions went out the window. Lizard brain—activate.

So I did what any hippie bee farmer would do.

I wound up, took a breath, and yelled, "Frack you!" before letting her rip.

The egg sailed in slow motion over the crowd as his face swiveled to the sound of my voice, those dagger-eyes running me through seconds before the egg popped him smack between them.

A laugh shot out of Bettie before she hollered, "Farm fresh, bitch!"

Yolk slid down his nose. His eyes stayed closed for a protracted moment that I suspected he needed to school himself.

When they opened, they locked on mine.

I'd never felt naked under someone's gaze until that moment, my lungs empty and extremities tingling. He'd pinned me to the spot from twenty feet away, his face unreadable. And though his eyes blazed like a thousand suns, his lips quirked into a tilted smile.

"Nice shot, Miss Blum." He retrieved his pocket square without breaking eye contact. "Hope it was organic."

In an out-of-body sort of feeling—and with the shock that he knew my name—I slapped on a smirk of my own, lifting my chin in challenge before offering a dramatic sweeping gesture, accompanied by a condescending nod. The crowd was chuckling and whispering, but the devil wiped the egg off his face and soldiered on, unfazed. But when he closed his speech and stepped back, he shot me dead with his eyes again, his smile sending a message clear as day.

Game on.

And oh, he had no idea just how on it was.

THE CLOSER

Grant

I should have won a fucking Academy Award.

Confusion and admiration rippled off the crowd as I spent ten minutes answering questions without flinching after getting hit in the face with a warm egg. With a long-practiced calm exterior, I ignored the tightening of my skin from the residue, particularly in a spot just left of the bridge of my nose that itched with particular ferocity. Two questions had been directed to The Egg Incident, both which I'd handled with a dry joke, a wry smile, and a pointed look in the offender's direction.

My only surprise was that I couldn't manage to make her shrink beneath the weight of my gaze, which I knew to be oppressive.

Instead, Jo Blum rose to meet me. What I couldn't tell was whether she believed her bravado or if it was just bald obstinance in the face of a challenge.

Either way, she'd break. They always did.

The Blum farm was one of six I'd been sent here to acquire rights to, and of the six, their farm had the largest shale deposit.

On visiting the farms to open up talks, I'd been denied by the Blums before I'd stepped onto their front porches. But I had a couple of aces up my sleeve.

Just had to play them right.

This part of the country was always the same—families living on the same plot of land for a hundred and fifty years or more, somehow able to survive the farming decline in the fifties, when everyone sold off their rights for oil to keep their businesses alive. It was rare that the state didn't own the mineral rights—on the sale of any old property, mineral rights transferred straight to the state—but to find this many hold outs along the vein of shale we'd found was unfortunate.

Which was why they'd sent me.

I was the closer, sliding in to get the job done when others failed. I knew a hundred towns just like this. Sure, they'd hold the line for a little while, but soon enough, they'd fold. Just had to find the weak spot and press. Easy enough.

I'd learned from the best, after all. My father was the original closer for Flexion and my boss. Mistakenly, I thought his mentoring me would bring us closer. But nobody should wish to get so close to a snake. You'd think I'd learn my lesson after all these years, but here I was in Lindenbach, Texas, dead set on closing the deal as quickly as possible in a thinly veiled attempt at impressing that cold-blooded bastard who raised me.

He'd taught me two things in life. No one would help me but me. Power was equivalent to control, and control was equivalent to happiness. In thirty years, life had only proven me right.

Some sought power with a fist. I acquired it with a velvet tongue and tried-and-true strategy. For instance, in Lindenbach, I knew at least half of my in was with the mayor—a base, misguided, tone-deaf man whose power was strictly his for what his forefathers accomplished. His Stetson gave him more power than his policies ever would.

for love or honey

Convincing the rest of the town was where the challenge waited. There was one sure-fire way into their good graces, and it rested somewhere in the Blum family farm.

Maybe in Jo's hands. Provided they weren't occupied by another egg.

My eyes slid over her again, noting the line of her jaw as her chin lifted in defiance. The stubborn line of her mouth that, even in its tempered rage, couldn't flatten the plump pout of her lips. The spiteful tightening of her eyes, as blue as a gemstone lit up by a burst of flame, lined with thick, black lashes. Her hair was the color of midnight—the same shade as her sisters, who wore equally hateful looks, though they barely registered next to the bonfire that was Jo Blum.

"If no one has any further questions or farm fare to throw"—I paused for a ripple of laughter—"we'll see you all at the farmers' market this weekend. Come by our booth. Bring all the eggs you want."

The fiery color rose in Jo's cheeks, a smudge against porcelain skin.

"Better wear a raincoat," Poppy Blum shouted.

My gaze shifted to her, tightening as I smiled. "Maybe we'll even make a game of it, Miss Blum."

There—the air went out of the youngest Blum just a little, just enough to know it was on my behalf, though she didn't quit the snarl on her face.

Satisfied, I adjourned the conference, turning to make my way up the steps with the mayor and a few others flanking me.

"Those goddamn Blum brats," the mayor growled. "They've been a pain in my ass since they were in middle school."

I shot him a look. "A trio of preteen girls were a problem for you?"

His weathered face flushed with defense and embarrassment.

8

"You didn't see what they did to my granddaddy's statue in town. It was indecent."

"Did it involve produce?"

"I'd have preferred it. They covered it in … with … well, they hung two dozen brassieres on him like a goddamn cross-dressing fa—"

"What color?" I interrupted, adding homophobic to my ongoing list of Mitchell's traits.

"The hell does it matter what color?"

I shrugged. "Just curious."

"All of 'em," he answered darkly.

I swallowed my laughter, though my face went stoic, nodding in feigned sympathy.

"Those Blum girls are trouble," he noted, seemingly on my behalf. "If anyone's gonna give you a hard time, it's them."

But a smile tilted my lips. "I was counting on that."

Puzzled, he glanced at me. "You're going toe-to-toe with the Blums?"

"It's why I'm here, isn't it?"

"Well, sure, but—"

"I can handle them. Question is whether they can handle me."

A wicked smile unfurled beneath his impressive mustache. "Fair enough, Mr. Stone. Let's see what you can do."

My cocksure smile sealed the count of my chickens before they hatched.

Because every egg was in Jo Blum's hands.

for love or honey

I just didn't know it yet.

BEE WITCHES

Jo

I pulled up to our house two days later, staring down at the two-seater Audi from my three-quarter-ton Hemi with no small amount of rage and disdain.

By my math, only one human in the county would drive a car like that, and he shouldn't be on my property, let alone in my house.

If the bed of my truck wasn't full of bees I'd just rescued from the junkyard, I could have fit that little German monstrosity between my wheel wells. Or I could have just rolled over it like The Beefeater at MonsterTruckopolis.

Satisfying as that might have been, I probably couldn't afford the hike on my insurance. Wouldn't have been worth it knowing he wouldn't give a shit. He probably had three more at home, wherever that was. Hell, I figured.

I threw the truck into park and slid out, slamming the door as hard as I could—which took both hands—before storming up the steps and into the house.

for love or honey

Our ranch had been in our family for coming up on two-hundred years, ever since the Blums immigrated from Germany, finally stopping here in the Hill Country. I had a suspicion it wasn't because they loved it here. More like it just kept getting hotter and hotter as they moved West, so they threw up their hands and threw down their stakes rather than continue to torture themselves or lose any more people to dysentery. But they would have been right about the weather—there was nothing between here and San Diego but desert and dirt.

My ancestors had chosen wisely. This was the last little oasis before a vast stretch of tumbleweeds, not to mention just how many of their countrymen were here. Germans had settled in this little patch of Texas, bringing beer and brats and broad shoulders to the Lone Star State.

Still couldn't appreciate their stupid, impractical little sports cars, though.

I was mad enough to spit (on The Suit's windshield, if my mother hadn't taught me manners), madder still when I heard him at the big formal dining table in the great room. My mother wore a polite smile, as did my eldest sister, Daisy. Poppy—the middle child—had on a smile too, though hers was more mischief than manners. She caught my eye, saying silently, Can you believe this asshole?

Sure can, I thought back.

Everyone turned when I made my noisy entrance. And the devil struck me down with icy eyes, a razor-sharp jaw, and a smile that could have convinced the Pope himself to eat forbidden fruit.

"What do you want?" I shot, ignoring the recognition that I sounded like a child. I folded my arms across my T-shirt that read Don't Mess With Texas.

He stood, never breaking eye contact as he smoothed his tie and stepped toward me. My chin lifted the closer he got, his height imposing. In another life, in another time, he lived out here in the sticks with an ax in his beastly hand or the reins of an oxen yoke clutched in his hammer fist. But I bet his hands were smooth as a baby's ass. I bet he wouldn't last one fucking day in the full sun doing real work. I bet he'd rather die than get in that shiny little sports car's bucket seats sweaty and peppered with dirt.

I warmed, either from his encroaching proximity or the mental image of him shirtless and chopping wood.

"I wanted to introduce myself since I didn't get a chance at the press conference," he said, extending that gargantuan appendage he called an arm. "Grant Stone." When I didn't take his hand, he added, "You threw an egg at me?"

"I recall. But you didn't just come here to meet me."

His empty hand returned to his side. "Then why did I come?"

"You're trying to butter us up. Come here being all polite as if that'll change our minds."

"Sounds like you have me all figured out."

My temper flamed at his milky reaction. "You realize we run a bee farm, right? You think we're going to let you run your diesel and pollute our flowers? Kill our bees? First it's bulldozers and backhoes. Then diesel trucks bringing machines and parts. Then your diesel rig and diesel trucks to haul your fuel off. And I swear to god, if you say one word about clean diesel, I will chase you off my property with a whole crate of eggs."

"Funny to hear all the green talk coming from the girl driving the Hemi."

My eyes narrowed. "Can't exactly pull a trailer with a Prius, can I?"

"Can't exactly get fuel for your Hemi out of the ground without diesel, either."

I shifted back to my point. "That's not even to mention what you'll do to our water. I'll tell you what my family was too polite to say—we don't want your money, so please get the hell out of our house."

He assessed me for a drawn out moment, his face unreadable. I was just about to repeat myself a little louder and a little slower when he said, "You don't think I understand."

My face quirked. "How could you? Isn't your daddy some big oil guy? Didn't you grow up somewhere on the East Coast with seersucker and bow ties? Yacht club and boat shoes? So tell me—what do you know of small towns and the working class? I don't even know how you can drive on half the roads in this town in that car."

"And what's wrong with my car?"

"It's useless and out of touch, especially around here. I don't even know how you can fit in it. What are you, like eight feet tall?"

An amused sound through his nose. "So if I came here in a pickup truck wearing a Stetson, you'd listen?"

"No."

"That's reasonable." He turned back to my family. "I'll see myself out. It's been nice to meet you. Thank you for the coffee."

My mother offered another smile, this time apologetic. "Pleasure to meet you, Mr. Stone. Good luck."

I didn't know if he caught the little bit of snark in her well wishes, but my sisters and I did.

He nodded once, then turned back to me, his eyes lit with the embers of challenge. As he passed, he leaned in, his lips close enough to my ear to feel his breath. "I'm afraid you've underestimated me, Ms. Blum—I understand you better than you think. So get ready. I'm coming for you."

I braced myself against a shiver of anticipation that wriggled down my spine. But rather than shy away, I turned my face toward him, forcing him to retreat or risk our lips connecting.

"Let's see what you've got, Stone," I said with a wry smile. "You have a nice day, now."

"Oh, I will."

With a mirroring expression on his face, he headed out. The second his back was turned, I scowled at him the duration of his walk to that stupid car, laughing when he realized the back of my truck was full of bees. He hurried into the HotWheels like his pants were on fire. I had to admit that the rumble when he started the engine did something funny to my insides, but I never would have said so.

"Iris Jo," Mama scolded, though she fought a smile. "I cannot believe how rude you were."

"Really? I threw an egg at him on live television two days ago. Was I really supposed to pretend like I was happy to see him in my kitchen?"

"Well, no, but you could have at least told him off politely."

"I can't even believe you entertained him."

"What were we supposed to do, send him off when he came here being so nice?" Mom asked.

"Yes," I answered.

"Oh, relax," Poppy said. "I put a laxative in his coffee."

Mom spun around to face her with her mouth open. "Poppy June—you did not."

Poppy shrugged. "No, I didn't. But I thought about it."

for love or honey

"Am I the only one who thinks he's dangerous?"

"He's only dangerous if you give him power," Daisy said, hooking her arm in mine. "So don't."

I sighed. "Fine. But don't let him in the house again. You'll mislead him into thinking he's got a shot at our rights."

"He brought an awfully big number with him," Mom said as she cleared his place. "Lots of zeros. Enough zeros to make us rich."

"And kill our business. If Grandpa didn't sell to oil in the fifties when the farm was actually in trouble, why would we do it now when things are fine?"

"I didn't say we should," she noted.

I made a derisive noise as Daisy towed me toward the coffee pot, ignoring the prick of fear that I didn't have as much of a say as I liked to think I did. Mama owned fifty-two percent, and we each got a split of the remainder when we turned eighteen. At the end of the day, all we could do was tell her what we thought and what we wanted. And though I knew she'd listen and honor our wishes if she could, it was still up to her.

Daisy leaned against the counter as I poured myself a cup.

With the jerk of my chin toward a vase of fresh flowers on the counter, I asked, "Did Billy or Bobby Jenkins send those?"

She sighed. "Billy. It's been five years those twins have been courting us. They just won't learn. And I don't think they've discovered the line between persistent and creepy."

"Listen, any boys dumb enough to think that if they came after all three of us at the same time, one of us would cave, deserves every Tuesday's bouquet rejection."

"I just feel bad, but they won't take no for an answer. If they weren't a couple of sweet little puppies, I'd worry."

Poppy snorted a laugh. "I'm pretty sure I could take them both at once. They can't weigh more than two fifty combined."

The truth was, Billy and Bobby hadn't addressed a single bouquet to me in a year. And as much as I'd like to say that it was because they'd somehow focused their attentions, the truth was that in most cases, none of the town boys came after me anymore. I'd become the prickly, unapproachable sister when it came to suitors, now directing my attention at warning everyone off who wasn't worthy. Which was all of them.

But somehow, it'd only isolated me from my sisters a little bit more.

"How'd it go at Crowe's?" Daisy asked.

A smile flickered on my lips. "Oh, man—you should have seen it. The colony had set up inside the rusty carcass of an old '74 Super Beetle. It was huge. I filled two full brood boxes. I thought Old Man Crowe was gonna have a coronary right there on the spot."

Daisy laughed. "Well, the sight of you scooping up handfuls of bees without gear on can be alarming to the unpracticed eye."

I shrugged, taking a sip of my coffee. "Well, we are the Blum bee witches, aren't we?"

"How we didn't burn in the pioneer days is beyond me," Poppy said. "Although we did end up cursed, so I guess we didn't escape unscathed."

The joke was an old one, and we laughed automatically, though I wasn't sure we even thought it was funny anymore. Our men suffered one of two fates—desertion or death. But despite being the town Black Widows, Poppy and Daisy were still pursued by the same boys who tried to date us in high school. We seemed to be the only ones who took it seriously.

for love or honey

I didn't mean to say we believed in actual magic, more like some deep and unbreakable bad luck that followed us around like a thunderhead waiting to strike. If we didn't fall in love, everyone was safe. Our hearts were safe.

Loneliness was preferable to heartache any day of the week.

Of course, there was the pact we'd made a million years ago to stay single as long as Mama did. If she didn't date, neither would we, and there was approximately zero danger of her dating, not with the same old town fare as she'd ever had. She'd devoted her whole life to raising us, and the thought of leaving her here alone disturbed us.

But one day, Poppy and Daisy would find someone, and off they'd go. But not me. I'd be here with Mama indefinitely.

Daddy wouldn't have left her alone, and neither would I.

I'd heard it said that every child is different, physically and personality-wise, and though my sisters and I were very clearly sisters, we lived up to the adage. We all possessed a healthy sense of sarcasm, but Daisy was softer, sweeter than Poppy and me. I was on the opposite end of the spectrum, too salty to be sweet. And Poppy fell somewhere in the middle, which was how she ended up the glue of our trio.

But where Daisy was just like Mama, I was the spit of my father.

As long as I could remember, it was all anyone ever said. I had the strong jaw and determined chin. I had the skeptical eyebrows and tilted smile that reminded everyone of him. I didn't know if my expressions were genetic or learned—I spent all of my time at his elbow. He taught me everything about bees and farming flowers, showed me what hard work meant and the difference between sarcasm and being an asshole. He even let me sit in his lap to drive a few times under the promise I'd never tell Mama.

I was nine when he died. My family came unraveled, left frayed and threadbare. There was a moment at the house, on the day of his wake, that a realization dawned on me, giving me purpose.

I was just like my daddy. So I was uniquely equipped to take care of them. Just like he did.

Mama used to joke that I was the man of the house, but I wore the title with pride. I was a champion spider slayer and the mistress of fixing squeaky hinges and stuck windows. I'd lobbed off the heads of many a snake, and once, when I was twelve, I shot a coyote that'd cornered Mama outside the chicken coop.

I cried for a week over that coyote, but never where anybody could see.

I'd made every big decision in my life on what Daddy would have done. And I knew one thing for certain—he wouldn't sell to Flexion's well-suited goon. He wouldn't sacrifice anything for the sake of money. And he wouldn't leave Mama here to fend for herself alone, either.

So neither would I.

"Think Stone will be back?" Daisy asked, and I realized I'd missed part of their conversation.

"I think he was sent here to get our rights, and he won't leave until he's done it or we run him out of town," Poppy answered.

And I smiled. "Then we'd better sharpen our pitchforks."

HELLFLOWERS

Grant

I sat on the small back porch of the short-term rental, sipping terrible coffee from a mug that read Rosé All Day, wondering if my father had sent me here to set me up for failure.

This town was too far off the highway to havte a hotel, and the one motel in town wasn't fit to take my shoes off in, so here I was in a tiny studio rental off the back of Salma Hayak's old Victorian near Main Street. No, not that Salma Hayak—this one was so old that her age was indeterminate. She was nothing but cotton fluff hair and clacking bones, but she was kind, and the sheets were clean.

Doilies saddled ancient furniture, including a television that looked to be from the 70s, complete with bunny ears connected by foil. The kitchen, which was in the same room as all the other rooms, hadn't been updated since the fifties, nor had the bathroom—the showerhead hit me in the kisser. The bed was an iron contraption made before mattresses had standard sizes, so someone had rigged up the frame to accommodate a double mattress, which worked fine, so long as you didn't move too quick. It'd already fallen through to the floor twice.

After a few nights in Salma's house, driving an hour from San Antonio was looking shinier than it had at first glance.

The back porch was secluded enough, facing back to trees. We were on the edge of town—a solid two blocks off the main drag—but you'd think no one was around for miles, as quiet as it was. Besides the warbling bird in a nearby tree that thought we should all be up with him well before the sun was out.

I'd been to towns like Lindenbach plenty of times but was always surprised by the alien culture in places like this. Jo wasn't wrong about my upbringing—I'd grown up in the DC area where my father worked for the Flexion's East Coast offices. I attended private boys' school in Connecticut, and though I could tie a number of sailing knots, I'd never actually sailed on my own, preferring yachts with crews and a bar to any sort of manual labor.

Most times, the key to cracking the code on small towns was making sure the check I offered was big enough to get them to throw their principles away. Everybody waved around their morals until you shook a bag of money at them. But when that failed, my job was to convince them I wasn't the enemy. To earn their trust, I had to relate to them and make them feel like I was on their side. They didn't need to know the only side I was on was my own.

If that didn't work, subterfuge would. All I had to do was find the chink in the armor and exploit it. Like turning brothers on each other. Or a couple's divorce, which was one of the instances here in Lindenbach. Seduction was always an easy one, and sometimes there were ways to squeeze a farm into a situation they couldn't get themselves out of.

To my credit, I'd never done anything illegal. But I'd done plenty of manipulating to achieve my goals, motivated by a lack of subjectivity and a very, very large bonus on clearing a town of resistance.

But Lindenbach was different. I knew the second I drove into town that this would be hard, maybe the hardest job I'd ever

for love or honey

done. They were going to make me work for it.

And I had to be ready for anything.

I took another sip of the brackish coffee and made a face, heading inside to dump it in the sink, daydreaming about that imaginary hotel in San Antonio. I hadn't unpacked anything, leaving the window open on my commitment. But I sighed, turning for the bedroom, resigned. If I was going to convince this town I had their best interest in mind, refusing to stay here wouldn't earn me any points. I could already hear Jo Blum ranting in the diner about it.

And I wasn't going to hand her ammunition.

Of the six farms I was here to acquire rights to, the Blum farm would be the hardest, and thanks to the size of its shale deposit, it was also my top priority. Leaving here without it would mean leaving with nothing, if my father had anything to say about it. Which he would.

The easy paths to their shale had been blocked. Charm was useless—the Blums valued honesty, and they didn't believe a word I said. Money seemed to be no object—anyone who turned their noses at seven figures was probably beyond the reach of my checkbook.

The way I saw it, there was only one way in. One of the sisters.

And only one of them held the keys to the kingdom.

Jo.

She was the smartest shot—if I took any other angle, she'd bar me with the ferocity of a cornered animal. But if I could figure out how to disarm her ... well, that was another story altogether.

I realized I was smirking as I pulled a pair of khakis and a navy Flexion button-down out of my garment bag.

Because taming Jo Blum was going to be a damn good time.

Khaki was as close as I got to casual, and paired with rolled-up sleeves and my lack of tie, I almost pulled it off. I'd work the festival booth today, turn on the smile, and see if I could win over a few townies. Flexion had sent a few people over to smile and hand out pamphlets and merchandise, so we could be seen and be seen as something safe.

Appearances were everything, and this was my second shot at giving an impression. In the first, I'd ended up with actual egg on my face, and though I handled it, I could use an egg-free day.

Hopefully, the Blum girls didn't have any produce up their sleeves.

Once groomed, I gathered my things and headed out. The day was warm already—September was just an extension of August, after all—but showing up to the fair in my Audi wouldn't have impressed anybody. My father didn't understand why I'd driven it here from Georgetown, enjoying the open road, the days of solitude, the radio and the rumble of the engine carrying me across the country. He'd suggested I take a Flexion jet and rent an Escalade when I got here, but in this, I didn't care if he understood.

In everything else…well, that was another story.

Hand in my pocket, I walked toward downtown, staying in the shade as best I could. When I reached Main Street, eyes followed me to the coffee shop, nearly suffocating me once I was inside. They were curious and suspicious—not only was I an outsider, but culturally, I couldn't fit in any better than they could at dinner at the yacht club.

I smiled. Nodded. Used my best Yes Ma'am/Sir. Held the door open for a mother with two squiggling children in tow. Let the crowd look unimpeded and hoped they noted what I'd done and that it was to their satisfaction. But I knew they'd never see me as one of them. I was imposing by default, though I didn't know if it was genetic or learned. My father called it charisma, and though he insisted I was lacking, I could hypnotize a room

23

for love or honey

just as well as he could.

We'd see if I could hypnotize a town. Or at least the gatekeeper.

I saw her as I crossed the street, setting up a booth directly across from mine with her sisters and mother. Their display was quaint but modern—racks of bouquets flanked shelves of honey, and in front of them sat trays of biscuits and samplers. They didn't wear branded clothing—they did however have on anti-fracking T-shirts—and they didn't have a sign. They didn't need one. Everyone here knew them and had been buying their honey right here, in this spot, for nearly two-hundred years.

But in all the time I'd spent assessing their booth, none of them had looked at me. They were too busy scowling across the way. At my booth.

Which, at present, was manned by three blondes who I suspected were too young to drink in Flexion crop tops, jean shorts short enough to catch a hearty view of their asses, and T-shirt cannons in small, tan hands.

I schooled my temper as I approached, listing out the names of what idiot had signed off on sending co-eds to shoot fucking T-shirts into a small town festival. Because somebody was catching hell for this.

If I'd needed help convincing the half of the town that would be happy to see half-naked girls bouncing around to Whitesnake, it'd be one thing. But I needed to win over the half that would look at our booth just like the Blums were. All except for Jo, who had spotted me long enough to have harpooned me with her gaze.

I smiled. Her eyes narrowed. I tipped an imaginary hat, and she rolled her eyes hard enough to see the swing set behind her.

So rather than head to my booth, I strode to theirs.

Nearly in unison, the rest of the Blums looked in my direction, stiff as a matching set of rulers.

"Morning, ladies."

"Morning—ow!" Daisy scowled at Poppy, who said, "Can we help you?"

I scanned the honey samples, each sitting in front of a different jar. Wildflower, clover, lemon, even a habanero honey.

Curious, I asked, "May I?"

"Of course," their mother, Dottie, said with a pointed look in her daughters' direction. She picked up a plate of cut-up biscuits with toothpicks sticking out of the top.

"Asskisser," Jo said. Daisy pinched the back of her arm, and she yelped.

"I'm sorry," Dottie started with a tight but apologetic smile on her face. "Forgive my children. They have never been morning people."

I set down my coffee and chose a moderately sized one even though I wanted a big one, but before I picked up a tiny paper cup of habanero honey, Jo handed me one.

"Careful, it's hot," Dottie warned.

"I appreciate the warning," I said.

Jo wore a wicked smile.

I held her gaze as I dunked the biscuit and put it in my mouth, pleased when her eyes flicked to my lips. And within a second, it took the rest of my attention to stop myself from reacting. The heat hit the back of my throat like a hot coal.

"Oh, shoot," Jo said sweetly, "was that the extra hot? I swear I thought I gave you mild."

Sweat pricked my hairline as a trail of fire scorched my esophagus, but I smiled like a goddamn professional and picked up my coffee.

for love or honey

"What are you feeding those bees, hellflowers?"

Daisy brightened. "Actually, we flavor them afterward with— oh. You were kidding."

"I'll take a jar of the extra hellfire habanero and a jar of wild-flower honey," I said around my fat tongue, reaching into my back pocket for my wallet. "And can I get a bouquet?"

Jo's face read suspicion. "Didn't take you for the type to have flowers in the kitchen."

I handed Daisy a fifty. "Guess you don't have me pegged after all."

"Or are you going to take them to your Flexion groupies?" Jo asked. "They're awfully chipper this morning. And I'm pretty sure the one in the middle will take her shirt off if you ask nice."

Her family eyed us warily.

Said groupies bounced behind me.

"I thought I'd give them to Salma. Pay her back for the three loaves of zucchini bread she left on my porch yesterday. Think she'd like the pink ones?"

Dottie picked a yellow and white bouquet. "These are her favorites. That's awfully thoughtful of you, Mr. Stone. Isn't it, girls?"

Two of them mumbled agreement. Jo just scowled.

I took my change, then my goods. And then I said to Jo, "Anything to make a lady smile."

She snorted a laugh.

I smirked, sharing a look with Dottie. "See?"

Daisy rolled her lips to stop herself from laughing, but Poppy didn't even try to hide her amusement. Jo's scowl deepened.

"You ladies have a good day, now. Hope it's a success."

"You too," Dottie parroted, her manners bred into her too deep to deny.

And I turned for my booth, walking away with my head high. The Flexion groupies turned their attention on me, and I realized that the middle one would take off her shirt. I might not even need to ask, let alone nicely.

"Hello, ladies. I think there was some confusion about what today's booth was going to be. Thank you for setting up. You're free to go."

They frowned. Well, the middle one pouted, but all three were disappointed.

"What do you mean?" Lefty said.

"We drove all the way from Austin," Righty whined.

"Are we still getting paid?" Middle asked.

"Yes, you'll still get paid, and I'll make sure you get a little extra for the trouble."

Lefty held up her T-shirt cannon. "Should we leave these here?"

Middle gave me a coquettish look. "Are you sure you want all of us to leave?"

"Yes, leave the cannons, and yes, I'm sure."

With more pouting, they grumbled around to the back of the booth where their purses were, occasionally looking in my direction, mumbling and giggling. I made myself busy moving things around the table without purpose so I could effectively ignore them. But when they said their goodbyes, I thumbed through my cash to pay them, handing them an extra fifty with the suggestion they swing by the Blum's table to buy themselves flowers.

for love or honey

And as her mother sold the poor girls some flowers, Jo and I waged a silent battle across a grassy aisle that she had no idea she was going to lose.

TNT

Jo

I'**D** almost forgotten all about Grant Stone as I strummed my guitar next to my cousin, Presley, up on the town hall stage.

The Blums had been a Lindenbach staple at town hall dances for near two hundred years—Blums were born with an instrument in hand and sang like larks. My ancestors would pile their seven kids in a wagon and head into town every Saturday night to entertain, and though the weekly dance tradition died down in the 60s, we still put on a show from May through September, for old times' sake.

Daisy played the fiddle on the other side of Presley, Poppy played a little trap set behind us, and Mama, who couldn't carry a tune to save her life, played the stand-up bass.

Most of us could play all the instruments—other than the fiddle, that was all Daisy—but Poppy preferred to bang on the drums, and since it was difficult to sing and play the violin, I was the one who typically fronted the band. But when Presley came to town, we put a guitar in her hand and shoved her in front of the microphone, figuring the town would appreciate us mixing things up.

for love or honey

The dance floor hopped in front of us, full of people two-stepping to the honky tonk we preferred. You wouldn't find any Kenny Chesney here—we were all Patsy Cline and Hank Williams and the like, with a little bluegrass thrown in for good measure.

Watching everyone happy and dancing cleared my mind of Grant Stone after a full day of staring at his stupid face at the market. As thankful as I'd been that he'd sent the cheerleaders packing, I wondered if it wouldn't have been better to watch them than have to ignore the icy gaze of the asshole who wanted what was under our land. My family didn't see him as that much of a threat—we'd declined and figured that was that. But he wasn't going to let it go. He'd said so himself.

Of course, they thought I was just being prickly. And I was, but not just for the sake of it. He was dangerous, and I didn't quite understand how I was the only one who saw it.

I knew this so well, in fact, that when he walked into the building, every nerve in my body shifted in his direction.

He was wearing khakis again, though nothing like people around here wore. No, his were tailored to fit him perfectly, the leg slim without being skinny, fitted without being tight, accentuating the lines of his thighs—which were substantial enough to note—and the curves of his ass—which was a marvel Michelangelo would have committed to marble. His button-down shirt was fresh, though, and cuffed at his elbows, revealing unholy forearms. The fabric of his shirt clung to his shoulders, broad chest, and rolling biceps without looking like it was too small for him but somehow still tight enough that, should he have to shake hands with another alpha male, it'd shred to pieces.

Those cool eyes found me as quickly as I'd found his, which was less surprising, as I was on an actual stage with a guitar in my hand, but I felt their weight all the same.

When the Loretta Lynn song Presley had been singing ended, the dancing paused for a round of clapping. Thirty seconds ago, I wouldn't have minded taking my turn on the microphone. But as Presley took a bow and stepped back, nodding for me to go ahead, dread gripped me by the guts. I must have shown it too because a smile flickered on Stone's face as he came to a stop at the edge of the crowd and folded his arms expectantly.

So I threw on the bravado I used as armor so often and stepped up to sing, wishing he hadn't walked in before this particular song.

Poppy called the one, two, three, and we played the opening, my sisters and Presley doo-woppa-dooing in harmony to kick off "Dynamite" by Brenda Lee, looking everywhere but at Stone as the dance floor bopped, and I sang about the magic of infatuation and how its spell turned every kiss into an addiction. Brenda was subtle enough about it, wishing for dynamite kisses and getting knocked out. About TNT and chain reactions and making history, what with, you know. The dynamite.

I decided I'd preferred to blow Stone up. Knock him out. And not with a kiss, but actual gunpowder and a fuse and a push handle box like Wile E. Coyote favored.

By the time the song ended, I was smiling. Partly at the impossibly happy beat, but mostly at musings of my new nemesis with dynamite up his ass.

I thought—as I had many times over the past couple of days— about the origin of my deep loathing for a man I didn't even know. Maybe it was what he represented—wealth, excess, privilege, soulless corporations, greed. Maybe it was that Flexion hadn't taken no for an answer, sending their golden boy to do what the last lackey couldn't. Or maybe it was just that he was foreign to me. I couldn't fathom the life he lived any easier than he could fathom mine.

He didn't belong here, and everything he stood for threatened my town, my way of life, my farm, my bees. As such, the odds of me behaving any better than a rottweiler at a junkyard gate were pretty low, even if he did have a steak in his hand.

I was on for another song, this time a ballad that Daisy took

for love or honey

to the piano for, "Gonna Hurry (As Slow As I Can)" by Dolly, brought down to a key I could manage. The lights were low, but I could see Stone just fine. A passive effect of his charisma, I supposed. And the town singles were flapping around in his orbit like moths. He was new, shiny, rich, and this town's dating pool was stagnant and covered in pond scum.

There were two ways to find love in Lindenbach—either you married your high school sweetheart or you left town and brought somebody back with you. So an eligible bachelor with a sports car that cost five times the town's median income would get noticed. Recently divorced, middle-aged Dolores James, who'd quit paying attention to fashion somewhere around 2002, literally adjusted her boobs—hands in the cups and everything—before sauntering over to him, lashes flapping and smile on full blast. He didn't even look at her when she bumped into him.

He was too busy staring at me with a smug look on his face.

Dolores looked at him looking at me, then looked at me and narrowed her eyes. Then she tapped him on the arm and told him something—about me, judging by her spiteful eye contact with me—when he finally acknowledged her. She was gossiping. He slurped up whatever she'd said like a bowl of ramen noodles.

I saw his face turn to mine in my periphery—I'd looked away like I didn't care. Which I didn't. But also fuck Dolores.

Instead, I watched the couples in the town take their turns around the dance floor, cheek to cheek under golden Edison bulbs. And around them in a half circle stood everyone else, looking in on their love with some longing, some envy, and a whole lot of loneliness.

I wasn't sure where I fell in the mix. Curiosity perhaps. Detachment. Because what they had, I could never get. No point in wishing for the impossible—I'd rather be practical about it. Own it, as it were. I wasn't mad or anything, just resigned to the facts. Because even if I wanted to fall in love, I wouldn't get to keep whatever I found.

Really, it was just math, even though Mama said we hadn't actually been cursed. My grandmother told a different story, blaming the town witch and some sort of grudge over a man.

Slim pickings bred all kinds of drama.

When my song was over, they paused and clapped again as we bowed and curtsied. Poppy hopped on her mic, informing everyone that we'd be taking a short break, after which Johnny Cash came on over the speakers by way of my playlist.

They'd have loved some of that Kenny Chesney we denied them, but they were getting honky tonk if they were getting anything.

We set down our instruments, converging to walk down the stairs, greeted by townsfolk on our way to the bar. And yes, we had a bar in our town hall. Truth be told, more would get done if they used it while they legislated. As it stood, nothing was getting done. We were in the midst of political gridlock, the town split down the middle, thanks to our mayor and his misguided agenda. We'd only just thwarted his attempt to bring the megastore, Goody's, to town, and though he was busy licking his wounds, he was planning something else, determined to make a mark on the town. Even if the mark he made was with a sledgehammer.

The fact that he was up Stone's ass surprised me zero percent. They deserved each other.

Somehow I ended up at the back of the pack after getting pulled over by sweet old Melba Hernandez, who told me a quick story about the time she met Dolly Parton—a story I'd heard about a hundred thousand times since I was five—and when I gave her a squeeze and turned for my sisters, I found Grant Stone instead.

God, he was tall, a tank of a man in khakis. He looked as at home in them as he did in Lindenbach, which was to say, not at all. Somehow, even khakis were too casual for him. But he wore them well, despite the disdain that either I projected or he exuded. I chose to believe the latter.

for love or honey

For a moment, we just stood there, staring at each other—him still smug, me still annoyed. If he hadn't been standing directly in front of me, I'd have just gone around. But his position left me pinned by propriety, a trait bred into me from birth by my mother, despite my recent behavior.

"Can I help you?" I asked.

He jerked his chin in the direction of the stage. "I heard the Blums could sing, but I didn't expect you to be that good."

My face quirked. "That was almost a compliment. It didn't hurt, did it?"

A single laugh through his nose. "I heard another tidbit about the Blums. Something about a curse."

Goddamn Dolores. But this was a dance I'd done before. I put on a wicked smile and leaned in a little.

"We're the kiss of death. Black widows. Get tangled up with one of us, and—" I cut my index finger across my neck.

"Sounds dangerous." He looked more intrigued than worried.

"Wait—are you one of those rich guys who jumps out of planes and builds rocket ships to go to the moon to fill the void where your soul should be?"

That earned me a genuine laugh. I hated that I very much liked the velvety, easy sound. Snake charmer.

"I'd rather be on a beach in France than jumping out of a plane, though I do enjoy a good hike."

"I know the perfect one. So you're going to hop on the highway and head east about fifteen hundred miles. You'll know it when you get there."

All I wanted to do was make him mad, but all he did was smile at me like a son of a bitch. "I'm curious as to why you hate me so much."

"How come you care so much?"

"Humor me."

"Really? You're really questioning this?"

An elegant shrug of one shoulder. How anyone could shrug elegantly had been beyond me until that moment. "I get that oil is the bad guy. But that doesn't explain why you hate me."

"Fair enough," I admitted. "I suppose I don't know you any better than you know me, but I know you want what's under my farm. And as such, I don't trust you." He opened his mouth to speak, but I cut him off. "And if you have some sort of line on your bifurcated tongue about how much more environmentally friendly fracking is these days, just keep it to yourself."

"For someone who's adamant that I don't understand you, you've made a lot of assumptions about me."

"It makes it easier to hate you."

"Hate is a deep emotion for somebody you don't know."

"Smugness is premature for a situation where you don't have the upper hand."

"Why not just acknowledge your mistrust and let it go?"

"Let it go?" I shot. "You told me—whispered in my ear like a creep—that you were coming for our farm, and I'm supposed to let it go?"

He didn't even flinch. Instead, his smile lifted higher on one side. "I never said I was coming for your farm, Jo. I said I was coming for you."

for love or honey

Heat slithered down my body and cold shot up my spine. The way he'd said it, the look in his eyes … despite accusing him of being a predator more than once since he'd rolled into town, his words hadn't felt predatory at all.

It was a promise, one he'd known I'd consent to before I did.

The realization shocked me mute. I'd have ridden his face like a pony without disturbing my wholehearted disdain for him.

Until that moment, I hadn't known both emotions could be present at the same time.

Before I found my words, my sisters pushed around him to intercept the exchange, greeting him, making some small talk. And all the while I just looked at him, perplexed by the shape of his lips and the knowledge that I'd love to have them on me.

At least it would mean he wasn't talking.

They swept me away, blaming Billy and Bobby for not being able to get back to me.

Poppy leaned in. "You're welcome for the rescue party."

"You just saved my life," I admitted in earnest.

"I know."

But she didn't.

She had no fucking clue.

BISCUITS AND MAYBE

Grant

"MORNIN', Mr. Stone."

Salma shuffled in my direction with a smile on her face and biscuits in one hand, holding up a bit of her zippered bathrobe in the other so she didn't trip.

"Morning, Mrs. Hayak." I rose, taking the biscuits from her and cupping her elbow to help her up.

A flush on weathered cheeks. "Oh, you just call me Salma. Only people who call me Mrs. Hayak are the ones who think I'm that pretty actress."

"Ever mess with people about it?"

She exhaled a dry chuckle. "Used to more, 'specially when I'd go into town. I can get a reservation into any restaurant in Austin with a name like this." When I laughed, she went on. "Made some biscuits this morning, thought you might like some."

"They smell like heaven."

for love or honey

"Let's hope they taste as good."

"Thank you. I have a few jars of Blum honey I'd like to try." I held the screen door for her and followed her into the house.

"Oh, Blum honey is just the sweetest thing in a hundred miles."

"All I've had so far is a sample of the habanero."

She turned to give me a sympathetic look. "You alright? There's Pepto under the sink if you need it. Yankee stomachs aren't meant for habanero anything."

I chuckled, setting the plate on the small table before moving to the kitchen for a jar of not-habanero and a honey dipper I'd found in a drawer of utensils. "I think it was a test."

"Did you pass?"

"I'm not sure, but I'll let you know when I figure it out."

"Those girls," she said fondly, shaking her head. "Always getting into trouble. Iris Jo fell out of my pear tree when she was eight and broke her arm. Didn't even make a sound other than the racket when she hit the ground, and a half-dozen pears flew out of her arms. When I caught her, she was trying to run off with them. Told her I didn't care a lick about the pears, but I had six boys and was well acquainted with broken bones, and that one needed a doctor. Little devil still wiggled away, even managed to take the pears with her." She chuckled. "Boy, when I heard how bad the break was, I couldn't believe she was upright, never mind running away with an armful of fruit. My son Eugene had a break half that bad, and you'd think somebody'd pulled his arm off and beat him to half to death with it." She shook her head. "If that little girl has one thing, it's determination."

"I've run up against that myself." I pulled apart a biscuit, releasing a plume of steam.

"I suspect you have, what with you looking for their rights. They won't sell," she noted as if she was saving me from some heartache.

"They might if the opportunity is right."

"You don't know the Blums very well. I've never met a more headstrong pack of women in my life. They could scare off a tornado with pitchforks and a few well-placed words. And, no offense, Mr. Stone, but I don't know that you're as mighty as a tornado."

"You wouldn't be the first person to underestimate me," I said with a smile before taking a bite of Salma's biscuit. It disintegrated in my mouth, and a burst of buttery honey spilled out.

An unbidden moan rumbled deep in my throat.

She smiled at me, folding her bony hands in her lap. "I only mean to help. I'm sure you're a busy man. Wouldn't want you to waste your time barking up the wrong tree whether there were pears in it or not." When she made to stand, it surprised me. I reached for a napkin and moved to stand myself.

"No, don't get up—you just keep enjoying your breakfast. I've got to see about a few things, just wanted to make sure you were fed before you go about your day."

I got up anyway and followed her to the door. "Thank you, Salma. They're … well, I've never had anything like them."

"That was the honey," she said with a knowing smile as I opened the door for her. Carefully, she crossed the threshold, then turned to give me an approving look. "I don't care what they say about you. I think you're just fine."

"Well, look at that," I teased. "I've been aiming for just fine my whole life. Looks like I finally made it."

"Looks like it. You have a nice day now, you hear?"

"Yes, ma'am."

for love or honey

Once she was safely down the stairs, I made my way back to my biscuits.

Salma was probably right about more than I'd have liked to admit. Because acknowledging that would mean defeat. And defeat wasn't really an option.

But I had a bag of tricks, and every one of them had to do with Jo.

I'd spent two days reliving the look on her face when I'd told her I was after her. When she realized just who she was dealing with. I'd wondered a few times what expression had been on my face when Jo had opened her mouth and music came out. I knew how I felt—awed, surprised, struck. Like I'd been hit by lightning, leaving nothing but a dash of soot on the ground.

She was a siren, calling ships into the rocks and a watery death, if the town was to be believed. But I wasn't superstitious. I didn't believe in fate or curses or destiny—life was what we made it. We had what we took.

And I was going to take that farm.

Jo too, if I played it right.

The challenge was acquiring their rights, sure, but now that I'd gotten a glimpse of Jo Blum, the game had new stakes. I didn't realize I'd enjoy flipping her so much, but already I looked forward to seeing her when we were apart, if not just to find new and interesting ways to prove her wrong. Mostly to enjoy the volley of conversation that felt more like foreplay than an argument.

I'd listened to the Blum sisters sing all last night, and every time Jo took the microphone, that strange sensation rooted me to the spot. She'd avoided me the rest of the night, and I didn't chase her down, opting instead for the occasional snag of her gaze, turning my tractor beams up to eleven. By the way she kept eyeing my lips, I knew the window was open. And I knew I wanted to know what her lips tasted like just as much as I had a feeling she wanted

to know the same.

For the first time since getting to Lindenbach, I had a shot at everything I wanted—the rights to these farms, the outrageous bonus, and a romp with Jo.

My phone rang as I was bringing the last bite of biscuit to my mouth, but on seeing my father's name on the screen, my appetite disappeared. Dread took its place in my gut.

"Checking up on me?" I asked.

"I drew the short straw. What's taking so long?"

"The bee farm. They're going to take some work to flip."

"And the others?"

"The right number of zeros on the check should do it. Just not the bee farm."

He scoffed. "Hippies. What's your plan?"

I sat back in the chair to a creak. "The youngest sister is the way in. Just need to get past her, and I'm in."

"I need to know how much time it's going to take."

"Sorry, I left my crystal ball in my other pants."

"Smartass," he spat. "They're impatient to get moving, and this is on your shoulders. I'm not going to save you."

"When have you ever saved me?"

"Only every day of your miserable life, Grant. Just get it done for once, on time."

"Yes, sir," I said, the words flat, dry.

for love or honey

Which pissed him off, as intended. "I don't know why I ever agreed to groom you for this."

"Because you only had one kid to abuse."

"Didn't get a chance for more, did I?"

Because you killed her, was the subtext. And there was never a time it didn't hurt. Not once.

"Well, it's been great catching up," I said, outwardly unfazed.

"Don't call me if you need help."

Before I could respond, he hung up.

I slid my phone across the table and picked up the last of my biscuit, but rage had boiled my guts and dried my mouth, the environment inhospitable for food.

So I pushed back from the table, storming to my suitcase for running shorts and a shirt. It was a thousand degrees outside, but if I didn't run, I was going to damage Salma's property. She didn't deserve a fist-sized hole in the wall just because my dad was an asshole.

Shoes on, I took off. I'd left everything but what I was wearing in the house, needing one stretch of time when I was untethered. Within the span of a minute, sweat was sliding down my body. I turned up a gravel road framed by barbed wire split rail fencing, focusing on the rhythm of my breath and the crunch of my shoes against rock.

You killed her.

He'd done this since I was a child, using her death as leverage on my sense of self and purpose. Maybe it was a means to control me. I could never be sure.

An embolism killed her within minutes of my first breath, leaving my father alone in the world with me.

I had few childhood memories of him—my happiest memories involved either the troop of nannies who raised me or my friends at boarding school and college. I'd spent holidays with friends or at school alone until I was eighteen, and ever after, I traveled with those same friends, most who had parents like mine. Absent at best.

All the closest of those friends had gotten married and moved away, too busy with their new families to go to Italy for a month during the holidays. And the people I was left with were proximity friends—they were nearby and single. The women in my life fell into the same pool of convenience. I was too busy to form real, lasting relationships and out of town too often to try to date. I'd never found anyone I cared about enough to drag through long distance even though a few wanted to. Which was a sign on its own to bail.

I'd mostly been alone, but I'd never felt lonely, at least not since I moved out of the house I shared with him to go to college.

When I graduated, my father sat me down and offered to teach me, mentor me in his career.

I was stunned to silence.

It was my only use to him, I figured. If by some chance he did love me, this would be the only way he knew to show it. He never remarried, never so much as dated that I knew, which admittedly wasn't much. But I'd caught little glimpses into who he was before she died. A box in the back of his closet full of photos of them, of movie stubs and birthday cards, of concert flyers and little notes for mundane things like dinner reminders and simple I love yous. Once, I'd caught him in the living room on his side of the house late one night. I'd come in from a party to find the flicker and noise and floated in its direction, pausing in the doorway, instantly sobered at the sight of my parents on their wedding day, the picture of hope and bright futures. And my father silently sipped his scotch, wrinkled and worn, from a

for love or honey

leather couch.

In that moment, I understood.

So when he offered to teach me, I said yes.

It had been much of the same for the last five years, with glimmers of respect amidst a sea of disappointment.

You'd think I'd get used to it.

But somehow, I never did.

ELEPHANT PARADE

Jo

Sweat rolled down every inch of me as I trotted to a stop at the foot of our driveway, panting.

It was too late for a run in this heat, but I loved the people in my life—none of them deserved to get their neck snapped just because I didn't let off my daily steam. Hands on my hips, I paced in front of the mailbox, catching my breath, going through the checklist for today. The biggest item on the list was a bee relocation I had out on Wyatt Schumaker's ranch, which was why I got to sleep in. It was the grand trade-off—I wrangled bees so they didn't have to, and in exchange, I didn't have to do my chores.

Truth was, I loved bee relocations. Mama said it was because I was a wild animal, which was largely true. But I think the trick was that I understood them, somehow. They lived their whole lives to build a home and care for their queen. To make and to work and to give to their family. Honey was the product of all that love they gave, and honey was the product of mine.

The thought of them building that home, protecting their queen, and being exterminated made me sick to my stomach. So whenever anyone in town found a hive where one shouldn't be, they called us, and I'd go down and move them into brood boxes where they'd live out their days here on the farm. They'd be safe here. They'd have a home here.

Nothing was more important than that.

Sweat somehow trickled into my ear despite my earbud, and I pulled the device out to rub the itch away. Which was when I heard the crunch of sneakers on gravel just down the road a ways.

Frowning, I turned my head to the sound, immediately sweating what was left of me into a puddle around a pair of empty sneakers. And not for the heat.

The unrecognizable man running my direction was shaped like a god, bare chested and tan and shining, with muscles I could count and name from fifty feet. Rolling shoulders. Pumping arms. Abs contracting and easing with the rhythm of his feet. Narrow waist, black running shorts slung low on his hips, shirt swinging from where it was tucked in the back. Rectangular thighs, thick as tree trunks, dusted with dark hair, driving him in my direction like a freight train. His jaw, sharp and tight and bunched at the joints. Lips an unyielding line, eyes tight, black hair lank with sweat, pasted to his forehead and unruly everywhere else.

I know him. How do I know him?

I scanned his body again, pausing when I reached his hips as if I could use what was there to identify him. How I'd not noticed his substantial swinging dick on the first scan was beyond me. It was like watching a baby elephant caught in a stampede. I stared much longer than I should have before remembering myself, my gaze jumping back to his face now that I really needed to know who that belonged to.

I could see his eyes now that he was closer, eyes as blue as the center of a flame.

Grant fucking Stone.

Grant fucking Stone with no shirt on. And those shorts on. And that thing between his legs.

I didn't think he'd seen me. His eyes were fixed down the road, his concentration so deep, I wasn't sure he was even on the planet.

His presence in front of my farm had to be for show. A joke. A ploy. Why else would he run by my driveway when he had twenty miles of nothing available to him in every direction? He was pretending not to see me—it was the only reasonable explanation.

With a mighty scowl, I popped my other earbud out and closed it with its twin in my fist.

"What the fuck are you doing?" I yelled in his direction.

His face jerked toward me, colored in confusion. He glanced around like he didn't know where he was, his stride slowing gracefully.

"What are you doing?" I said slower, though with no less accusation.

"Looks like the same thing you are," he panted, hands on his hips like mine had just been.

"Don't gimme that bullshit. I hope you're not here to—"

"I went for a run, Jo," he said darkly. "Not everything is about you."

I jerked back, affronted. "Charming, really."

He glared at me, chest heaving. "You're mad if I'm nice to you and mad if I'm not. What do you want from me?"

"To be left alone."

"Fine." He picked up to start running again, leaving me with a strange feeling. Equal parts annoyance, rejection, and a bizarre sense of longing.

for love or honey

It must have been the elephant in his pants.

But rather than take it back, I put my nose in the air and stepped up to the mailbox to collect its contents.

His footfalls stopped behind me.

"Really?" he said. "That's it?"

"You're mad when I tell you how I feel and you're mad when I don't. What do you want from me?" I stacked mail into the crook of my arm with a little bit of violence.

A haughty laugh. "Whenever do you keep how you feel to yourself?"

I slammed the mailbox shut and turned on my heel to face him. "You think you're privy to all my thoughts and feelings?"

"No, I just didn't think you were capable of keeping anything to yourself."

"Well, I don't think you're capable of telling the truth."

"Because you know me so well."

My eyes wanted to roam down his chest and lower, but I drilled my gaze into his eyeballs so they couldn't. "I know all I need to. You want to come in and snatch what you can, then leave and never think about us again. You don't realize that Lindenbach is a living creature, and you're just a virus we caught."

"A virus."

"Yup. A greedy virus trying to suck the life out of our town."

"That's a little dramatic. I'm not going to ruin your town."

"But you'll ruin my farm without blinking."

"I'm not going to ruin your farm either."

"Damn right you're not, because you're not getting your fangs in it."

He watched me for a moment, the massive discs of his pecs rising and falling and glistening and begging me to look. I didn't. This was a big deal.

"I'm not going anywhere, Jo. You're not going to run me off."

A wicked smile brushed my lips. "Wanna make a bet?"

"I don't take bets I know I'll win. Takes all the fun out of it."

I snorted a laugh. "Chicken."

"You think I couldn't possibly understand hard labor or living a modest life, is that it?"

That earned him a full-blown bout of laughter as I imagined him working land. "You wouldn't last a day."

Something came over him quietly, filled him with purpose and challenge that drew him a few inches taller, his broad shoulders stretching wider. His smile held a thousand promises, and I told myself I didn't want a single one of them, even though I could think of five off the top of my head that he could convince me to take.

"Well, then—maybe I should learn. And since you seem to know everything, maybe you should be the one to teach me."

I laughed again, hoping he didn't catch the oh, shit my nerves sang beneath the sound. "I don't have time to babysit you."

"Chicken."

"Am not."

"Are too. Put your money where your mouth is, Blum."

for love or honey

I assessed him a moment, considering how this could benefit me. The biggest draw was the thought of humiliating him—there was nothing I'd like more than to see him fail. There was also the newfound allure of the firehose between his legs that, although I'd never know biblically, I wouldn't hate to catch the occasional glimpse of. Strictly for educational purposes, of course.

Because really, it wasn't fair that he should be that hot, that rich, and that hung. It upset the balance of the universe.

He'd said I couldn't run him off, but if I did this, that statement might change. He thought he could hang, but while his jock did all kinds of hanging, his constitution through the hell I could put him through had yet to be determined. And while I believed he was stubborn as all hell and would stick it out longer than any normal person would, I knew for a fact that I was more stubborn.

So I smiled. Narrowed my eyes. And said, "You're on."

And with a smile from him that told me he had no idea what he'd gotten himself into, he said, "Good."

I turned for the driveway, not bothering to speak over my shoulder. "Lessons start in two hours. Wear something that can get dirty."

"Yes, ma'am."

As the gravel crunched and his pace picked up, he ran back in the direction of town, and I snuck one more glance just to see if the back of him was as cut as the rest. He was looking right at me with a knowing smirk that had me rolling my eyes.

But not before I found out the answer was yes.

MASOCHISM AS A SPORT

Grant

Water sluiced down my back, hitting the bottom of the clawfoot tub with a slap.

Absently, I wondered how many showers I'd take today. If Jo had her way, three wouldn't be enough.

I smiled to myself, reaching for a bar of soap, considering the roaring hellcat, living her life offended by my presence while somehow managing to send me signals she'd deny until she was in the dirt. But I saw her. I saw it in the look on her face, in the roaming of her eyes, in the way I'd caught her sneaking a final glimpse of my ass as I ran away.

Now all I had to do was let her torture me.

Smiling wider, I wondered what she'd put me through first and decided I'd rather not know.

When I'd washed the layer of Texas sweat off of me, I turned the squeaky faucet until it closed and reached for a towel.

I hadn't realized that I was in front of her place until she spoke. I'd been running blind, so deep in my thoughts that I wasn't sure I was even still piloting my body. The heat, the tearing of my lungs, the burn of my muscles—it'd all been dim and distant until she called out to me. Had the tables been turned, I'd have assumed she'd done it on purpose too. And it would have been a great plan, if I'd intended to accidentally run into her.

Instead, it was an honest accident, though no less effective.

Once dry, I padded into my room, digging around in my suitcase for the few articles of clothing I owned that didn't get hung in my closet. Other than exercise and sleep clothes, the most casual thing I had were chinos. Rummaging through my workout clothes, I fought to find something suitable. My running shorts all had a three-inch inseam—a dubious choice, depending on what she had in store for me. The chances of me needing to cover my legs were high, so I picked out the best I had.

A pair of gray sweatpants.

Hopefully she didn't ask me how much they cost.

I stepped into them with a vague sense of warning. I was going to pass out from heatstroke wearing sweatpants. This was a first—I'd never had to get dirty to win a contract—so I hadn't considered bringing anything more casual. But without any better options, all I could do was go with it.

A knock rapped at the door, and I strode across the room to answer it.

When I whipped it open, Jo's fist was raised like she was about to knock again. Her face shot open like a firecracker had just gone off her hand, and that hand pressed the words Get The Frack Out into her breastbone.

"Jesus," she said. "Who'd you think that I was, the police?"

"Are you always this dramatic?" I asked, turning into the house with the assumption she'd follow.

"Without question." She paused. "You're going to die of heatstroke in those sweatpants."

"I was only expecting to pass out. Should I call the funeral home and make arrangements?"

"Ha, ha. Don't you have anything else to wear?"

"What do you suggest?"

"Well, a shirt, for one."

I shot her a smile over my shoulder. "You don't really want me to wear a shirt."

"Does that bullshit really work on girls where you're from?"

"Every time."

She rolled her eyes. "You don't own a pair of jeans, do you?"

"Not one. It's either this or running shorts."

I couldn't see her from the dresser in my room as I dug up an old Cornell T-shirt and grabbed my running shoes. The bed squeaked when I sat on the end to get my shoes on.

"What are we doing?" I asked.

"It's a surprise."

"A bad surprise." I guessed.

"Probably."

I could hear her smiling, which put a smile on my own face.

"Good."

"Good?"

"I'm just happy for a chance to prove you wrong, that's all."

"You're so sure of yourself, aren't you?"

"That's the key to success," I informed her. "It's fifty percent being sure of yourself."

"And the other fifty percent?"

"Self-loathing. Every successful human lives by that ratio. Unless they're a sociopath."

"Hm. And I was so sure you were the latter."

Once my last shoe was tied, I made my way back to her, pulling on my shirt as an experiment. When my head was out of the neck, I found success—Jo's thirsty eyes slid down my body like they'd slipped on a banana.

I paused, smirking. "Did you get all that, or should I go back and do it again?"

The flush in her cheeks belied her scoffing. She turned for the door.

"Come on, let's go," she said.

"Am I driving or you?"

"Please. Your toy car is never going to make it into pastures. I'm driving."

"Pastures, huh? Are we doing something with cows?"

"Nope." She exited the house, not bothering to hold the screen door, which nearly hit me in the face.

I caught it, giving the back of her a flat look. "Sheep?"

She opened the door to her truck and climbed up on the rail, turning to me with a smile. "Nope."

"You're not even going to give me a hint?"

"You want a hint? Really?"

This time, I gave the front of her a flat look that was met with a smug smile.

"All right, fine."

She disappeared, digging around in the back of the cab for a wad of white material. I frowned. And when she threw her burden at me with both hands, I caught it, though it'd partially come unfurled in transit. My eyes widened as I realized what it was.

A beekeeper's coverall.

The satisfaction on her face shouldn't have been legal.

"Get in, asshole. We're going to save some bees."

GOOD VIBES, BAD VIBES

Jo

We bumbled and bounced up the long dirt road that led to Wyatt's ranch house. I wore a smile. Grant tried to cover his suspicion, his gigantic hand hooked in the Oh, shit handle and a beekeeper suit in his lap.

The sight made me want to cackle like a Disney villain.

This was a preferential reaction to the one I'd had when he answered the door shirtless in gray sweatpants. There was no logic behind the exponential hotness of a man in gray sweatpants. It was just a law of the universe and one I was very, very thankful for at the moment. Although I really was concerned about him heatstroking or passing out. There was no way I could get him back in the truck alone if he swooned.

When we reached the house, Wyatt came walking around from the back, turning the corner like a model for the promising future of FFA kids. Sunbleached cowboy hat, short-sleeved plaid with pearl snaps that was so tight around his biceps, I was pretty sure it would tear if he so much as opened a jar. Wranglers snug as all hell, boots worn and rugged. Rugged like his square jaw and strong nose and eyes that promised a deep and serious fucking.

Eyes that were locked on Grant and a smirk that backed that promise up, times ten.

Grant didn't even flinch under his gaze. Instead, he held on to it with a smirk of his own, which left me wondering what happened when gay men waged the battle of the tops. It also left me wondering if Grant was as gay as Wyatt, and with my disappointment at the thought, the hope that he was bi.

I blame the python he called a dick. I'd been dicknotized.

I rolled down my window and hung out by my elbow.

Wyatt hooked his arm and shouted, "Come on—I'll show you where I found them."

With a nod, I settled back into my seat and waited while he hopped into his truck and backed out, and we took off down a trail.

Wyatt's expansive cattle farm was left to him by his father. He'd learned to ride bulls here, and he had a wall full of rodeo trophies to prove his skill. He was the catch of the century, so long as you had the right equipment. Which sadly, I did not.

I glanced at Grant, smiling like I was teasing him. "Wyatt's something else, isn't he?"

"I don't think I've seen many cowboys who look like that."

"Wait until you see him in a slutty cow skirt and top."

A laugh shot out of him, an honest, happy sound that surprised me. "I'm surprised he doesn't catch hell around here. I mean, I'm assuming he's gay."

"He's so very gay. And honestly, it used to be bad, but when you've won as many rodeo competitions as he has, a certain clout comes with it. He could ride down to Main Street in nothing but a red leather Speedo and red cowboy boots, and even Pastor Coleburn would be out whistling at him. Wyatt's impossible not to love.

And anybody who'd challenge his sexuality would be run out of town—likely bleeding—or at least shamed into shutting up." I snuck another glance at him. "You interested?"

His face turned to mine, one brow up to match that rising corner of his lips. "What would you say if I answered yes?"

Damn. "That I wouldn't blame you. I don't know that there's a human in town who wouldn't hit that, and the ones who say they wouldn't are liars."

He assessed the back of Wyatt's truck for a second. "He's not my type."

"Because he's a man?"

"No, because he's got a boyfriend."

My mouth popped open. "How do you know that? Is that some secondary mode of gaydar?"

"I ate at Abuelita's last night and saw him with one of the cooks."

I paused, processing. "So you're gay?"

He shifted to face me, resting his hand on the back of my seat. A cursory glance revealed that goddamn smirk again. "Would you be disappointed if I was?"

Yes.

Ew, shut up.

"It would make things a lot simpler," I admitted.

Under his gaze, I felt like a deer in the sights of a mountain lion. "Would it?"

My cheeks warmed. "Only because you run around town with your dick swinging like a firehose somebody let go of."

Another laugh, this one hearty enough that he looked out the window to hide his face.

"I'm just saying—four women live in my house, and when a man comes running by with a thing like that untethered in his pants, it feels like an advertisement."

"Funny, I didn't think anyone in that house would entertain me for another glass of sweet tea, never mind handling my firehose."

I snorted a laugh. "Would you answer me already?"

He shrugged, glancing at Wyatt's rear end again. "I like what I like."

Still unsure, I asked, "And you like what's in Wyatt's Wranglers?"

At that, he gave me a promissory look that sent a shock of heat straight between my legs. "Among other things."

Message received.

"Ever hear of the Kinsey scale?" he asked.

"No," I admitted, annoyed that he knew anything I didn't.

"It was a study done in the 40s that determined that everyone's sexuality fit in a section of a scale—zero is strictly hetero and six is strictly homosexual. It's a little dated now, but the idea is that there's no one or the other, but a gradient. I'm somewhere in the middle."

Surprised but mostly relieved, I said, "I always say everyone's a little gay under the right circumstance."

When he laughed, I knew he knew I was relieved and cursed myself for all but admitting I'd pony up.

But rather than prolong my embarrassment, I changed the subject. "Now that we know how you feel about Wyatt's ass, how do you feel about bees?"

He glanced out the window, considering. "I think I'm indifferent. But ask me again when I'm face-to-face with a hive."

"They're only scary if you're scared."

"Never would have guessed."

"What I mean is, if you trust them, they trust you. If you walk into it scared, they know and will likely see you as a threat. Which is when you get stung."

He rearranged his suit in his lap. "Where's your suit?"

"I don't have one."

"You don't ... have one?"

"Don't need one," I said with a smile in his direction as I put the truck in park next to Wyatt.

Before he could ask any more questions, I opened the door and climbed out.

Wyatt stood next to a shed, looking at the door dubiously with his hands on narrow hips.

"Heya, JoJo," he said, still eyeing the shed.

"Hey. You gonna help me do this?"

"Hell no. You're on your own, kid." He nodded toward the shed. "Opened it up yesterday and got swarmed. I dunno where they even are in there."

"You ran," I said around a snicker.

"Fuck yeah, I ran. I ain't even ashamed. Mighta screamed a little too." He glanced back at the truck. "The hell's he doing here?"

"Oh, Grant? I'm gonna scare the shit out of him."

A laugh cracked out of him like a whip as Grant walked up, his beekeeper suit awkward in his hands and his eyes on the shed like there was a bomb inside.

Wyatt reached around me, extending a hand to Grant. "Name's Wyatt. Good to meet ya."

Grant took his hand and pumped it. "Grant," was all he said.

Probably because I'd walked up to the shed door and opened it without pause.

A cloud of bees zipped out, some hovering and lighting on me. "Hey, babies. Don't worry—I won't hurt you."

"Well, that's my cue," Wyatt said from his open truck door, which was too far away to have gotten to at a normal human pace.

"How the hell did he—" I muttered.

"He ran," Grant answered.

Wyatt was waving out the window. "Come find me when you're done, kid."

I just waved and chuckled. He was already too far gone to hear me making fun of him, so I kept it to myself.

The shuffling of material drew my attention back to Grant, who was stepping into the suit.

"Here, let me help you," I said, moving behind him to help him into the arms.

"Are you sure this gonna fit me?"

"I'm sure."

"I don't know—oh!" he said when it was fitted nicely on his shoulders. "Why do you have a suit this big?"

I stepped around to the front of him, showing him the loops for his fingers in the sleeves to keep the wrists sealed. My eyes fixed on my hands, and a placid smile touched my lips. "It was my daddy's." Before he could respond, I hitched on my tiptoes to arrange his hood. "You're gonna want to make sure this is all zipped up. You might be a little claustrophobic, but try to keep breathing and remember you're safe in there. I mean, maybe not from the heat, but the bees won't get you."

A pause while he let me get him the rest of the way in the suit. "If I'm scared, will that mess the bees up for you?"

"Worried about my safety?"

"Shouldn't I be?"

"How about you just let me handle them, and you hang back a little. We'll see what they do."

I pulled the zipper closed on his hood, still avoiding his eyes. He smelled like mint and soap and man, and I decided I should never be this close to him again.

It was real hard to hate him when I wanted to climb him like a jungle gym.

I reached into his front pockets, surprising him as planned. I dangled elbow-length gloves in front of him and left him to fend for himself while I unpacked the brood boxes from my truck and headed for the shed.

He grabbed me by the arm before I reached it. "Hang on. Don't you need smoke or something?"

One of my brows rose. "Are you questioning my authority?"

"No, I just—"

"I think I've got this, Stone." When he didn't remove his hand from my person, I added, "If you don't mind…"

He let me go and exhaled audibly as he peered into the dark shed. And with a smile on my face, I ducked into the den, humming.

The shed housed equipment that didn't look like it'd been used much in recent years. It was big enough for an ancient tractor—though not much else—with old bales of hay stacked in a corner and rusty hoes and rakes and other various tools hanging on one wall. The space was filled wall to wall with the hum of a massive hive I needed to locate.

I set the box down and opened it up, assessing the space as I turned my baseball cap around so I could see better. Light cut into the shed in slices thick with dust motes, just enough to show me what I was dealing with.

I crept around the tractor with bees flitting around me. "Hello, friends," I said in the voice I used only with bees and babies. "Look at what a good job you did building your house." I crouched to look under the tractor but saw no sign of the hive. "Wyatt needs his shed back, though. Wanna come live with me? The place is lousy with flowers."

Carefully, I tested the tractor's hood and found it unlatched. Even more carefully, I lifted it enough to see the massive hive inside.

"There you are," I whispered, putting it back to rest so I could figure out how the hell to get them out. I stepped back and assessed the situation. There was no motor, so the bees had taken the shell for a home, attaching their honeycombs to the hood, which meant I couldn't open it all the way without breaking the combs. I had to figure out how to prop it so I could separate them from the metal.

"Grant—I need your help."

I glanced back to find him hovering near the door with his eyes on the tractor.

for love or honey

"Grant."

He found himself and looked at me.

"I need you to hold up the hood so I can cut the honeycombs out."

"All right," he said with confidence I almost believed.

"It's gonna be awkward. Hop into the tractor and reach over the wheel. I'll pass you the hood, and I need you to hold it right there so we don't break the structures."

He was already climbing into the tractor. "Good thing this one's old and doesn't have a windshield."

"Heaven forbid we have to use a ladder." I nodded to the wall where a ladder hung.

"You think you're so smart."

"There's no thinking about it," I said, retrieving the A-frame ladder from its rusty nail and opening it. Once set up, I inspected the rungs for rot before climbing on. "Okay, lean this way."

He did, and I opened it as far as I could before indicating he should take it.

"Watching you stand there without gear on is terrifying."

"Grant Stone, scared?"

"My heart's a jackhammer. Have you ever been stung?"

"Of course," I answered, pulling my knife out of my pocket. Tenderly, I held the comb with one hand and began to saw the first row out. "But not since I was little. Daddy taught me all the secrets."

"Care to share with the class?"

"Mostly what I told you. It's all about trust."

"Interesting, since you don't seem to trust anybody."

"That's not true." When I'd angled the honeycomb out, I climbed down and fruitlessly inspected it for the queen before sliding it into the brood box. "I just don't trust you."

A laugh through his nose.

"But bees are different. They have no grand designs, no greed to speak of. Hoarding, maybe, but not greed. They just want to live their lives and protect their home—simple needs. And if they know that I want to protect their home too, they let me in to help them."

"So it's mind over matter?"

I smiled. "That, and we're witches, remember? We can charm them with nothing but our voices."

There was a look of recognition and appreciation on his face. "Genetic, then? Do your sisters do this without gear?"

"Sometimes, but not in instances like this." I worked on the next comb, squeezing into the small space made by the lift of the hood. "I haven't worn gear in ages."

"But why?"

I chuckled. "Because those things are hot as fuck, and it's hard to move bees with gloves on. I know I don't need it, so why bother?"

"So you don't get stung to death."

"They won't sting me." I slid the second honeycomb in the box and went back for more.

"You've never come up on pissed-off bees?"

for love or honey

"Some hives are more aggressive than others, but … I don't know how it works. They just don't sting me."

"I just read a study about brain waves. What you're doing, what you're feeling emits different kinds of waves, and they think it's possible that some people are more sensitive to them than others. Real-life vibes. Maybe it's that. Maybe they just like your vibes."

I smirked up at him. "You keep denying our powers with the dark arts."

"If you were witches, you'd already have run me out of town with a spell or broken my legs by way of a voodoo doll."

"Who's to say we don't have something brewing?" I got another free, removing it carefully. My hands were barely visible for all the bees.

"I think I'll go with science."

"The science of good vibes?" I scoffed. "You realize you're trying to frack your way into their environment. You think they can feel my brain waves, but your drilling and diesel won't affect them at all? That's some logic."

I could feel him frowning as I inspected the comb for the queen. I was just about to attach it to a frame and slide them into their new home when I saw her in the midst of a cluster and smiled.

"There you are." So gently, I laid the comb on top of the box and reached into the fray to scoop up the knot of bees. They didn't want to break from her, but I managed to separate them so I could put the queen in a clip. Now that I had her, the bees still in the tractor would migrate to the box where she was.

Grant let out a breath. "Christ. I haven't been so nervous since I saw a guy put his head in a tiger's mouth."

"Oh, that's nothing. Watch this." I climbed up on the tire, dipped a hand into the hive, and came back with a wriggling, tickling handful. Hanging onto the tractor with my free hand,

I leaned toward the box, flicked my hand toward the opening, and shot the whole lot of them in without incident.

"Witch."

"Told you," I said on a laugh.

He was quiet as I climbed back on the ladder and got to work on another honeycomb.

"What if," he finally said, "we didn't have to drill on your land? We just need what's under it, and the cache we found extends into your neighbor's land."

"No."

Another pause. "I know you think there's no way to do this without disrupting your bees—"

"Because there isn't. Even having you on other farms affects us. Now shut up, because if I get stung today because of you fucking with my vibes, I'm cutting a hole in your suit and locking you in here."

That did the trick. And I found my smile again. There was nothing so heady as holding power over a man who thought he ran the world.

On the other hand, I was glad he mentioned the reason he was here. For a second, I'd forgotten he was the devil. Which was exactly how the devil got in, I supposed.

That was his plan, after all—to try to wiggle into my good graces. He still hadn't figured out I wasn't won over so easy. That, and I'd outlast him without fail.

He'd realize it soon enough.

But hopefully not until I'd fucked with him well and thoroughly.

DAT ASS

Grant

I didn't know why I was shocked to find thirty anti-fracking signs stuck in my small front yard the next morning.

Jo was my first thought in the way of perpetrators, though on consideration, it could have been anyone. Especially given that she had new and cruel ways to punish me. Signs were nothing when she could force me into an enclosed space full of bees.

With a sigh, I walked past the signs. Having played this game before, I knew that removing them would only multiply them— I'd wake up tomorrow with more.

As I headed toward town in search of a hot meal, I thought about what else she had in store for me, deciding that it was unimaginable and pointless to try. One thing I wouldn't dare tell her was that yesterday was more fun than I'd had in a long, long time.

We'd cleared out the bees, and Wyatt fed us pulled pork and sweet tea while we sat in his kitchen talking, laughing. Mostly,

I listened, observed as they told stories of the town, of their youth, with a little gossip strung in for good measure.

I had friends, people I did things with. But these people were a part of each other's lives in a way I found fascinating. It was a thing I'd only seen on television, a concept that felt about as real as a Norman Rockwell. I watched them like a voyeur, feeling more like an outsider here than I maybe ever had.

Her honesty held its own appeal. I lived in a world of mirrors, where people behaved like they thought you wanted them to behave. Where genuineness was not rewarded—it was punished. It left a window for being taken advantage of, a window I'd taken many a time. But this time was different. I didn't know how, exactly. Probably to do with Jo's and my arrangement and the time we'd spent together. It was easier when they weren't humanized. When the things they wanted were merely bargaining chips to get what I wanted.

But yesterday, I watched a half-pint woman with inky black hair and a backward baseball cap scoop up handfuls of bees like the hive was a basket of kittens. While she talked shit to me.

It was hard not to be impressed.

You have a job to do. So do it.

My father's words in my head steered me toward my day as I reached the edge of Main Street. That voice had followed me around my whole life, cold and distant. I hated it. But that voice inspired me to prove him wrong—a potent motivator. Pissing him off satisfied a quiet, deep-seated desire to hurt him. Even deeper than that, deeper than I liked to acknowledge, was a kernel of hope. It'd happened here and there—he'd toss praise at me like the scattering of breadcrumbs, and I'd lived off those crumbs my whole life, keeping me in his sphere, starving for affection I'd never get.

But on the flip side, I enjoyed my job. I liked to be useful, to be successful in my goals. To know that when a task was set to me, I accomplished it despite whatever odds were against me. I looked forward to seeing these towns, noting the differences between my life and the people I came across. A tallying of what I had and what they had, not monetarily, but in a spectrum of worths and desires. A seeking, almost. For what, I didn't know. All I knew was that I hadn't found it.

As for Lindenbach, I had rounds to make at a couple farms I hadn't signed yet and dinner at the mayor's house. Like the rest of the country, Lindenbach was divided, and the mayor represented one side of the coin. Mitchell had grand ideas, misguided though they were. He wanted to elevate the town, but he was coming at it crooked, mistakenly believing that capitalism was the only way up.

I found him crass, and not because he was from the country. But because his ego could barely fit in Lindenbach. Every word he spoke had an unspoken expectation that you'd agree with him, and if you didn't, then fuck you.

It wasn't my job to get involved in local politics. I had deals to close, and then I could go home. What Lindenbach did after that was none of my concern.

When I turned onto Main Street, it was to find more anti-fracking signs posted in establishment windows. Someone had been busy. The new development struck a chord of urgency in me—it was the point when I should take my time and hurry before they took to legislating regulations to kick Flexion out of town.

Hands in my pockets, I strode toward Bettie's Biscuits, the town's diner. Eyes followed me. I met passing gazes with a smiling nod or an easy Morning, taking the flak where I had to. This was the job. Eating the shit sandwich.

Fortunately, I'd been bred not to care. When I left here, I'd never see any of these people again. What they thought of me only mattered in relation to how it affected the contracts I needed to get signed.

Everything I did here was for show, I reminded myself.

Jo's face popped into my thoughts with the subtlety of a jack-in-the-box. Objectively, whatever happened with her was for show too. Subjectively, the undercurrent of intrigue flowed beneath the façade of indifference. In that place, so far beneath the surface, lived the beginning of something else, something other. Something decidedly not objective.

I made myself feel better by insisting my interest was nothing more than the challenge she presented and the fine packaging she came in.

Whatever helps you sleep at night, a voice in the back of my head snarked.

But I shook it off. This was my domain, and I reigned supreme. I knew what I was doing. And I didn't have feelings to hurt, to consider, or to even manage. Which was why I was so perfect for this job.

The bell over the door dinged when I entered. I was met with Hank Williams and the hum of the breakfast crowd, the smell of bacon and coffee in the air and the clink of silverware against plates.

I took a seat at an empty booth by the window and picked up a menu from the condiment caddy, skimming it for something that sounded good, which ended up being all of it.

"Hey, sailor," came a raspy voice from my elbow.

I looked up to find ninety-year-old Bettie herself standing at the end of the booth, pouring my coffee with a smirk on ruby lips and a shirt that read Oh yes I can. She'd knotted it at her waist, sporting a pair of wide legged black slacks and, if I wasn't mistaken, a pair of red Converse.

I shot a smirk right back at her. "Morning, Bettie. What's farm fresh on the menu today?"

A laugh slid out of her. She propped a hand on her hip and gave me an approving look from behind chunky red glasses. "So you knew that was me, did you?"

"You can assume I know everything."

"Everything, huh? That's a mighty statement."

"It's my job to know. Particularly who wants to humiliate me on live television."

"Well, you handled it like a pro."

"Also in the job description."

She made an amused sound. "Is handling bees in your job description too?"

"Only this time. Anyway, Jo handled the bees. I wasn't allowed to touch anything."

"Look at that. You're not even surprised I know."

"It's a small town. Of course you know."

"I heard your ass looked great in that beekeeper suit. Surprised I know that?"

"I wondered if she took a picture of that. Did she send it to the group text?"

"Honey, I'm royalty around here—she sent it straight to me."

It was my turn to laugh as she watched me with a curious smile on her face.

"What are you doin' with her?"

It wasn't an accusation, which surprised me.

"Proving a point."

"Sure, sure—but what are you really doing with her?"

Poker face firmly in place, I answered, "I'm sure I don't know what you mean."

"Oh, I'm sure you do. You don't put a straight man who looks like you and a hetero girl who looks like her together without something happening."

"How do you know I'm straight?"

"Touché."

"I promise you—my intentions are good."

"That, I seriously doubt," she said on a chuckle. "I'd just remind you of two things. The first is that she's not gonna flip for you, so if that's your angle, you'd best rethink it. And second is the advice I'll give for you to watch your ass. That girl is beloved by this town, and if anything happens to her? Well, if you think you've been trolled by all those signs in your yard, I'm here to warn you that you ain't seen nothin' yet. So be good, cowboy."

"Yes, ma'am."

"Now, what am I feedin' you, kiddo?"

"Biscuits and gravy, thank you."

The bell over the door dinged, and we both looked to the sound, greeted by the sight of Jo.

Her hair was loose and long, shining as bright as her eyes and her smile as she strode in, looking to the counter for a friendly face. When she didn't find one, she scanned until she found Bettie. And subsequently, me.

Her smile faltered, though not in dismay, only surprise. Color smudged her cheeks.

"Let me get that started for you," Bettie said with a smile of her own before swinging by Jo, leaning in to whisper something that made Jo giggle. Their eyes darted to me.

I laid a hot look on her that would have split an iceberg, a look that told her she didn't want to fuck with me, lest I devour her. The color in her cheeks rose higher. But rather than shrink away or go back to her business, her chin rose, and she sauntered over like she owned the place.

"Well, howdy there."

I sat back in the booth and reached for my coffee. "I didn't realize people actually said howdy anymore."

"If you're under eighty, it's only a novelty." She leaned on the other side of the booth, folding her arms and looking down her nose at me. "You recover from your bee trauma yesterday?"

"If you think that was trauma, I wonder how charmed your life is."

"And if you think that's the worst I've got to dole out, you've got another think coming."

"Bring it on, Blum."

"Tomorrow. I'll pick you up at seven."

"You keeping this one a secret too?"

"No, because you need to go get some appropriate clothes."

One of my brows rose.

"That's right. You're going to Cavanaugh's to get yourself some jeans and boots. And a hat if you're smart. Otherwise you're gonna get fried working cattle on Wyatt's ranch."

I didn't react other than saying, "Fine, but you're coming with me to shop."

"You're a big boy. You can do it by yourself."

"Oh, no, you don't. If you're going to be the boss of this, own the title. I'm not risking ending up in the emergency room because I had the wrong shoes on."

She sulked a little, but said, "Fine. Meet me there in an hour. I've gotta take breakfast back, and then we're getting your burly ass in a pair of Wranglers."

I shook my head at her. "How much do you love this?"

Her smile widened. "So, so much. See you in an hour, rube."

Before I could think of something clever to say, she pushed off the booth and headed for the counter where a waitress met her behind the register with a couple of bags of food. I tried not to stare, but I couldn't keep my eyes off Jo. She wore a navy T-shirt with the Cub Scout logo big on the front and a pair of frayed cutoffs just long enough to cover her ass. She was strong, her arms trim and thighs toned, too fair for a deep golden tan, only a sun-kissed glow.

And I realized with no small certainty that I was going to enjoy myself with her thoroughly.

***

An hour and a half later, I stood in a dressing room that smelled like leather, listening to Garth Brooks over tinny speakers, and frowning like a son of a bitch in my underwear at the clothes Jo had picked out. They hung on the wall like a curtain of hell made of denim and plaid.

"Quit pouting and put those Wranglers on," she commanded from the chairs just outside.

for love or honey

"I don't pout," I said, reaching for a pair of stiff, dark wash jeans.

"Have you ever even worn jeans?"

"Of course I have."

"What'd they ever do to you?"

"Besides being coarse and unforgiving?"

A pause. "What kind of places do you get your jeans from?"

"Nowhere like this." I stepped into one leg, then the other.

"I can't imagine being a little kid and having to wear khaki and slacks all the time. Didn't your mama ever send you outside to play?"

I pulled them over my ass and immediately felt constricted "She's dead. So, no."

A pregnant silence. "I ... I'm sorry, Grant."

"Don't be. I didn't know her."

"Still, she ... she was your mother. Couldn't have been easy not to have her."

"Hard to miss what you never had," I deflected. I buttoned the fly, turning three-quarters to look down my silhouette. And hot damn.

"Are you and your dad close?" she asked.

An unbidden laugh puffed out of me. "No."

"That was definitive."

"He's a definitive asshole."

"Oh. Do you have siblings? Any other family?"

"Nope."

"So you're alone?" Her tone was gentle, sad.

"It sounds an awful lot like you're pitying me," I warned, turning in the mirror.

"I'm sorry—I don't mean to. It's just that my mama and sisters are the best thing in my life. I don't know what I'd do without them, and when I thought about it just now, it made me sad."

The rock in my chest warmed and softened at the earnestness in her voice. "Don't be sorry. But don't be sad either. Look at what a successful adult I am—I can afford that car you hate so much and an apartment in Georgetown that's so bougie, you wouldn't be able to stomach it."

"But who do you have?"

The question slithered under my skin, wrinkling me up. In my desperation to change the subject, I decided for guerrilla tactics, reaching for the door handle.

When I stepped into the waiting area in nothing but a pair of ungodly tight Wranglers, she shut up, though her mouth didn't close. It hung open like a trout as she scanned my naked torso, the hem of denim low on my waist, the shapes of my thighs on down to my bare feet.

"They're too long," I said, turning to look in a mirror behind me so I could discreetly knock her on her ass at the sight of mine.

I snuck a glimpse at her in the mirror as I pretended to mess with my hair, pleased to find her dangerously close to drooling. Her tongue slid out of her mouth to wet her lips.

My jeans got a little tighter.

She cleared her throat and sat up, averting her eyes. "They're not too long—they're meant to be worn with boots. Did you try on one of the shirts?"

"Not yet. Wanted to make sure the pants were right."

"Oh, they're right," she said salaciously, catching herself with a laugh. "Seriously—go put a shirt on. I'm gonna find you some boots."

I shook my head, turning for the dressing room, muttering, "How the fuck did I let you talk me into this?"

"Because you think you're so smart, and you'd do anything to prove it. Even let me dress you up like a real-live cowboy."

"So I'm a sucker?"

"Without a doubt." Her voice trailed away.

Why I was smiling at the insult, I'd never know. But there I was, cheerily putting on a plaid shirt with pearl snaps with my ass clad in denim.

What has she done to me?

Don't ask questions you don't want the answer to.

It was for the job, I reminded myself as I snapped buttons. I thought the shirt would be hot, but the fabric was surprisingly airy, and as I cuffed the sleeves, I had to admit there was something to the whole look. I couldn't have told you what it was— maybe the unadulterated masculinity it evoked. Or the look on Jo's face when she saw me in the jeans. I'd never have admitted it, but I'd have my nuts crushed into these pants if it meant getting Jo out of hers.

When in Rome.

"Here," she said from the other side of the door before chucking a pair of tan suede boots under the door.

Emboldened by the jeans, I stuffed my feet into the boots, taking a second to arrange the excess denim over top of them. They were tight on my feet—so I could break them in, I figured—but I was glad she hadn't chosen the kind with a heel on them. These were more work boots than the fancier sort one would wear to church or a wedding.

I snorted a laugh at how casually I imagined wearing boots to a wedding.

"Something funny?" she asked.

"Am I supposed to tuck the shirt in?"

"Not without a belt."

"You get me a hat?"

"Of course I got you a hat."

"Guess we should see the whole look then," I said before opening the door.

A small crowd of women had gathered curiously near Jo, and knowing I had an audience, I tilted my smile and strode toward them.

Stunned, they tried to eye me up and down subtly, but their manners had given way for base objectification. Apparently manners couldn't hold up against a man in tight jeans.

Enjoying the attention a little too much, I kept on walking up to Jo. Her eyes rose as I approached, her cheeks hot when I leaned in, holding her gaze while I took the hat out of her hands. As if no one was watching, I turned for the mirror, tipping my head to put the hat on. And when I looked up again and checked the gaggle behind me, they'd nearly fallen out of their chairs.

Several of them turned on their heels and hurried off, one of them fanning herself with a brochure for the feed store.

"Is my hat on right?" I asked innocently.

"You know damn well it is," Jo answered. "You're going to give poor Martha Ann an aneurism, strutting around like a rooster."

"I've been called a cock enough times that it seems fitting."

"Think you can sit down in them?"

At that, I frowned. "I don't know."

"Well, come on over here and give it a try."

So I did, taking the seat next to her with care. They were tight and restricting. The only way I could sit was with my legs spread out or else I'd either split a seam or crush my balls.

"Don't worry," she started, snickering. "They stretch out."

"Are you sure I don't need a bigger size?"

"Absolutely certain," she said so quick and definitively, I gave her a look. She shrugged. "You just need to wear them in—the boots too. Which means you should probably wear them all day today. Maybe walk around Main Street a couple of times. Get your steps in."

"To break in the jeans and boots."

"Of course," she said sweetly. "Why else?"

"To humiliate me."

"You don't need my help with that—you do just fine on your own."

"You don't mind helping."

"No, I do not," she said on a laugh.

I looked down at her, smiling with my lips together. "You've been nice to me."

"I've been laughing at you."

"Hey, if that's what it takes to have a conversation."

"You really don't care about all this,"—she gestured to me—"do you?"

"Why should I?" I asked as I stood.

"Because you're proud and rich and I imagine don't like looking stupid."

"Sure, but you're the one who's a snob."

I caught a glimpse of her affront as I closed the dressing room door.

"I am not a snob."

"Sure you are. Snobbery isn't just by the rich. You hold my status against me. Decided it makes me lesser in your book, out of touch. I don't understand, right?" I pulled open the shirt with a string of satisfying pops.

"You are out of touch. And you don't understand."

"Not any more than you'd understand my world, but I don't hold it against you."

"Well, you're trying to get something from me, so even if you did, you'd pretend you didn't."

She wasn't wrong, though I wouldn't admit it. "You already said no about the rights. Why do you think I want something from you?"

"Because you don't strike me as a man who takes no for an answer."

for love or honey

"You make me sound like a predator."

"Aren't you?"

I frowned so hard, my brows nearly touched. "I don't have to prey on women to get one."

"Not of women. Just generally speaking."

I conceded to that as I pulled off my shirt. "It's part of the job. I do what needs to be done. Don't you?"

"That's not the point. Point is, you're not just a harmless visitor. You want something from me, and if you think I don't know that this whole thing is an angle, you're mistaken."

My fingers paused on a snap of the new shirt. "Then why play along?"

"Because I enjoy making a fool out of you," she said lightly. "That, and I have the constitution to weather whatever you throw at me."

"I've enjoyed being made a fool of by you, if I'm honest."

That got her. At her silence, I smirked.

"Let's see how you feel after tomorrow." I heard her smiling.

And looking forward to her eating crow come tomorrow afternoon, I answered, "Deal."

DEAR DIARY

Jo

I could barely handle the fact that Grant Stone was sitting in the cab of my truck in a Stetson at seven in the morning.

Honestly, I'd been banking on him looking all wrong. I thought he'd complain mightily and expected his visible misery. And I was almost sad he wasn't. Almost—because when coupled with his swaggering bravado, he looked too fucking right to have any regrets.

I wished I'd only made it up in my mind. But he looked like he was born on the range. Like he'd been driving cattle since electricity was a thing, or building houses with his bare hands as a homesteader for two hundred years.

Like he belonged in a saddle and chaps with a lasso rope in hand. A natural.

That asshole.

He yawned and looked out the window toward the very break of dawn. The sky was blue and purple, with a sliver of pink on the horizon, the start of what would be a beautiful—albeit hot—day. One he'd spend getting his neck red.

My smile widened.

Wyatt was waiting out front when I pulled up, and on seeing Grant in his getup, Wyatt's face went carefully appreciative.

He held it together better than any of the females who'd seen Grant in Wranglers.

"Mornin'." Wyatt nodded to Grant's shoes. "You breakin' those in today?"

"Didn't have much notice," Grant answered.

"No, I suppose you didn't. Hate to tell you this, but you're gonna be hurtin' come tonight."

"Don't have much a choice there either."

"Sure you do. Nobody said you had to do what Jo said."

I crossed my arms. "You sure about that?"

"Did I say anybody ever told you no, squirt?"

I gave Wyatt a look, but he just laughed.

The farm was busy with workers, and his foreman interrupted for instructions before zipping off again.

"This way," he said, waving us to follow and giving a rundown as we went. "Jo said you needed a full day's work, so we're starting in the barns and will end up in the pastures. You'll be shoveling hay, stacking bales, herding. You know how to ride a horse?"

"I've ridden a time or two."

"Good. One less thing to learn." Wyatt nodded toward the nearest barn. "We'll start off over here, filling troughs and bedding."

I couldn't keep the smile off my face when I saw the look on Grant's while Wyatt rattled off instructions. I had big plans to watch him from Wyatt's back porch all day. I wondered if Grant would get hot enough to take off his shirt and hoped the answer was yes.

With every uptick of the sun, the temperature seemed to gain five degrees of heat. We'd just stepped up to the barn when Wyatt extended two hay forks that'd been waiting for us.

I made a face. "I'm not—"

"Yes, you are." That asshole smirked at me. "You didn't think I was gonna let you punish him all day while you sat on your ass and made fun of him, did you?"

"That's exactly what I was going to do."

"Idle hands are the devil's workshop." He shoved the tool at me.

Grant watched on, smirking just as bad as Wyatt.

"Don't look so smug," I said to Grant. "I do this shit every day. The only calluses you have are from the gym."

"Think you can outlast me?" he asked.

"I know I can," I lied, hoping I didn't push myself too hard trying to keep up with him. I really didn't want to vomit with an audience. Especially not this particular audience.

"Then let's go."

"All right. You start at that end, and we'll see who hits the middle first."

"Well," Wyatt started, "looks like you've got that all sorted out. I'll be back, and we can move to the hay barn."

That, I hadn't done. A small bale weighed nearly as much as I did. And though I was strong, there was virtually zero chance of me picking one up with hooks by myself.

Wyatt looked at me like he knew it.

Traitor.

Grant headed to the other end of the barn, and I headed to mine, all kinds of salty.

Salty and determined.

And I almost beat him.

An hour later, Grant was waiting in the middle of the stalls while I finished the last few of mine. He leaned against the last hay trough he'd filled and squinted up at the sun.

"It is so fucking hot here."

"Not hotter than DC. Isn't it all nasty and humid there?"

"I don't know if you realize this, but I'm not known to shovel hay much at home."

"I could have guessed. Outside the fact that you just beat me at my own game," I said, pitching a fork full of hay into a trough.

"Don't blame yourself. I have nearly a foot on you and at least a hundred and fifty pounds."

"But you don't even know what you're doing," I huffed, angrily burying my fork in the hay for another load. "You're supposed to be bad at this."

"Sorry to disappoint," he said with a smile on his face that told me he wasn't sorry one bit. And then he stood, pulling off his gloves so he could take off his shirt.

I groaned. "Keep your shirt on."

He didn't stop. "Why? It's too hot for this many clothes."

"You gonna take off your pants too? That's the real burden."

"I'm not above it."

I pointed my pitchfork at him. "I mean it. Put it back on."

He laughed. "You gonna impale me?"

"I might. I'm trying to get rid of you, you know. And I know a lot of ways to dispose of a body."

"What's your favorite?"

He didn't put his shirt back on, and I didn't lower my weapon. "Did you know that pigs will eat anything?"

His smile faded. "Anything?"

"Anything. Bones and all. They'll even eat your belt buckle, though they sadly can't digest it. It'll be the only evidence that I took you out for fucking with me."

"I never thought I'd find bacon unappealing. Thanks for ruining that for me."

"My pleasure. Now put your fucking shirt on."

"How about you take yours off and we'll be even."

"Fine," I said curtly, tossing my pitchfork into the hay.

He froze.

I had on a sleeved button-down to keep the sun off my shoulders, and I reached for the top button, unfastening it and working my way down, grateful I had on a cute sports bra with all the crisscross straps and not one of those old ratty ones I could never seem to get rid of.

"I find you interesting, Mr. Stone," I said, disrobing. "When I met you, know the first thing I thought?"

"No, but since it precluded you throwing an egg at me, I can't imagine it was good."

"I thought you were the devil. The real live Lucifer come to slither into our town and squeeze the good out of it. I wasn't wrong, either—you're some sort of temptation, just not the kind you intended, I think."

"What do you know of my intentions?"

I undid the last button and whipped my shirt off my shoulders, tying it around my waist. "I know they're motivated by your designs, which I assume are power and money. Am I wrong?"

I reached for the pitchfork to resume my task, pleased that he couldn't quit staring at my almost naked torso.

Payback's a bitch.

"You want to know the truth?" he asked.

"If you're capable."

"My father doesn't think I can do it."

I paused, fork midair. "Why?"

He shrugged one naked shoulder, squinting up at the sky again. "He doesn't believe I can do much of anything. I've lived my life as a disappointment to him—he's never masked his feelings about it. My mother was the only thing he loved more than himself. I'm the reason she's gone. He makes sure I know it, too."

"Grant—"

He shot me a sideways smile. "I hear that pity again."

I tried to school myself, not understanding how to convey compassion over pity. "I'm sorry," I managed.

"It's nothing to be sorry over, Jo. You asked why I was here, and that's the truth of it." He watched me through a small silence. "You didn't think I'd be honest with you."

"I didn't think the reason would be this, that's all."

"You expected it to be an ungodly sum for selling my soul? In the interest of truth, I should warn you I'm still getting that. It's just not what's motivating me. So what's motivating you?"

I took back to my pitchfork, throwing my wall back up. "Aside from the well-being of my family, farm, and town?"

"Aside from that. You've got a whole lot of spite for someone who's already solved the problem of her farm." When I shot him a look, he put his hands up. "It's not an insult, just an observation."

"I'm a bee farmer and you're an oil man. We fundamentally disagree."

"Who said I agreed with them?"

"You work for them."

"That doesn't mean I believe what I sell."

I stared at him for a second, shaking my head. "You are the devil."

"Daddy issues, remember?"

With a sigh, I shoved my fork into the hay and started filling the next trough. "You and me both, since we're being honest."

A pause. "Tell me about him."

for love or honey

"He was …" I thought through a fork of hay. "He was my best friend. Everybody said we were just alike. Looked alike, laughed the same. Our smiles went up on the same side, same sense of humor. Every day he'd get his Thermos and pack us into the truck to work the farm, tend the bees. He taught me everything I know." I drifted away for a moment before speaking again. "When he died, Mama was…well, we were all lost. I was the youngest of us, but I knew what he'd do, so I did it. I took care of them just like I always will, and the farm too. So if you really want to know my motivation, aside from my love for the creatures I care for, it's defending my home just like Daddy would have."

He was quiet for a bit, watching me shovel. "Do they know? Your mom and sisters?"

"That I take care of them like I think he would? I don't know. It's not a thing that's said aloud, but I think they have an inkling, or a feeling at least."

"Is that why you made up the curse?"

"I didn't make up the curse. It's been around since my grandmother stole somebody's boyfriend a million years ago, and now we don't get to keep who we love unless they possess vaginas."

"You can't actually believe that, though."

I stopped, stuck the fork in the ground, and leaned on the handle. "My grandaddy died in a tractor accident. Daddy died in a car accident. Daisy's high school sweetheart died in an accident too. Poppy's sweetheart went to New York and never came back. Presley's daddy took off when she was a baby. It's a thing whether any of us want to believe it or not."

"And you? Who did you lose?"

I picked up the fork and went back to my task. "Nobody. Because I wasn't dumb enough to ever fall in love."

When he didn't pick on me, I snuck a look at him, but his face was unreadable.

"What, you never fall in love either?" I asked.

"Hard to fall in love when you're soulless, wouldn't you say?"

"You're not soulless."

A smile. "Gotcha to admit it."

I rolled my eyes.

"Admit you kinda like me."

"Never in a million years."

"Admit I'm not the devil, then."

"Jury's still out."

"Then admit you don't hate me."

"I don't hate you," I answered, my eyes on my task.

"Admit you kind of understand me."

At that, I raised my pitchfork and pointed it at him. "Don't press your luck, buddy."

Faster than I could track, he grabbed the pitchfork and pulled it in his direction, hauling me toward him with it. He managed to keep the tool out of the way so there was room for me to get close enough that he caught me around the waist. And just like that, I was flush against him, our sweaty skin slick.

"Pressing my luck is my favorite pastime," he said, smiling down at me from the shade of his cowboy hat. "You like me. Know how I know?"

"You read my diary?"

His smile quirked higher on the one side. "Because I can see it. Looks the same on you as it feels in me."

I stared at his lips for a heartbeat, then found myself. "I shoulda stabbed you when I had the chance."

"Probably," he said.

He was about to kiss me, I realized. And I had no designs to stop him.

The sound of an engine snapped us out of the daze, and we broke apart like an eggshell as Wyatt pulled around the barn in his truck.

"Gimme my pitchfork," I said, hand extended and heart pounding.

"How about you let me finish your job." When I didn't agree, he added, "It's the only way I can make sure I don't get stabbed and fed to the pigs."

I laughed, and he took the response as an invitation to get back to work.

"You should probably put your shirt back on," he noted.

"Why? Wyatt's not looking at me, is he?"

"No, but these jeans are tight enough without your cleavage getting involved."

"Too bad for your nuts, then," I said cheerily, turning to strut toward Wyatt with no living clue what had just happened.

Or why I wished Wyatt had stayed away for just five more minutes.

***

The day was long and hot and full of conversation. Once in the hay barn, I was saved from carrying anything by driving a tractor pulling a trailer of whatever Grant had stacked. He looked like a stranger hauling hay with a bandana around the bottom half of his face, sweat sticking his shirt to him in all the right places, his brows drawn in concentration and exertion.

By the time we made it to the pastures, his shirt was hanging from his back pocket. From my perch on the fence, I watched him walk across the field in a hat and jeans, a bandana around his neck and leather gloves on his hands. Sweat and dirt were flecked and smeared across his torso, and he walked like a man who'd done hard work and would do more, that sure and certain swagger of a capable man in his element.

Except this wasn't his element. Honestly, he'd ruined my whole plan, and I wasn't nearly mad enough about it.

Wyatt had him off to the side, giving him instructions I supposed, as Wyatt gestured and Grant nodded. He pointed toward one end of the herd, then the fence. Stay close to the fence, was the golden rule. Because it was breeding season, which meant there were bulls mixed in with the females, and there was never any anticipating what a teenaged bull would do.

They parted ways, and Wyatt trotted to the back of the herd, circling slow while Grant walked around the other, mimicking predators to catch the cattle's attention and force them to bunch. I kept my eyes on the bull, who didn't seem to be paying attention to either of them, but I noticed had shifted to the outside of the herd on Grant's side. As he walked up, the warning jolt hit me in the chest, and everything happened in slow motion.

The turn of the bull's head. The burst of bucking, head down, pointed straight at Grant. Grant stopped, saw him. Faced him. Shifted into a lateral sprint. The bull grazed him, the force knocking him into the dirt so hard, he didn't get up. Wyatt whistling, calling the bull's attention. My name. I heard my name.

I snapped into action, running toward the herd as Wyatt distracted the bull, chasing it in the direction of the chute so I could get Grant out of the way. As I approached, he came to, realizing where he was. Fast as he could, he scrambled to his feet, and I grabbed his arm, pointing toward the fence. And we ran like all hell, picking up our pace when Wyatt yelled Run! over the noise.

We hopped that fence like a couple of Olympic gold medalists, whipping around to find the bull bucking the fence hard enough to knock one of the posts loose.

And then I was staring at Grant's filthy, naked back, one arm out to his side and the other guarding my flank.

"Run, Jo," he ordered.

"Not without—"

"Run."

The command shot me into action. I took off across another small field, getting over the fence to the other side, sure Grant wasn't too far behind me. But he was still at the fence, keeping the bull's attention while Wyatt got out the other side and sprinted to Grant. He'd picked up one of what I figured was many baseball bats, got in front of Grant, and started yelling at the bull, brandishing the bat like he was going to make ground chuck out of its face if it didn't back off. And after a minute, it seemed to realize that they were out of his reach and stamped his hooves, head low before finally backing away.

The men relaxed and turned in my direction. I caught flashes of teeth. Wyatt clapped Grant on the back like he'd just hit a homer.

I rolled my eyes, partly because I wasn't done being terrified and here they were, acting like dudes about it, all proud of themselves for not getting trampled to death.

With a jolt down my spine, the curse crossed my mind, the invasive vision of Grant being run down by a bull arresting my thoughts and my pulse. I wondered if it was possible that he could be hurt or worse just from proximity to me? Our track record was not promising, our luck too dark when it came to such things not to consider what might happen to him.

But it was silly. Not just the curse, which was its own level of stupid. Even if it were real, Grant wasn't mine and never would be. Except my brain wanted to spit out all kinds of bullshit to the contrary every time said curse crossed my mind. I was too young when Daddy died—at nine, that curse was a truth that kept me up most nights. Believing something so deeply in those early years was a curse of its own, and deep down, my wiring was set up to be afraid of this.

Yet another reason to be a spinster cat lady with Mama.

I marched in their direction as they headed in mine. When they caught sight of me, I yelled, "Assholes!"

They looked at each other, confused.

"Why are you laughing? You almost got gored by a bull, for Christ's sake."

"But we didn't," Wyatt said.

"And you." I pointed at Wyatt. "I wanted you to scare him, not get him killed."

Grant elbowed Wyatt. "Told you she liked me."

"Oh my god," I said through my teeth.

Laughing, Wyatt said, "Would you look at that? She sure does."

"Fuck y'all," was my answer as I turned on my heel to march back toward the trucks, fully intending on leaving Grant here with his new buddy.

Until I heard footfalls behind me. But when I turned to the sound, it was too late.

for love or honey

Grant bent, putting his shoulder at my stomach at the same time that he grabbed my legs and stood, slinging me over his shoulder in one swift motion to the tune of Wyatt's laughter.

"Throw her in the pond," Wyatt said. "I think she needs to cool off."

"Don't you do it," I yelled, slapping Grant's back and kicking my feet. His ass even looked good upside down. Fucker.

"Come on, Jo," Grant said. "I don't know why you're scared. I'm the one who almost died."

"It's not funny!" I kicked my feet some more so he knew I was serious.

"I'm not putting you down until you quit being mad."

"Guess I live here now."

"I could do this all day, you know." He started to spin in circles, and I screamed.

"And you think I can't?" I beat on his back with my fists, but to my dismay, I'd started to laugh and I couldn't stop.

There was only one way down, and I took it—I reached into his pants, grabbed the hem of his underwear, and pulled as hard as I could.

Immediately, the world quit spinning, and he roared so deep, it reverberated through my body.

Grant set me down hard enough that I bounced. He stuck a finger in my direction, but he was laughing too. "You fight dirty." His other hand was busy trying to dig his boxer briefs out of his ass. "Goddammit, these jeans are tight."

Wyatt was practically rolling around in the grass, he was laughing so hard. "You're gonna have to drop your britches if you want them outta your crawl. Next time, just skip 'em."

But Grant was already unbuttoning his pants so he could right his situation. I caught Wyatt peeking for a glimpse of Grant's substantial junk and snickered.

"Watch it, Blum," Wyatt warned. "I'm not as generous as he is—I'll throw your ass in the pond without blinking."

"Not if you can't catch me."

I took off, running as fast as I could with a couple of monsters on my heels, the three of us laughing hard enough that I knew without question it was the happiest I'd been in a good long while.

But for once, instead of overthinking it, I enjoyed it.

Maybe a little too much.

WHEN A COKE'S A COKE

Grant

The entire town had converged at the high school stadium that Friday night, donning the purple and gold of the Lindenbach Bears to pack into the metal bleachers under the floodlights and twilight. The clack of snare drums echoed. Cheerleaders calling Go with such an accent, it sounded like Geaux, getting tossed in the air like they weighed nothing. The murmuring crowd, the sharp whistles of refs, the clap of pads and the unified grunts from the line.

We were in the second quarter and whipping the shit out of the neighboring town, and I'd suffered this much of the game at the elbow of Mayor Mitchell. After a grueling dinner at his ranch, I hadn't had much choice, and as I'd sat here through the first half of the game, the split in the town had become almost visible. The way people either swept by Mitchell like he was a celebrity or cut dark looks in his direction, whispering behind hands, left no question as to who was aligned with whom.

As much as I needed to stay in Mitchell's good graces so as not to rock the boat, I needed to get away from him. Because buddying up with this asshole was never going to win me any favor with the other half of the town—the half I needed to win.

I'd kept an eye out for Wyatt or the Blums or anyone I knew well enough to get up and chat with, any excuse to say my goodbyes to Mitchell for the night, but I hadn't spotted anyone despite my searching.

Until Jo came walking down the lowest rise, the wide walkway against the railing over the track. She leaned over the rail with a purple Bears sweatshirt in her hand, tossing the bundle to a cheerleader with a red face and a grateful expression before she hurried off toward the bathrooms.

Smiling, I stood before even considering if I should follow her, turning to say my goodbyes to Mitchell with the shake of hands and tips of hats. And then I made off in the direction of that ass I'd just seen bent over the rail.

I'd worn the jeans and boots, feeling more at home in them of late, especially at events like this. I'd never had to adapt quite so well in order to fit in, well enough that what had started off a costume had turned into a preference.

No one ever told me that looking the part could lead to faking it till I made it.

The charm was in the novelty, I told myself, like playing dress-up on Halloween. It was fun to pretend, on top of the enjoyment I felt on seeing Jo's face when I didn't fail like she'd intended. Nearly getting gorged by a bull aside. That scared the shit out of me—and was simultaneously the most alive I'd felt in years. God, she was pissed.

A smile crept onto my face. Seeing Jo pissed had become one of my favorite things. Because when she was pissed, I'd usually just proven her wrong.

I could still feel the shape of her against me as I wrestled her into the pond, the two of us soaked through and laughing like maniacs.

It wasn't as if I hadn't done such things before. Only that it'd never been quite so honest as this.

So much of my life hadn't been quite so honest as this.

Don't get sentimental, asshole. Just get the job done.

I followed her all the way to the other end of the bleachers, like she wanted to put the entire town between her family and the mayor. I spotted her sisters and Wyatt with his boyfriend nearby, plus Bettie and a few other friendly faces. And they all saw me before Jo did. Their faces wore varied expressions, from amusement to mistrust.

"Hey, man," Wyatt said with a thick lilt, half standing to shake my hand and clap me on the shoulder.

"Some game, huh?" I answered.

Jo whipped around like a top.

"We might take the championship this year in our division if they keep up like this," he said proudly.

I extended a hand to Wyatt's boyfriend, who looked amiable enough, though I was a thousand percent certain would beat my ass. He took it and nodded.

"Grant. Nice to meet you. Your boyfriend tried to kill me the other day."

He laughed, pumping that hand before letting it go. "Manny, and he'll do that."

"Mind if I sit?"

Jo answered for him, sassy as all hell. "What, you don't want to sit by your new best friend, Mitchell?"

"If I'm being honest, I'd rather have been on this side of the bleachers all night."

"And when have you ever been honest?" she said with a challenge on her face but a smile on her lips.

"Don't make me dump your ass in the pond again," I warned. "I'll do it without thinking twice."

She rolled her eyes but blushed as I took the seat that opened up when Wyatt slid over, which was right in front of her.

"So," I started, actively ignoring Jo in an attempt to get her attention, "let me guess. Cowboys fan?"

"It's the only option 'round here unless you're not a Texan."

"Dak Prescott is on my fantasy team."

"He's looking good this year, if he'd quit getting hurt. You don't have any Titans players, though, do you?"

"No, why?"

"Because there's no greater offense in these parts than rooting for the team that used to be the Oilers."

"What about the Texans?"

His face darkened. "Don't even get me started."

A chuckle through my nose. "I haven't been following much this year, though. I've been here longer than I planned."

"You could still leave," Jo offered.

I smirked at her over my shoulder. "But we're having so much fun."

Wyatt shook his head at her. "Quit actin' like you don't love torturing him. I've seen it firsthand."

"Oh, what do you know, Wyatt?"

The look on his face said he knew more than she should push him to admit. "Plenty, JoJo." He turned back to me. "Who's your team?"

"I don't really have one. I like the Cardinals and the Chiefs. Always been a fan of Indie."

"No home team?" He seemed confused.

"Washington's fine, just never really felt like a home team."

"Huh," he answered noncommittally. "No college team?"

I shrugged. "I went to Cornell."

"So, no," he said on a laugh. "Ivy League, huh? You don't have some kinda law degree or something, do you?"

"Speech communications."

When I didn't elaborate, he asked, "What all goes into that?"

I waited for Jo to butt in, but she didn't.

"Preparation for communication positions in things like marketing and journalism. Studied methods of oral and written communication, rhetoric, that sort of thing."

"And your stake in oil is…"

Other than the connection to my father, I didn't have one, but I couldn't exactly say so. "It's a job. I'm good at it. And the money doesn't hurt."

Jo stood up hard enough her feet stomped. "I'm getting a Coke. Anybody want one?"

"I'll take a Dr. Pepper," Wyatt said.

She flipped the rim of his hat, knocking it off to reveal his smashed hair.

"Dammit, Jo."

"Anybody else?" she asked her sisters.

"Dr. Pepper sounds great," Poppy said.

"I'll take one too," Daisy answered.

"I'll come with you," I said, standing.

"Didn't invite you," she answered cheerily, already heading down the stairs.

"Well, now you made me out to be a creep," I told her back as I followed her.

"Quit following me, then."

I frowned, trotting to get next to her as we turned toward the stairs where concessions were. "What's with you?"

"Nothin'. What's with you?"

"Did I do something to upset you?"

"Other than exist?"

That did it. I stopped, snagging her arm gently. When she was facing me, I let her go, and she folded her arms.

"I mean it. What'd I do?"

Her arms rose and fell as she took a deep breath. "You came here with Mitchell."

"Not because we're buddies."

"Fooled half the town."

"I have to play his game."

for love or honey

"You're playing games with him and everybody."

You're playing games with me, her eyes said.

I was, and I wasn't. But I couldn't tell her that either. "Can I tell you something?"

"Depends. Can I hit you if I don't like what I hear?"

"Deal."

A pause. "Well, go ahead."

I took a step closer so I could speak where only she could hear. Where I could be honest in the greatest capacity I was capable of. "These days I've spent with you are some of the most honest days I've ever had."

Her hard expression softened, first at her eyes, then her lips, then her shoulders.

A smile tugged at one corner of my lips. "Gonna hit me?"

With a huff, she rolled her eyes, but she was smiling too. "Buy our Cokes, and I'll let you off the hook."

I followed her toward the concession stand. "I thought they wanted Dr. Pepper."

"They do. We just call it all Coke."

"What do you call Coke?"

"Coke. What do you call it? Pop or something stupid like that?"

"Pop is worse than calling all carbonated beverages Coke?"

"Pop's for Yankees and Canadians."

"Well, guess I'm in luck. We call it soda."

When we pulled up to the end of the line, she gave me a little smirk. "I'll allow it."

I shook my head. "That look spells trouble, usually for me. Which reminds me—what's my next torture?"

"Two-stepping, tomorrow night."

I kept my face still when my insides flinched. "At least it's not line dancing."

"Oh, you're learning that too. But we'll start with the two-step. Wear those jeans and your good pearl snap."

"They're all brand new."

"Then I guess you've got options."

"What about singing with the band?"

"Oh, they'll be fine without me. You, however, have a lesson to learn."

"And what's that?" I asked.

"That you're not good at everything."

"I'm good at most things."

"But not everything. And I'm gonna find your weakness and exploit it for all it's worth."

She laughed, and so did I, but the words rang true for a different reason for me. It drew a line beneath my intentions, underscoring the ugly root of its meaning.

Because I didn't want to exploit her, not anymore.

The realization was painful, twisting my stomach into knots. My plan, the plan I'd deployed time after time, town after town, might not get me through Lindenbach, but not for the reasons I'd imagined.

But because this town had somehow gotten its hooks in me.

And there was no plan in existence for that.

DON'T WORRY

Jo

"**S**o lemme get this straight," my cousin Presley said as we worked our way down a row of flowers in our fields, harvesting for bouquets. "When y'all were at Wyatt's, you took your shirt off, he nearly kissed you, and then you all jumped in a pond together?"

"After he picked me up and spun me around. Yes."

Poppy eyeballed me. "I cannot imagine where in the hell you lost your mind. He wants our farm."

"Technically, he wants what's under it."

"Oh my god," Poppy groaned. "Somebody talk some sense into her before I beat it into her."

Daisy laughed. "Oh, what's the big deal? We're not selling. There's no danger of Jo actually dating him since he's leaving anyway. Let her have fun, Poppy."

"Yeah, let me have fun, Poppy," I teased, enjoying the view of my sister all riled up.

Poppy squished an overripe mum head and threw a clump of petals at me that broke apart like confetti as it reached me.

"Daisy's right—there's no danger of anything serious. And if you'd seen the general length and girth of his anaconda, you'd be willing to set your scruples aside too."

"Must be some dick," Presley said.

"It looked like he had a baby arm just like—" I put my elbow near my crotch and waved my hand around to a chorus of laughter. "Listen, if he hadn't looked like he did in those jeans, I don't know if we'd be having this conversation."

"It can't just be about the way he looks," Daisy said.

"Can't it?" I challenged.

"No. Because you had fun with him at Wyatt's, and I saw you last night with him. You like him."

I sighed, snipping mums and depositing them into the basket I shared with Presley. "When he's all decked out, it's like … I don't know. I can almost pretend like he's someone else. He doesn't act the same either, not like when he's in a suit and has that look on his face like he wouldn't know happy if it bit him in the ass. But he … at Wyatt's he was having fun, and that changed just about everything about him."

"Well, it sounds like your grand plan to make him look like an ass is working out great," Poppy snarked, snipping her flowers with what I could only describe as hostility. "Sounds like he's just absolutely humiliated."

"Don't worry. His next lesson is in two-stepping. He's gonna fold like a bad hand." I paused in thought. "I oughta get him a bolo tie," I said.

"Yeah, that'll totally make him look like a fool," Poppy noted with no small amount of sarcasm.

"It's one thing to be out at Wyatt's farm in a cowboy getup. It's another thing entirely to be at town hall with the whole town, learning how to line dance."

"I bet he's good at it," Presley said on a laugh.

I shoved her. "Ugh, whose side are you on?"

"I'm not sure I know anymore."

I made to shove her again, but she dodged me. So I stuck my tongue out at her like a goddamn adult.

"I'm just saying," Presley continued. "You could sleep with Big Dick, take all that hate out on each other before he leaves town and leaves you empty handed."

"And empty vagina'd," Daisy noted, but when our laughter died down, she sobered. "I heard the Patersons signed their rights over to him."

"Goddammit," Poppy snapped. "You cannot get in bed with the enemy, Jo."

"What's the harm? Mama is the final say, first of all. And I'm not gonna sign his contract regardless of the size of his dick. I can't believe out of the three of us, you think it's me who would cave."

"Right. Ironclad. The one talking about sleeping with him would never be the one to cave." Poppy glared at me, her cheeks flushed pink. "There's no danger here at all. Silly me."

"Poppy—"

"Don't you Poppy me, Iris Jo. I don't think you realize the stakes of the game you're playing with him. I should tell Mama. She'll talk sense into you."

for love or honey

"Don't you dare." I pointed my shears at her.

"You're not the boss of me. I'll tell her if I want." She pointed her shears right back at me.

"Oh, stop that," Daisy said, snatching Poppy's shears. When I stuck my tongue out again, she reached over the bush and snatched mine too.

"Hey," I whined.

Presley just laughed.

"Some help you are," I noted.

She shrugged.

"Poppy," Daisy started, pointing both shears at us, respectively, "this is barely any of your business. Jo is the only one of us who never got involved with anybody—she knows exactly how to keep things casual. Don't you think you ought to leave her alone?"

"No."

Daisy rolled her eyes. "Fine, but do you really think if she's gonna fall for somebody, it's going to be that guy?"

She sighed. "No, probably not."

"Exactly. So let her do what she wants with him. Honestly, we all oughta be more worried for him."

"I just really want to see him in these mythical pants," Presley said with a certain kind of look on her face.

"It's a special sort of magic," I said, shaking my head. "Once you see it, the world will never be the same. So you should take one last long look at Sebastian and pray you're not ruined."

Presley patted my shoulder. "I think I'll be okay."

Which was fair enough. Her boyfriend was the most eligible bachelor in town, until she locked him down. If we hadn't sworn never to date anybody, he'd have been on the top of my list for at least ten years.

"Are you gonna see him before the dance today?" Presley asked.

"He has a bunch of meetings, and Mitchell keeps asking him to dinner."

"Red flag," Poppy said.

I laid a look on her. "Cut it out."

"I don't know that I can." Her nose was in the air.

"I'm not going to sleep with him," I said, done poking the Poppy-bear.

Three reactions happened at once—triumph on Poppy, pouting on Daisy, and disbelief on Presley's.

"Well, why not?" Daisy asked.

I frowned at her. "And why are you so anxious to get me laid?"

"Because of the three of us, you need it worst."

Poppy cackled like a witch, and I reached for Daisy across the bush, but she evaded me.

"You asked."

"But seriously, why not?" Presley asked. "Now I want to know."

"In a perfect world where things were simple, I'd ride his face like a drugstore pony. But we don't live in that world. I don't hate him anymore, I don't think—I mean, so long as he stays like this, at least. Maybe I never did. Maybe this was him all along." I shook my head to clear it. "But sleep with him? That has to be the worst idea in the history of anything. Especially knowing he wants something we have."

"I mean, is it the worst idea?" Presley said.

"It is. Probably."

"Well," Daisy started, picking up her basket, "I think you shouldn't overthink it."

We followed suit and headed back toward the truck.

"I think you should overthink the hell out of it," Poppy noted.

We know, Daisy and I said in unison.

Poppy rolled her eyes. We could have made an Olympic sport out of the expression.

"Don't say anything," Presley started, "but Renee canceled her last order with me because she's closing down."

Poppy skidded to a stop. "Oh no. Not Renee."

Presley nodded, her face sad. "We're just not getting enough traffic to town to support the shop anymore."

"That's the third shop this month," Daisy added darkly. "Half of Main Street is boarded up."

"We've got to do something," I said as we climbed into the truck.

"But what?" Poppy asked.

"I don't know." I nibbled my lip, starting the truck. "We need to get people to town to shop, and we need businesses to move in."

"Nobody will with Main Street looking like it does," Daisy said. "I can't imagine why they covered up so much of the old building façades in the 70s, but it's gonna cost a small fortune to set it back

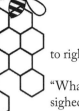

to rights."

"What if we could restore it somehow?" Poppy wondered, but sighed. "I can't even imagine what that would cost."

"I wonder if we could raise the money," I said. "We could talk to Mr. Meyers, see if Meyer's construction would give us a deal. And then we could do some fundraising. See if we could woo some donors."

"Call it Glow Up, Lindenbach," Poppy said, smiling.

"Sebastian would definitely be interested in helping. Not just in donations, but for organizing. Want me to ask him?" Presley offered.

"Absolutely," I said. "Maybe we could do a dinner here. We have the wedding space, and we could be the entertainment. There's Jesse's sister—I heard she was looking for work, straight out of culinary school and starting off her new business in town. We could see if she's up to the challenge…how fast do you think we could get it set up?"

Daisy bobbled her head. "A couple of weeks, if we can get her on board."

"We can get a bigger plan together once we talk to everyone." I paused. "Is there anything we can do to help Renee stay in her store?"

But Presley shook her head. "She's packing up and moving to San Antonio where her mom lives. I think she's going to open a new store over there, but not any time soon."

I sighed, my shoulders slumping. "More people moving out too. We're losing ground left and right."

"Doubt Mitchell will be any help," Poppy spat. "And he'd better not get in our way."

for love or honey

"No, he'd better not," I echoed. "Why he'd try to pull something is beyond me, but sometimes I think he's just a born contrarian."

"Ask your boy toy to donate," Presley suggested. When no one answered, she kicked the back of my seat.

"What, who? Me?"

"Mr. Tight Pants McMoneybags could do a lot around here." Daisy nodded.

"He's here to make money, not spend it."

"Except he's paying everyone for their land," Poppy added.

"He's not paying for anything."

"Don't you let him in your pants, Iris Jo," Poppy said.

"You're a broken record, Poppy June," I snapped. "At the end of the day, he's still the enemy."

The passengers snickered like I was a fool. Naturally, I tapped the brakes so they'd get whiplash.

Hating that they were right.

LIGHTS OUT

Grant

The second I cut the engine that Saturday night, I heard the music floating from town hall over the rain.

For a second, I just sat there amidst the scent of leather and luxury in a pair of Wranglers and cowboy boots, wondering how I'd gotten here.

It'd only been a couple weeks ago that I'd pulled into this town in this very same car, primed to get what I came for by any means necessary. In my cocksure certainty, I'd taken the window Jo provided, thinking I knew what I was doing. And here I was with a Stetson in my passenger seat, feeling like a foreigner in my own car.

I'd spent the rest of the football game talking to Wyatt, Manny, and the Blum sisters—minus Poppy, who dutifully ignored me— while the town looked on from the bleachers around us. A couple of days ago, I'd have been happy to perform for the town, to play the part of someone who belonged.

But now? Well, now I needed a new plan. Because for a minute there, I felt like I did belong, and I enjoyed it just a little too much for comfort.

I'd gotten attached like a fool, but I couldn't seem to help myself.

Maybe it was time to lean in. Maybe while I was here, while I had this moment, I could enjoy it. Maybe I could find a way to convince the Blums to sign earnestly, no lies, no catch.

Maybe, for just a little bit longer, I could pretend I belonged here.

You don't. And they don't want you, the real you. Quit dreaming and get your job done.

With that affirming pep talk, I sighed, grabbed my hat, and slid out of my car, hurrying for the door before I got soaked.

So far, I'd exploited a messy divorce on one of the properties for a signature and a second after the owner died and his kids began to split up his assets.

But the Blum farm was another beast altogether. I could feel the slow blooming of her trust and reveled in it, the joy well beyond the job.

It was a rare thing to want someone's trust, to crave it. At some undetermined point, I'd stopped wanting hers for the contract. I wanted it for my own. I wanted her for my own. And I might have figured out a way to have my cake and eat it with an unburdened conscience.

And all I had to do was be as honest as I could.

The muffled sound of honky tonk as sung by the Blums grew louder, opening up to vibrant clarity when I entered the building. Eyes found me, faces leaning toward others to whisper and watch as I sauntered into the room like a motherfucking cowboy.

Ignoring them, I searched the stage for Jo, but she wasn't there. Presley, who was singing, gave me a wink and a smile before her eyes cut to the other side of the room. And when I followed her gaze, there was Jo.

She wore a dress the same color blue as her eyes, deep and rich and dotted with little white flowers. The curves of her alabaster shoulders were only marred by the thinnest of straps connected to a neckline that hugged her breasts. Little buttons kept the corset tight all the way down to the skirt, which swayed with her body as she sang along from the edge of the crowd. Her legs were shaped like a woman who'd never met a trainer but knew a hard day's work, and on her feet were a pair of brown boots with cobalt blue stitching.

Thoughts of what I might do to her with nothing but those boots on invaded my mind.

And then her face turned to mine, and for a moment, she and I were all there was.

Color flared on her pretty cheeks, those eyes sliding up and down my body like mine had done hers. She grew in my vision until I realized I'd nearly reached her, pulled in her direction without will or consent.

When I was almost by her side, she flipped some switch, her face now colored in nothing but sarcasm and amusement.

"Well, look at you," she said, briefly glancing behind me. "I think half the straight women in town just lost their drawers."

"Which half are you on?"

"Wouldn't you like to know?"

"You have no idea."

She laughed. I watched her mouth.

Looking to the stage, I said, "You're not singing tonight?

for love or honey

"Nope. I have lessons to give." Now she only looked wicked.

"And you're the authority on two-stepping?"

"More of an authority than you, I'd wager."

"Remember when I said I don't take bets I know I'll win?"

One of her brows rose as I stepped into her and grabbed her around the waist, taking her hand in mine.

"I don't take bets I know I'll lose either."

She laughed, her hand clutching my bicep as I spun her in a quick circle. Every pair of eyes in the immediate radius were on us—she seemed to realize it the same moment I did.

Schooling herself, she put a little space between us before bringing us to a stop. She looked down at our feet, then back up at me.

"All right. It looks like you've got at least a little experience dancing. This shouldn't be too hard."

"You sound disappointed."

"I'll just pin all my hopes on you looking like a dummy when you line dance."

I must have looked worried because she laughed again.

"Okay. So the step goes one-two, one, two. One-two, one, two. On the one-two, step quick in the same direction, then step normal—right, left. So, right-left, right, left." She'd started to shuffle to her own directions, pulling me to follow, and I did through a few practice steps. "Ready?"

Rather than answer, I spun her onto the dance floor and stepped her rightly around in a circle to the steps she'd shown me.

"Like this?" I asked with a sideways smile.

Her eyes flicked to the ceiling to mask her flush and smile. "God, are you bad at anything?"

"I'll let you know if I find out."

I turned her around the dance floor, ignoring everyone watching us just as well as she did.

"Save any bees today?" I asked, wishing the song was slower so I could get closer to her.

"Not today. We worked in the cannery to fill a big order for a shop in Austin."

"Cannery?"

"It's not as fancy as it sounds. We're the only ones who usually work there since collectively, we possess plenty of hands. It's just where we process what we sell commercially so it meets all the FDA requirements. We can our own in the kitchen like professionals."

"How many generations of Blums have kept bees?"

"Six," she answered with pride. "The farm almost didn't survive the depression. My great-great-granddaddy used to make purses out of armadillos and take them into San Antonio to sell."

"Purses. Armadillo purses."

"It was a thing," she said, amused. "A thing of nightmares, but a thing nonetheless. Google it at your own risk."

"Now I have to."

"We've got a couple somewhere around the farm if you really want to lose your appetite."

"So they sold honey and armadillo purses?"

"And flowers. Half the town deserted, heading into the cities to find work. Farms were abandoned all over the county, but we were able to hang on. The Blums all stayed put. Family tradition, and all that."

"And they made it through the oil boom without selling out."

She shrugged. "We survived the hardest part. So long as the Blum offspring stays on the farm, we can survive just about anything. We're resourceful that way."

"As the purses prove." I shook my head. "Armadillos. How did they survive without getting leprosy?"

"It's one of the world's great mysteries, like how eels reproduce or the purpose of Stonehenge."

I chuckled. "I can't imagine having roots that run that deep. To live in the same house my predecessors lived in."

"I can't imagine having no roots at all. Seems like there's a lot of freedom in that."

"And a lot of loneliness," I admitted.

Her face softened. "I can only imagine."

I spun her around for a second so I didn't have to speak. "I bet you're never alone."

"It's a rare and blessed occasion," she joked, but her eyes were still all big and warm. "What do you do for the holidays?"

"Leave the country."

She laughed, then realized I was being serious. "For all of them? Really?"

"Why not? I'd rather be on a beach in Brazil than in Georgetown alone on Christmas."

"You're not alone in Brazil?"

"Not usually." I didn't elaborate, taking the shift in song to a ballad as an opportunity to pull her closer.

"When was the last Christmas you had with your family?"

"I've never had one."

Her feet came to a stop. "Never?"

I urged her on until she moved with me again. "There's that pity again." When she tried to wipe her expression clean, I chuckled and turned us around. "Like I said—hard to miss something you never had."

"That makes me want to adopt you for the holidays."

"Why, so you can ruin them forever? Pass," I joked.

"So you can know how it feels. Everyone should know how that feels."

"Tell me," I said softly, willing at least for this small torture.

She thought for a moment, her face as open as her heart. "It's the comfort of being in a place where people love you. Where you laugh and eat and celebrate your affection and appreciation for each other. Where you fight a little and bother each other, and somehow, it only makes you love the others more. Days spent in the kitchen with the lingering scent of cinnamon and apples from the pie or the buttery onions and celery sautéing before they go in the stuffing. The joy of not only finding gifts that mean something to those you love but to watch their joy when they open them. It's … I don't know. It's magic. Everybody deserves a little magic."

"I've had more magic here in Lindenbach than I've had in a long, long time."

for love or honey

She gave me a suspicious look.

"You don't believe me."

"Can you blame me?"

"Guess not. Still hurts a little."

Now she assessed me. "Tell me," she said with more skepticism than I had.

I considered for a moment, holding her close as we moved around the dance floor. "It's rare that I'm outside of my comfort zone, and you've made sure that's the only place I'm allowed. And it's been … fun."

"Dammit, I was going for torment."

"It's been some of that too," I said on a laugh. "I appreciate a challenge."

"And I'm happy to oblige."

"I appreciate that too." For a moment, we were quiet. "You've given me a glimpse into another life, the kind of thing you see on television or in movies that's too fantastic to ever be real. And you have it here in your town, in your family, in your farm. So thank you. Thanks for showing me a little of it."

Again her cheeks were smudged pink, but she wore a smart smile. "You're really putting a damper on my plans to run you out of town."

"You're doing a terrible job. Because I keep getting the feeling I'd rather stay."

Her smile faded, lush lips parting in surprise. A long peal of thunder rolled, the sound heavy enough to rumble the floor. Faces turned up to the ceiling.

"You don't want to stay," she said quietly, half to herself.

"I can't. But that doesn't mean I wouldn't like to."

A laugh as she pushed the thought away. "Quit messing with me, Stone. I'm not buying what you're selling."

"Who says I'm selling something?"

"Aren't you always? Don't you always have an angle? Wasn't the whole point of this to be some kind of an in?"

"At first. Not anymore."

"Wouldn't you say that either way?"

I took a breath and shook my head. "I wake up every morning wondering if I'll see you, when I'll see you. My time is spent thinking about what you'll put me through next, not just because I want to beat you at your own game. Not because I want anything. But because when I'm around you, that magic is there too. I've been starved for that magic my whole life, and you take it with you everywhere you go."

Her feet slowed, her eyes searching mine for a fissure, a flaw, without luck.

Because this the only way to win Jo. So for once, I gave the absolute truth.

"I'm not staying," I said again, "which works for you, doesn't it? Easy to avoid your curse if you know from the start I'm temporary, right? But I wonder how much more magic you have to give. I wonder if you find magic in me."

She couldn't seem to find words, which was its own oddity.

Another long tear of thunder rattled the building, bringing our eyes up as if we could see through the roof. Before it ended, the room went dark, the music cutting to silence. All that was left were murmurs and instructions called in the distance. I heard nothing but her shallow breath.

I found her face in the dark, cupped her jaw, lifted it. "Tell me you want me," I whispered against her lips. "Tell me—"

I was silenced by her lips, her soft, sweet lips against mine in the dark. The absolute darkness, a void with us in the center. With my fingertips in her silky hair and the scent of lilacs on her skin. With my heart hammering my sternum and her body against mine. I breathed her like I'd never breathed before, like I'd been starved until here, until now, until her.

A noisy inhale brought us flush, my arms squeezing her hard enough to nearly lift her off the ground. How was I supposed to let her go?

Why couldn't I fathom it?

What had she done to me?

It was that magic, the make-believe. The fantasy I'd found my way into by sheer luck. The deep and quiet idea that I somehow belonged here after a lifetime of belonging nowhere, to no one.

And though it was as outrageous as me ever being a cowboy, I decided not to shatter the illusion.

Instead, I leaned in.

She broke the kiss, panting in the dark, her hands on my chest and her forehead against my lips.

"Come with me," I whispered.

She hesitated.

"Don't overthink it, Jo. Come with me."

She drew a breath, then another while I held mine.

And then her hand slipped into mine before she said, "Try to keep up."

By the time the lights came back on, we were already gone.

NO WAY

Jo

We ran through the rain for his car hand in hand, and there was only one thought in my head.

Don't overthink it.

This thought played in a loop like a prayer. This was a stupid, terrible, dumb idea. And I didn't care.

Grant might be a liar, but my bullshit-o-meter was well-tuned and well-practiced. I knew an honest answer when I heard it. And I knew an honest kiss even better.

No way could he have faked that.

I laughed, running for the passenger door, soaked through. My dress clung to every curve, so wet it was transparent in crucial places. And I didn't care about that either.

We ducked into the car, closed the doors, and launched ourselves across the console in search of each other's lips. I tossed his hat in the back window so it was out of my way, our mouths a seam, our tongues a tangle, our hands roaming.

I'd just pulled his shirt out of its tuck and was about to deep dive into his pants when he caught my wrist and broke the kiss.

"I can't fuck you like I want in this car."

I whimpered. He kissed me again, a kiss deep enough that I was reaching for his belt again.

He laughed into my mouth. "Sit," he said, starting the car with a rumble and roar that I felt all the way to my uterus.

"Oh my god," I whispered, wide-eyed and smiling.

Grant smirked at me. "Not making fun of the car now, are you?"

I bit my lip and shook my head, buckling up like I'd been told.

And we took off in the rain toward his house.

I panted in my seat, partly from the run, partly from the kissing, partly because the vibrations of the car from the outrageous engine might grant me my first of what I hoped would be many orgasms of the night.

"Jesus Christ, Jo," he said in a tone I'd almost call tortured.

"What?" I asked, turning to him.

And goddamn if I didn't almost come just from the look on his face.

He was going to devour me. And I'd die happy.

His eyes shifted back to the road, and he sped up a little, but his closest hand reached for me. First for my face, his fingertips on my jaw. Then down my neck, my sternum, to fondle my breast, his thumb circling my nipple, visible through the thin fabric of my dress. Down my stomach and to my core, that wicked thumb stroking me where I needed him. I spread my thighs, my lids heavy as he flipped my skirt up so he could touch my flesh, groaning deep in his throat when he found me pantiless.

Afraid he'd stop, I held his wrist in place, rolling my hips in time with the slow tease of his fingers. It'd been a long time since I'd been touched, a long, lonely time. My eyes closed tight, my heartbeat all I could hear as heat crawled down my body to where we were connected. Lungs pinched, back arched, lips parted, mind empty of all but this, the orgasm sprang from deep inside me and pulsed in relief, letting go of my ribs so I could breathe. And when I did, it was joined by mewling.

He took a hard corner, and my eyes opened just a little, my hand still on his wrist and his fingers stroking aftershocks from me.

He was darkness, shadows but for the sallow glow from the dash and the glint of light in his eyes. His jaw was clenched hard, his eyes hungry when they caught mine for only a second.

Another hard turn, and he said to his driveway, "Thank fuck."

We skidded to a stop in front of his place. And he unbuckled us both at the same time.

"Get the fuck in the house. Now."

It was a command, not a demand, thick with lust and promises. I smiled and nearly fell out of the car on jelly legs. Apparently I didn't move fast enough because there was Grant, crushing me with a kiss, lifting me up so I had no choice but to wrap myself around him. As if there was anywhere else I'd want to be.

He pushed into the house—I didn't know if he'd opened his eyes, because mine were closed, every thought on the feel of his lips against mine. How did they fit so well? How did they know mine? I'd kissed plenty of men, but never like this. Never like him.

Grant dumped me onto the bed, climbing up after me, kicking

his shoes off on the way. I made to kick mine off, but he stopped me, saying with a smile against my lips, "Those stay on."

And then he captured my lips, teasing me with his tongue as I pulled open his shirt and reached for his belt.

This time, he didn't stop me.

Instead, he flicked open the buttons of my dress front, baring me two inches at a time. I slipped my hands into his pants, and when I found what I was looking for, he flexed into my hands, searing me with his kiss.

And then his lips were gone. I made a noise of disapproval before I realized those lips were following his hand where it cupped my breast, teasing my nipple to a peak before he closed that hot mouth over me.

A sigh emptied my lungs, my legs hooking his thighs, pulling until his shaft brushed the aching tip of me.

The flick of his tongue, the moan deep in his throat, his hand abandoning its post to touch the place where I wanted him, where I needed him.

But he only teased me, caging me with his body, my wet hair splayed across the bed, my breasts bare and dress draped around my waist. When I reached for him, he shifted so I couldn't have what I wanted.

"Jesus, Grant—fuck me like you promised," I panted.

"Oh, I'm gonna."

My eyes rolled back in my head when he gently flicked my swollen clit.

"Don't fuck with me," I mumbled, though my hips betrayed me, rolling against his hand. "Do that later. Because if you don't get in me, I'm going to come again."

for love or honey

"I missed the part where that's a bad thing."

"Because if you're not inside me when I do, I'll never forgive you."

He laughed. He kissed me. He released his hold on me to reach somewhere for a condom—I didn't care where. I rose to taste his body with my lips and tongue and fingertips, dropping his pants to reveal his substantial ass and that cock that had taken up residency in my filthiest dreams.

When he had what he needed, he stood at the foot of the bed, shucking his shirt and stepping out of his pants, our eyes locked. My legs spread gently, my fingertips brushing the nipple still slick from his mouth as I watched him fist his shaft and roll the condom on.

And then he moved too quick to do anything but meet him with my lips, with the warmth between my thighs as he breached me, flexed slow, filled me as deep as he could get. The kiss broke—he breathed deep and heavy, his eyes on my lips, his own parted as he retreated, then advanced again. My eyes closed, my head lolling, exposing my neck. And he took the invitation for a moment until he lost what little hold he had. His body moved in a wave, his hips stroking and grinding against me and inside me at once. I clawed at his back, his weight pressing me into the bed, crushing me in that way that left me defenseless, powerless, as if he were the master of my body and needed to prove it.

Again the tingling heat, the scattering of nerves toward the core of my body. The firing of electricity behind my eyes, dulling every sense but the one he drew from me with every thrust.

He swelled inside me. I contracted around him, my neck snapping off the bed as I whispered yes and please and don't stop into the shell of his ear. His hand pinned my hip, his pace speeding with my pulse, my thighs falling open, making room for him to come deeper, deeper.

A flash of lightning in the dark, and I came with a rush, a gasp, a heaving sigh. And that was enough for him to let go of the tether he had on his own release. He was so swollen, and I gripped him so tight, my eyes shot open with a sharp gasp, hanging onto him as he buried his face in my neck and his cock in me.

He slowed but didn't stop. Relaxed into me, shaking and spent. For a long while, we lay there together, with his arms around me and his lips lazily kissing my neck, my breast resting easy in his palm.

I waited for him to retreat completely, but he never did, somehow still hard and still fucking me slowly, his intent more focused by the minute.

My lids fluttered closed as I lay beneath him, and I smiled. "No way," I muttered.

"Hmm?"

I met his thrust with one of my own. "No way."

He rose just enough to look down at me wearing a smile of his own. "You didn't think you were sleeping tonight, did you?"

When I laughed, he kissed me.

And kept me up all night.

HOUSE OF CARDS

Grant

My new favorite place in the world was the velvety space between Jo's thighs.

Those thighs were slung over my shoulders in the golden stretch of dawn, her fingers in my hair and her chin lifted to the ceiling. It was time well spent returning the favor I'd woken up to—her lips between my thighs and just north a click.

Over the course of one night, I'd learned the shape of her body and the taste of her desire. I'd learned what she wanted and where, exploiting the knowledge to elicit uncountable moans, trembling limbs, and long, sweet releases.

We'd slept here and there, dozing off only to wake hazily, reaching for the other to take, to give in the dark of night where the world was empty beyond the confines of this room.

I should have been tired, but all I could muster was a languid sort of contentment, a quiet sort of peace. As if this was all I'd ever known and all that ever was, yesterday's agenda wiped away and today's a blank page.

Her fingers tightened in my hair, her center squeezing around my two curled fingers inside her. With the tip of my tongue, I teased the tip of her, easing her thigh up and open to give me more space, but as she came closer, her legs flexed, bringing us together harder. A long suck and she gasped. A flick, and she moaned. With the gentle shake of my head and the stroke of my fingers inside her, I was granted another orgasm, a hot wave of pleasure against my tongue.

I slowed at her pace, unlatching my lips to brush kisses across milky thighs, up soft stomach, against pale nipples, to rosy lips. Her hand splayed around my neck, the kiss long and lazy and languorous. When I broke it to look down at her, she smiled up at me.

And laughed.

I watched her with one brow arched, amused. "Not exactly the reaction I was hoping for, Jo."

"I'm sorry." She cupped my jaw, testing the feel of my stubble against her palm. "I just … I have seen so much of you naked."

"Complaints?"

"No, just wondering how we ended up here." She still had an entertained, admiring look on her face.

"I think it had something to do with me in Wranglers."

She tipped her head back and laughed. "That didn't help."

I kept on smiling down at her. "What are you doing today?"

"No, what are you doing today?"

"No plans."

"No farms to finagle into submission?"

"Nah. I'm too busy finagling something else into submission." My hand, which was still near her breast, cupped it to demonstrate.

"I have your next torture lined up."

"Oh?"

"We're going to make honey."

"Sounds sticky."

"Sometimes, but not generally, if you do it right."

"Which you're hoping I don't."

"Listen, a girl's gotta have goals. I'm going to find something you suck magnificently at, and it's going to be the best day of my life."

"Good luck with that."

"So are you in?"

"Can't back down from a challenge."

"I mean, you could …"

I gave her a look.

"But you'd catch all hell for it."

"Because you can't back down either."

"It's not in my nature. What time is it?" she asked, looking in the direction of the nightstand.

"Near seven."

"I should go."

I reveled in the disappointment in her voice.

"You could stay."

"If I thought I could walk after what staying would mean, I'd take you up on that."

I chuckled.

"They're going to know I didn't come home, and the longer I wait to get back, the worse the heckling."

"What are you going to tell them?"

"The truth. Why would I tell them anything else?" She was genuinely confused by the question.

"Because you're sleeping with the enemy."

"They already told me to." At what must have been surprise on my face, she clarified, "Daisy and Presley did, at least. Poppy remains firmly in the no column, but she won't start any fires or anything. Probably."

"But why did they tell you to?"

"Have you looked in a mirror recently? That's reason number one. Also, there's no chance of you getting the farm, and they had the same take on things as you—you're leaving, thus making you even more safe. Daisy also said I needed to get laid, so there's that."

"Well, I'm eager to help."

"Help? I just saw more action in one night than I have in … well, never mind in how long. You broke the record."

"You're welcome."

With another laugh, she rose enough to kiss me briefly, then shifted. I moved out of the way so she could get out of bed.

"What time should I come over?" I propped up some pillows and

for love or honey

sat back, watching as she pulled on her dress and buttoned it up.

"I've got chores and need to get everything set up in the kitchen. And gossip about your dick with my sisters."

I flinched, compressing my smile. "Naturally."

She straightened up, sobering. "Shit. My truck is still at town hall."

"Can I give you a ride?"

She sighed, buttoning the last button. "It's not that far. I can walk."

"Walk of shame in Lindenbach? It'll end up in the papers."

"Oh, everybody already knows by now my truck was there when I wasn't. And likely that we left at the same time." Boots in hand, she sat at the end of the bed to put them on.

I moved until I was close enough to kiss the smooth skin between her shoulder blades, resisting the temptation to slide the strap over her shoulder. "You sure we don't need some sort of cover story?"

"I'm sure. No point in hiding it, although I would like to be home before church starts. I don't love the thought of being discussed during Bible study."

I swept her hair out of the way to kiss the curve of her neck. "Are you afraid of anything?"

She leaned back a little until she was resting against my chest. "Not generally. Are you?"

Only this. "Not generally."

"Didn't think so." She turned her face to kiss my cheek, then hauled herself up. "So I'll see you in a few hours?"

"I'll text when I'm on my way."

"Good," she said with a sealed, happy smile before sweeping toward me for a brief, tender kiss. "Unlock your car so I can get my things?"

"Keys are right there." I jerked my chin toward the table, and she unlocked the car with the fob. "Sure I can't give you a ride?"

"I'm sure. It's too pretty not to enjoy the day for a minute before I get home and answer a thousand questions about how the devil got me into bed."

A chuckle. "Come here."

She did, still wearing that smile. I angled for her lips, and she leaned over to meet them. Her mouth opened, her tongue sweeping my lips, and when the kiss deepened, I pulled her into my lap with a yelp and a giggle and a long, hot kiss. When she leaned back and looked into my eyes, she held my face in her palm.

"I'm going," she said firmly, but everything about her was happy. With a final peck, she slid off my lap and headed for the door, her skirt swaying as she went. "See you in a bit."

"You will."

With a final smile over her shoulder, she was gone.

For a minute, I leaned back, my gaze focused on nothing as I replayed what had happened and how stupid it'd made me. Not in that I'd made a poor decision, only that she'd reduced me to a swooning imbecile.

I didn't know that I'd ever swooned. If I had, it'd been nothing like this.

I realized that over the last few days, my plan had shifted into a tactic I'd never employed—honesty. It was the only way to Jo and the rest of this town, who were so different than anywhere I'd been before. It was the people themselves that set Lindenbach apart—they were a family, tightly knit and fiercely protective, even when they disagreed. What they valued had to do with the whole, not the individual, and the truth was the only way in.

Only the truth needed a slant to make it through their armor.

What I didn't expect was to enjoy that honesty so much. I'd lived my life in a world of double talk and deception, where nothing was taken at face value. Here, everyone said what they meant and what they wanted. I didn't think I could make it five feet into the Blum's house without hearing about someone's feelings. And that left me feeling refreshed, comforted.

I could be myself, even if I wasn't exactly sure who that was anymore.

Either way, I still needed to do my job. And if there was any chance at flipping the Blums, it would need to be done incrementally, seed by seed.

I flipped off the sheets and climbed out of bed, pulling on sleep pants before padding into the kitchen to make coffee. I was filling the pot at the sink when I heard the screen door open and close.

Instantly, I was smiling again. "Forget something?"

A deep, dark voice answered, "No, don't think I did."

My chest locked at the sound, my throat clamping shut as I turned to find my father standing just inside the door, looking around the house with thinly veiled disdain.

He was one of the few people who met me at eye level, his tidy hair more salt than pepper, his eyes sharp and icy when they met mine.

"Look at you, slumming it," he said.

"This was the only place in town—"

"I'm not talking about the house."

My temperature spiked. Don't blow it. Let him run his mouth.

Again he looked around, striding like a jungle cat toward the musty old couch in front of the tube television. He flicked the doily on it. "Although the place does have its own … charm."

I went back to making coffee, with my senses on alert, awakened by his presence. "What are you doing here?"

"What do you think I'm doing here?"

"Not sure. I didn't ask for your help."

"I didn't come for you."

I drew a breath to steady me, but it did no good. "I don't get the hurry. I've almost sealed the deal on the second farm, and the Blum contract is coming."

"Looks like the youngest girl is coming too."

I gripped the handle of the pot so tight, it squeaked against my palm. When I didn't answer right away, too intent on managing my instinct to hit him, he continued.

"I'm here because I got a call from the top. I'm not taking the flak if you fail, so I'm here to back you up."

"You're here to help? That's a new one."

"I'm here to get this done so we can both go home. I didn't know you'd fucked your way into the young one's good graces."

Don't hit him. Lie. Get him out of here. "By any means necessary, right?"

"Whatever it takes. But that will help us lock down the deal. What's your next move?"

"Earn her trust, show her how signing will help her. Convince her we're not so bad."

"So to lie to her."

I turned the pot on and faced him, leaning back on the counter. "Just giving her the company line. Was there something else you'd suggest?"

He glanced at my boots lying haphazardly on the floor. "Looks like you've gone all in. You've even got a red neck."

"And a Stetson in the car."

A single laugh through his nose. "That I'd like to see."

"Stick around, and you will."

"I'm not leaving the state until you close the deal, so I'll have something to look forward to. That farm has the biggest shale deposit of the six. If you don't secure it, that's on me. So I'm here as … let's call it insurance."

"And what's your plan?"

His smile was a knife slash. "Depends on how you do over the next week."

"Can't help you if you don't tell me."

"Unlike you, I don't need help." He turned for the door. "I have business in Austin and San Antonio while I'm in town, so don't fuck anything up when I'm not here. I'll expect you in Austin for dinner tonight at my hotel. There's nothing to eat in this shithole town but diner food and enchiladas."

"Can't. I have plans." Which I didn't, exactly. But I planned to.

"Cancel them."

"I can't—"

He whipped around and pinned me with a look, the same look I'd learned from him. "You will. Plan to be in Austin by eight. I'll text you the place."

My jaw clenched so tight, the muscles ached. I couldn't speak without telling him to fuck off, so I nodded.

"Good," was all he said, leaving me with nothing but rage and a bitter taste in my mouth.

The coffee pot sputtered and wheezed as I stormed to the bathroom and turned on the shower, dropping my pants and stepping in before it was hot—a blessing in disguise. I was mad as all hell and needed to cool off.

I was building a house of cards, and he was a gust of hot wind.

Which meant I needed a new plan. Or maybe just a new timeline.

Plans were in motion for the farms in my docket, but the Blums would be the last and hardest, even knowing I'd earned some level of trust from Jo. I had to work fast and smart. Because I didn't know what my father would do, but I knew it wouldn't bode well for the Blums or me.

And all I could do was put myself between them and hope it was enough.

SHOWER WARS

Jo

Grant's massive hand covered the bottom half of my face to keep me quiet as he fucked me slow and easy on a counter in the cannery.

The honey spinner was loud, but for a second, I'd been louder. The last thing either of us needed was for somebody to hear me and come inquiring after the sound.

I'd worn a sundress again in the hopes that this would be a part of our day, even though I was still aching from the long, long night we'd spent together. I found his presence inspired an entirely different ache that was far more needy.

This morning, I'd walked to my truck with my cheeks high and sore from smiling, having fully embraced the art of not overthinking it. Drove home with my windows down and my hair in a sloppy bun on my head, belting "Saddle Tramp" by Marty Robbins, an old honky tonk song that spoke of a man who wandered from town to town on horseback—much like Grant—but its title felt more like my physical condition.

The number of orgasms I'd had in a single night confused and elated me, though he'd had to work for the last few. Never had I witnessed a man with such stamina, and though I knew he was a scientific anomaly, I couldn't help but feel proud of myself. As if it were my irritability that had conjured the boner to rule all boners and not some freakish genetic condition or maybe a fortuitous malfunction of some crucial hormone-producing organ.

Either way, I'd made it home floating like a balloon to find my sisters waiting for me in the kitchen to whisper-hiss at me, demanding an explanation. Shifty-eyed and on the lookout for Mama, I'd shooed them outside and followed, the three of us going about our chores while I regaled the tale of the evening, the morning, and our plans. Daisy had grinned, all teeth and bright eyes. Poppy only scowled.

When we came in, Mama had gone to town, and I rushed to shower and change before Grant got here. I wondered if he'd show up in a suit and wished for it in the hopes that the sight would put a stop to what was clearly a deep infatuation with him—or at least his dick—but I had no such luck. He'd climbed out of that tiny sports car in those fucking jeans and boots, and pop! went my ovaries.

It was my own damn fault that he even owned them, thanks to what could only be called the backfire of the century.

My suspicions had quieted about him, but they'd been fewer and farther between for some time. I just hadn't been able to admit it to myself. He'd been vulnerable, honest, and I could see how foreign it was on him. He could lie without trouble, but the truth? That meant exposing his soft underbelly. That meant being real, and I got the sense that he generally avoided letting anyone that close.

I understood that well enough. Neither did I. So I guessed it was a bigger deal for both of us than we'd likely admit out loud.

That didn't change the fact that he had a job to do or that I was a part of that job. But it sure did make it a lot more pleasant to bear.

for love or honey

We'd driven out to the bees, heading to the next hive set to harvest with him all suited up and me collecting honeycombs, this time with smoke so I could easily part the bees from their bounty. This was the time of year we harvested our last until spring, and was easier to handle in stages than all at once. We'd brought them back and stored all but the nine I put into the spinner. With those nine, I showed him how to uncap the honeycombs using a comb meant for this purpose, carefully separating the wax cap from the cells teeming with honey. And into the spinner they went, a centerfuge machine that whipped all of the honey out without disturbing the honeycomb's shape.

And I discovered Grant's preferred method of killing time while we waited.

The counter thumped as he slammed into me, his hand still over my mouth. My lips parted, my tongue tracing a slow line on his palm that sent a shuddering groan through him. His other hand tightened its grip on my thigh, pulling me into him so he could get deeper. But the sound of his pleasure sparked the rising flame of mine, and with a well-placed thrust, I came, my nose puffing noisy breath and my cries muffled by his palm. And he was right behind me, his head bowed and body arching over mine.

Only then did his hand fall from my lips so he could capture them with his. Both arms wrapped around me and squeezed, the kiss bruising.

That kiss didn't end until the spinner stopped, and with secret smiles on our faces, we set ourselves to rights.

"Wash your hands," I said with a laugh, pushing him in the direction of the sink. "We've already violated the health code once today."

"Worth the fine."

"I'll send you the bill if we get busted."

Side by side at a big stainless sink, we washed our hands.

"What are you doing tonight?" I asked, hoping I didn't sound clingy.

Something in him closed when he answered, "I have a dinner thing." But he brightened back up when he shot me a smirk. "Call you after?"

"All right."

"Might be late."

"I can wait."

He leaned over and kissed my temple, but that uneasy feeling didn't quite go away.

"So what kind of dinner thing?"

"Just a work meeting, nothing big. But it's in Austin. Don't wait up if it's too late, okay?"

"Don't tell me what to do." I bumped him with my hip.

He was quiet for a second while we dried our hands. "Are you sure you're okay with people knowing about us?"

I frowned at him. "Your continued questioning is starting to make me wonder if it's you who doesn't want people to know about us."

"I don't mind at all, but my feelings about it don't matter."

"Sure they do. Why wouldn't they?"

"Because I don't live here. These aren't my people—they're yours."

I considered that as we moved over to the spinner, where I worked on setting up a bucket and strainer beneath the tap.

"I know how the rumor mill here works—hell, we practically power the thing. People are already talking about us, and they have been since you came with me to Wyatt's to save those bees. They think we've been hittin' it all this time. Why bother trying to hide it? The most vicious rumors are the ones that are assumed. By tomorrow morning, the whole town will know, thus absolving me."

"Interesting logic."

"They'll still embellish, but I've learned time and again that there's no way to keep a secret in this town. Every human in the city limits knows Blums don't date, so I figure they'll either blab about me breaking the code or they'll call me a whore."

"And you don't mind being called a whore?"

"Not when it comes out of the mouths of assholes like Marjorie Flint and her toadies, all high and mighty, toting her Bible around to whack people with. And she's one to talk—she cheated on her husband with his brother, divorced her husband, married the brother. But I'll guarantee she's already calling me a whore to any ear she can get ahold of."

"She sounds like a delight."

"The jewel of Lindenbach, revered by all. Anyway, unless you have some reason to be sneaky, I'm not so worried about it that I'm willing to work to keep it a secret."

"I was more worried about you than myself."

I clutched my hands to my chest. "My hero."

With a chuckle, he slapped my ass and turned to the spinner. "Let me guess—turn the tap and filter the honey?"

"You're a natural." I did just that while explaining. "There's plenty of wax still in the honey from uncapping the honeycomb, so it'll run through this sieve, which will get the big stuff out. Then we'll seal it for a couple days to let it settle, and when it's finished, we just skim any wax off the top and bottle the rest."

"So we're going to sit here for two days while it settles? Whatever will we do with all that time?" He grabbed me around the waist, and I giggled. He actually had me giggling.

"I've got some settled containers up at the house, Romeo. We can bottle there."

"Damn." He laid a hot little kiss on me before letting me go. "Lead on."

So I did. We hopped in a golf cart and zipped to the house. It was a windy day—my hair was getting whipped around even at the whopping ten miles an hour we were cruising at—and I could smell change in the air. Maybe we'd get a cool front or maybe it'd rain. Or maybe it was some bigger intuition. Maybe it was Grant, who smiled at me and tucked a wild strand of hair behind my ear only for it to fly loose again.

Maybe it was a good change coming.

Or maybe it was another sort of storm altogether.

When we stopped at the back of the house, he climbed out. "Come with me somewhere. Next week, Wednesday."

"You assume I don't have plans."

"Do you?"

"No, but that's not the point."

A chuckle. "Come with me after your chores that day."

"Where?" I asked.

"It's a secret."

for love or honey

My eyes narrowed at him as I opened the kitchen door. "Suspicious."

"What, a guy can't surprise the girl he's fucking?"

Snickering had our heads snapping in the direction of my sisters, who'd been leaning against the big island.

"What are you gonna surprise her with?" Daisy asked with mock innocence.

"That monstrous pipe you're packing?" Poppy guessed.

And Grant smirked. "Nah, that one hasn't surprised her in at least twenty minutes."

Daisy almost choked on the drink she'd sipped, which had proved to be a grievous error. She pinched her nose. "Jesus, that burns."

"You earned that, Daisy Mae," I said. "Now scram so we can bottle."

Daisy shook her glass so the ice rattled. "Mama said no drinks in the living room." She took a seat on a barstool.

"Then don't go in the living room," I suggested.

"She said no eating in there either." Poppy sat next to Daisy with a bowl of popcorn between them and a couple of terrible smiles on their faces.

"God, you three look alike," Grant noted.

At the same time, the three of us said, "I'm the pretty one," and busted out laughing.

It was true. We had identical black hair and sharp blue eyes and pouty lips. When she was little, Presley was convinced that Elvis was our grandpa even though it was mathematically impossible. But with the way we looked and the fact that we could all sing, I could see the reach.

But there were differences too. All of us had long hair—more out of laziness than credo—but Daisy had thick bangs and a heart-shaped face. Poppy rarely wore her hair down, had a smattering of freckles across the bridge of her nose, and sported a subtle cleft chin, courtesy of Mama's genetics.

I gave them both the hairy eyeball.

They laughed.

"We don't have to do this part if you don't want to," I said to Grant.

"Why? Worried they're going to spill your secrets?"

"Oh, I know they will."

"Then we should definitely stay."

"I like him," Daisy said with her mouth full of popcorn. "When he's not selling something, at least."

Poppy leaned to look around the island. "The jeans lived up to the hype too."

I rolled my eyes so hard, I was lucky they didn't detach from my optic nerves. But I otherwise ignored my sisters with the practiced patience that only the youngest sibling can muster.

I picked up a jar and handed it to Grant before getting one of my own. "This is the easy part. Just fill 'er up."

He filled his first, holding it up to the light when it was full. "You don't do anything to it? Like, sterilize it?"

"The jars are sterilized, but the honey doesn't need it. Honey is too acidic for bacteria to grow, so no raw honey is pasteurized."

"Huh." He screwed a lid on and fixed a label to the front. "Like this?"

for love or honey

"Just like that."

"All right." He looked to my sisters. "Spill it."

The three of them were smiling so evilly, I wanted to fling a handful of honey at each of them, splat, splat, splat. Grant's curiosity was warranted, but I gave Poppy and Daisy warning looks.

"Don't be scared," Daisy said sweetly, which was her whole cover. Everybody thought she was such a peach. But "everybody" didn't have to endure her torment.

"You're an asshole," I answered.

"Have you always gotten along this well?" Grant asked.

"You should have seen us as kids," Poppy said, tossing a few pieces of popcorn in her mouth. "Like the shower wars."

Daisy and I groaned.

"Shower wars?" He screwed the lid on another jar.

"I don't even know how it started," Poppy said.

"I squirted the last of the shampoo into the shower so I could make bubbles," I reminded her.

"Oh my god, yes—Daisy's good stuff, the all-natural crap from the mall."

"Mama said it was expensive," Daisy defended. "I didn't want to get in trouble."

"That gene apparently skipped me," I noted.

"So Jo got in trouble, and Mama got us each our own shower stuff in a little caddy with our names on it so we wouldn't use each other's stuff. Except that Jo kept taking ours and dumping it out."

"It smelled better than mine."

Daisy rolled her eyes. "Poppy got so mad, she took Jo's shampoo, put it in a Coke bottle, and stuck the pump nozzle in the neck of it."

"And then Jo got so mad, she emptied Poppy's entire shaving cream onto the wall and wrote Poppy sucks in it."

"I got my mouth washed out for that one," I said.

"It went on like that for years. There was other stuff too," Poppy continued. "Like nobody will own up to wetting wads of toilet paper and sticking them to the ceiling."

"Because it was you," Daisy noted.

"Was not. And anyway, what about Daisy's hairballs?"

I made a gagging noise. "She'd stick her hair all over the wall, and when you showered, they'd wave in the breeze like spider legs. When she got in trouble for it, she just balled it up instead and left it in our soap dishes."

"I swear one time I thought it was a goddamn rat," Poppy said with a shudder.

"Ew, what about the vacuum cleaner and the—"

"Hello?" Mama said, struggling to get in the door with her arms full of groceries.

We moved in unison to help, but Grant got to her first.

"Let me help you with that, Mrs. Blum," he said.

Mama's smiling face was redder than an apple as she handed them over. "Well, hello there, Mr. Stone."

"Please, call me Grant." He moved to the counter next to the refrigerator to set down his haul. "Are the rest in your truck?"

for love or honey

"Sure are, in the back seat."

He nodded, gave me the most discreet wink, and headed outside.

"So it's true," Mama whispered, rushing me.

"How did you know?"

She waved a hand. "Oh, don't look so surprised, Iris Jo. Marjorie saw you walkin' to your truck this morning with your hair all ratted, wearing your clothes from last night. You know the first thing she did was call the phone tree."

I realized then that maybe I did give an eensy-weensy shit about my reputation and wished I'd been more careful.

"So did he say he didn't want the farm anymore?" she asked.

"No."

She blinked. "Then why in the world would you spend the night with him?"

"Do you think I'd believe him if he said he was giving up on the farm?"

"I suppose not, but that doesn't answer my question."

"I don't know, Mama," I huffed, unable to find the words myself. "We … well, I think we became friends somewhere along the line, and last night, he made some good points. He's leaving. I don't want anything serious." I paused. "Okay, when I say it out loud, it does sound stupid. But I swear, I've got it under control. In fact, maybe I can convince him to quit working for people who are going to put polar bears in the obituaries. Or at least question his morals."

She gave me a look. "Honey, he really does look good in those jeans, but you are smarter than this."

"I'd never get serious with a guy like him, Mama. Just trust me—"

The door opened, and in he walked with his arms full. The four of us met him in the middle of the kitchen to help him, but I hung back so they were occupied.

"Let me help you with the rest," I offered.

Grant's eyes shifted to my wary family, then back to me. "Sure."

When the door was closed behind me, I let out a mighty sigh.

"That bad?" he asked.

"It's just going to take some explaining. We hadn't told Mama this morning. Figures she'd hear about it at the grocery store."

When we reached the truck, he stopped on the inside of the open door and pulled me into him.

"She doesn't trust me."

"Should she?"

"You do."

"Against my better judgment, I do. A little."

"Then I'll convince them, too."

"Think you're up to the challenge?" I asked.

And with smiling lips close to mine, he answered, "I was born for it."

HERE, KITTY, KITTY

Grant

Jo sang along to the radio from my passenger seat, the windows down and her hair flying as we made our way into town a week later.

And what a week it'd been.

When I wasn't with Jo, I was running around town, working on deals with the farms on my docket, besides the Blums, but I'd made no ground with any of them. One of the farm owners was in bad health and had recently been admitted into the hospital. His son was circling like a vulture, even going so far as to reach out to me for dinner to probe me for numbers, should his father die. A few weeks ago, I would have only seen it as good fortune. But thanks to a newly found conscience, the exchange left me feeling unclean. I sent a Texas-sized gift basket to the hospital and hoped the son wouldn't get any of the Moose Munch.

I'd been summoned to Austin a couple times by my father, but I hadn't seen him in Lindenbach since the day he arrived, which was almost worse. I'd spent an inordinate amount of time wondering what he was going to pull and how it would hurt, so much that it bordered on paranoia. But I kept telling myself it was a good thing. Maybe he'd left me to my own devices as a sign of faith. Maybe he'd let me do my thing, his appearance strictly an act of observance.

I only wished I didn't know better. And that I'd made more progress.

But every night, Jo was in my bed. Every day, she was in my thoughts. I'd begun to gently plant those seeds regarding her rights, though thus far, we'd never made it past joking. In fact, it'd become the joke, since it took a dangerous thing between us and made it small. Better than ignoring it, I figured, assuming she felt the same.

We were on our way to an event downtown for Glow Up, Lindenbach. The Blum sisters had launched a whole campaign, were in the process of planning a fundraiser dinner, had shirts and signs and bumper stickers printed up, and had gotten together with one of the local construction companies to start revamping Main Street. The money wasn't there yet, but it was imminent, and today was the first collection.

Donations would be accepted while the town got together to start unboarding shop windows and cleaning them up. The Blums had come up with displays for all the windows that marketed to new businesses. We'd be pulling down signs and sweeping out spaces. Cleaning windows and setting up displays. Poppy was working on sourcing local businesses in the nearby metro areas to open up shop in Lindenbach.

The swiftness and efficacy with which the town had mobilized was astounding. Just like everything else here.

When we pulled into a spot near the park at the end of Main Street, the sidewalk was full of people in work clothes heading into town. A pack of guys near Jo's age spotted us, leaning in and whacking each other on the arms. One of the guys seemed to have been nominated to approach and sauntered over, leaning into her window.

"Heya, Jo."

"Hey, Chris," she said politely—and with as much disinterest that she could manage—while she gathered her things.

"Haven't seen you around much."

"When do you ever see me?"

"Aw, come on. I've been trying to see you since freshman year."

"Are you for real?" I shot.

He acknowledged me with the jerk of his chin. "Nice car. But it takes more than that to hook a Blum girl."

"Are you drunk?" she asked.

"Why, want a sip?" He reached into his pocket for a flask.

"It's nine in the morning," she noted.

He shrugged, then tipped it back.

"And I'm sleeping with Grant."

He ducked when his drink shot out of his mouth, which was lucky for him. I'd have put him in traction if he'd spit bourbon all over Jo and the interior of my car.

Chris stood and wiped his mouth with the back of the hand. "Jesus, Jo. Marjorie said you were whoring around, but I didn't think you'd show it off."

I'd unbuckled my seat belt and was half out of the car when she opened hers hard enough to knock him over, in part because he was trashed and in part because she was out for blood.

"Oops," she said, slamming the car door behind her. But she bent over him as he sluggishly tried to rise and said, "Watch your fucking mouth, or next time I'll let Grant at you. You don't want that, do you?"

He shook his head stupidly, shooting me a dirty look. I'd have laughed if I wasn't doing everything I could to keep myself from separating his limbs from his torso.

She patted his cheek hard enough that it was more like a series of curt slaps. "Good boy."

And then she was smiling her way over to me and tucked in my side.

"You just saved his life, do you know that?" I asked.

"I do. Although I can take care of myself, you know."

"Doesn't mean I don't want to take care of things for you."

"Look at you, Mr. White Knight."

We walked for a second in silence. "Does it bother you? What he said? What people are saying?"

"You'd think it would, but not really. Thing is, I don't have boyfriends—I date. They've called me a whore since junior high."

"And that's something someone can get used to?"

"Not used to, more like I know they're all assholes, so what do I care what they think? I'm not running around sleeping with strangers I never see again. I just don't do commitment, so guys like Chris weaponize it when they realize I don't want to date them. Until they figure that out, they think they can score. Then they get told no, and suddenly I'm a whore. It's a bullshit double standard, and I don't have time for bullshit. Anyway, I told Chris ten years ago, and he's been ignoring that no ever since."

"How many men in this town have tried to date a Blum?"

"All of them. Age aside. At one point, Daisy even had a DILF after her so hard, I'm surprised he didn't just up and propose."

"Too much gray hair?"

"Psh. Listen, I've got no qualms with a silver fox, and the daddy jokes were endless, but he used to date my mother in high school."

I gagged, laughing.

"Billy and Bobby buzz around my sisters like flies, but they won't pick one. Both of them are going after both my sisters at the same time. Dummies. A dozen more are actively trying to get in our pants, which is astounding since we haven't said yes to anybody in town in forever, but it has its perks. A Blum woman hasn't had to open a door for herself in at least a decade."

"So the curse doesn't stop everybody."

"Oh, they think they're immune. The smart ones stay away."

"You callin' me stupid?"

"Nah, you're smart enough to know to leave."

"Love 'em and leave 'em. Is that our motto?"

"Guess so. You don't have all the girls waiting for you back home?"

"I don't date either, but I don't have a curse to blame."

"Then what is to blame?"

"Never wanted to. Maybe I've avoided it on purpose. It's easier when there's no expectation, isn't it?"

"It is." We were quiet a second before she said, "Sorry Chris spit on your car."

"He's lucky he didn't spit on you, or his teeth would be in his esophagus."

"Well, I wash off, but if he'd gotten it in the car? What would

STACI HART

you even do? Just throw it away and buy a new one?"

"Hey, you could dive around in a vault full of doubloons too if you'd sign."

"Can't I just dive in yours?"

"Sure, but it hurts less if it's your own. Doubloons aren't easy to swim in. I've tried."

"Shame I'll never know."

"It is. Do you know the secret to being rich?"

"I'm afraid to ask," she said.

"Middle class makes money to spend and save. Rich people make money to invest."

"It's that easy?" she joked.

"I don't live on what I make. I live on dividends of what I've invested. Just think—if you had the money, you could make it work for you, then you'd never have to work again."

"And what if I enjoy working?"

"So do I—my job is my whole life, same as yours. Doesn't mean you have to stop. You just do it because you want to."

"I'm not signing your papers," she said in a sing-song voice.

"I'm keeping my pen warm all the same." When she didn't respond, I added, "I just like seeing you taken care of, that's all."

"Well, I do just fine with that on my own, but thank you for your concern." She smiled up at me, her face tilting for a kiss that I granted.

And that was that.

for love or honey

For now.

***

The town was out in earnest that day, and by the afternoon, we'd tackled nearly every façade on the street. At the moment, we were outside what was once a five-and-dime. A twenty-foot ladder was propped against the roof where we'd just lowered the worn sign, and inside the window, the Blums and Presley were putting the finishing touches on the window treatment, which was in both of the big display windows on either side of the door. Inside, Presley's toddler daughter, Priscilla, was chasing a collarless kitten that I didn't think anyone had noticed lurking around the back of the store.

Wyatt and Sebastian had hauled the sign off to one of the dumpsters, and I took a seat on the tailgate of the Blum's truck with a water bottle, observing the town. Music played from a setup near the park just a few shops down, and as people finished their work, they'd begun to mill around, chatting. Poppy had a concession stand with pretzels and popcorn and cotton candy for the kids, and a few of the local teens had been hired to watch people's children so they could help out.

Though the town had been in some upheaval of late, you'd never know it on a day like today. Everyone was helping everyone, the common cause bringing them together, if only for a day. And I wondered over them as I was like to do, this little town that made such a big impression.

They seemed interested enough in me too, making it a point to walk by and nod their hellos or come and catch up with the Blums, watching me out of the corner of their eyes with bald curiosity. Maybe they hadn't expected me to show up, or maybe they hadn't expected me to work. Maybe they hadn't expected the jeans, though that seemed unlikely—the whole town had heard about those. A few people did take it upon themselves to speak with me, asking about Salma and prying gently for information about the farms I was here to acquire to see who'd sold. But with each other, they were all hugs and smiles and how's your son and how's your grandmother.

It was the kind of place I'd dreamed of as a kid. The kind of place where you'd ride your bike until the streetlights came on and everybody knew your name and pedigree. Where the same doctor that delivered you would deliver your children. Where lifelong traditions made up the fabric of every life.

I was watching a couple of kids chase each other in figure eights around a cluster of adults when I heard a little voice say, "Here, kitty. Come here!", except all the Rs sounded like Ws.

Frowning, I looked in the direction of the store to see Priscilla clearing the top of the ladder and heading up the steep pitch of the roof.

I was on my feet and to the ladder in a heartbeat. "Hey, Priscilla," I said gently, my pulse hard enough to nearly choke me. "Hang on, kiddo."

She ignored me like a seasoned professional, climbing a little higher on all fours as the cat sauntered on in front of her like it figured the child had as many lives as it did.

"Oh my god," someone said from the direction of the park. A gasp from below, more exclamations. I kept going.

"Priscilla Marie!" Presley said from the foot of the ladder, her voice shaking.

At that, the little girl stopped and stood to look back, not realizing how high up she was. Her little face opened wider in fear, and in her hesitation, her foot slipped. A small scream came from above, many from below. The music had stopped.

"Hey," I said as I reached the top, trying to keep my cool, smile on my face. "This is pretty high up. Can I help you down?"

Torn, she looked back in the direction of the cat, who had taken a seat on the peak of the roof to watch us blandly. "Kitty ran up the tree, and I can play with her."

I climbed onto the roof, careful of my footing, almost close enough to grab her. "I think kitty might be done playing for today. Can you come here? I'll help you down to your mama."

She glanced down at her mother, who looked scared shitless, pale as a sheet and hands over her mouth. Sebastian came running up with half the town.

"Hi, Mama!" she said, waving. "I'm okay."

"Come down with the nice man, baby," Presley called up.

"Can I have a pokkacicle?" she asked.

A nervous roll of laughter. "Sure. You can have as many popsicles as you want. Just let him bring you down, okay?"

The little girl with ebony hair eyed me for a second. "You has candy?"

"No, but there's a cotton candy machine over there."

"So I can has pokkacicles and cotton candy? But no kitty."

I could have grabbed her, but I didn't want to scare her into thrashing and send both of us over the roof. "Yup, no kitty."

She sighed, looking back at the cat. "Bye, kitty." And then she held her arms open in the universal sign for Up, please.

I hitched her to my hip, and the crowd below collectively sighed. Carefully, I found my way onto the ladder, then down as Sebastian held it steady. When I was close enough, I handed her over, and her parents converged over her, scolding her gently, smoothing her hair, and making in the direction of the concessions.

My knees were weak when my boots hit the ground, and when I turned, I hoped to find Jo there. Instead, I found myself in a knot of townspeople and a quiet chorus of clapping.

Surprised stupid, I accepted handshakes and well wishes and hands to chests and thank the Lords. Someone put a can of Miller Lite in my hand, others clapped my back. And then Jo was smiling at my side, interjecting to thank them for their thank yous for some reason, before leading me toward the park.

"You okay?" she asked after a second, smiling.

"Yeah, I just didn't expect all that."

"People thanking you?"

"Or to climb a two-story building chasing a small child."

"Well, Cilla gets herself into all kinds of trouble, so I don't think anyone was surprised. Scared to death, but not surprised. She'll be drunk on popsicles in the hour. Honestly, that might have been her plan all along."

I couldn't help but laugh. "Is she scared of anything?"

"Not a damn thing, and it might kill her mama and daddy."

We were interrupted by a few more people before walking on again.

"You've made quite the impression," she said. "I haven't seen Jemima Jenkins smile at anyone but Priscilla and now you in twenty years."

"Good to know I still got it."

"You didn't even realize what you were doing, did you? You moved up that ladder like a cat yourself."

"I didn't think about it. Jesus, that scared the shit out of me. And that cat watched on like it was plotting to kill us both."

"There's no telling what she did to the poor cat before it made it to the roof. She's been known to love things a little too much."

for love or honey

I must have had a disturbed look on my face because she laughed.

"She doesn't pull heads off mice or anything, just gives insistent hugs."

"Me and her both." I pulled Jo into my chest, smothering her in my chest as she laughed and wriggled, swatting at me. When my grip eased, she lifted her face to mine, and it was the color of joy.

So I kissed her, hoping a little bit of it would rub off on me.

I didn't want to lose the feeling.

DINNER WITH THE DEVIL

Jo

A couple of days later, my sisters, Grant, and I were chopping vegetables for fricassee in my family kitchen. Mama had run to Mariel's to pick up a couple important things we'd forgotten, like ice cream.

The sun hung low on the horizon, the days getting shorter as time marched toward October with the unrelenting pace it favored, sweeping us along with it.

It'd been nearly three weeks ago that I'd first seen Grant standing at that podium in a black suit and an intensity that'd hit me like a brick wall from thirty feet. And somehow, the man next to me was that same person. His hair was a little longer, his jaw dusted with stubble since he only shaved every few days. I'd gifted him my favorite baseball cap—a blue Ranger's cap that was the color of his eyes—simply because it looked too good on him. No point in keeping it to myself when I could admire him in it instead. Daddy had gotten it for me at a ball game when I was little, saying I'd grow into it. But I'd worn that cap ragged the bill all frayed on the edges and the blue faded from time. I didn't mind seeing it go, not when I had a dozen other hats, most that were my father's and all that I'd be keeping for myself.

And then there were those jeans and boots, already worn in since they were the only pair he had. Somehow he'd turned into a guy who wore the same pair of jeans every day rather than the sort who wore a pair of khakis once before he probably just threw them away for a new pair.

The same guy who, after rescuing Priscilla from the roof of the old five-and-dime, had been the recipient of half a dozen pies, a couple of casseroles, and a pile of cookies taller than me. The whole town had known his name for weeks, but now they spoke it with a smiling pride I never thought I'd hear in conjunction with those two strong syllables that made up his name.

"Did Melba make you her snickerdoodles?" Poppy asked, nodding to the mass of sweets he'd brought over.

"Which one is Melba again?"

"She's the one who dyed her hair pink so nobody'd call her a blue-hair," I answered.

He chuckled, his eyes on his hands as he chopped a carrot, click, click, click. "That's right. I don't think I've ever had a cookie so soft. Thing fell apart in my hands."

Poppy dropped her knife and was off to dig around in the mish-mash of cookies. "I live my life for those cookies."

Daisy chuckled. "We call them crack cookies around here."

"Oh my god, there are brownies in here," Poppy breathed.

"Good thing Mama's bringing Bluebell," I said.

"She's bringing back flowers?" Grant asked. "What's that have to do with brownies?"

The three of us stopped and stared at him.

"The ice cream? Bluebell?" I half asked.

"Oh, I think I've heard of that."

"You're about to have your mind blown, Mr. Stone," Poppy said, shaking her head as she popped the rest of her cookie in her mouth and started up with the celery again.

"This has become a regular thing when I'm around Blums."

I smiled up at him from his side, and smiling back, he leaned in for a quick little kiss.

"Ugh, you guys are gross," Poppy noted, pointing the tip of her knife at him from the other side of the island. "If you weren't leaving, I'd never let you near my sister."

My heart squeezed at the reminder that he was temporary. I kept forgetting. He'd fit himself into my life a little too perfectly, a little too comfortably. And I was liking the thought of him leaving less and less by the day.

It's for the best.

I wondered if I said it to myself enough times, I'd believe it.

"Oh, leave him alone," Daisy said. "For the record, Grant, I was on your side from the beginning."

"Because she's a sucker," I noted.

She gave me a look. "I'm a sucker? What about—" Daisy's face changed into something unreadable when the door opened behind us.

Frowning, I turned to find Mama making her way in.

With a man behind her.

A man in a suit who looked an awful lot like Grant. I looked to the latter for confirmation, and on finding his face as dark and dangerous as it had been the day I threw an egg at him, I knew.

for love or honey

Mama was all smiles as she walked into the kitchen to set down her haul, talking. "Look at who I ran into. Y'all, this is Grant's dad! He just got to town, had his cart half full, found me picking up boxes of Rice-A-Roni I'd knocked over in aisle four like a klutz."

"Merrick Stone," he said with a smile I didn't trust. "Pleasure to meet you. Hello, son."

Grant's expression didn't change. He muttered hello and got back to chopping, his eyes shielded by the brim of his cap.

The power shift was unnerving. Grant had the gravity of a star, holding everything around him in orbit by sheer force. But his father was a world eater, a black hole capable of consuming a star whole without even making a dent in its appetite.

And he was smiling at my mother.

Worse—she was smiling back.

Grant's eyes were trained on his hands as he kept working.

"Anyway," Mama was saying, "I thought it'd be nice if we all had dinner, seeing as how you two are ... what do you kids say now? Hanging out?"

Grant and I shared a look.

"Mama, can I talk to you for a minute?" I asked, setting my knife down and taking her arm before she answered.

"Do I have a choice?" she joked as I hauled her away. "Excuse me, Merrick."

My sisters followed silently until we were around the corner and out of earshot.

"What are you doin', Mama?" I hissed when I let her go.

She had that mom look on her face, all stern and indignant.

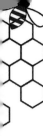

"What do you mean what am I doin'? Same thing as you're doin', as far as I can see."

"What is he doing here?" Poppy whispered at me.

"I don't know."

"Grant didn't tell you?" Daisy asked.

"No, but that's a whole other problem," I said. "Mama, he can't have good intentions. He just can't."

"But Grant does?"

"Well—"

"Don't you dare go making excuses for him because I could use the same ones for Merrick. That man was not only kind but he's smart and charming too. I was thinking—what if you tried to turn Grant around?"

"It's not a bad idea," I admitted, "but—"

"We can hit them from both angles? Maybe we can flip both of them."

"But he's not like Grant, Mama. He's different. He's … he's … well, he's just worse."

"How so?"

"Well, I don't know. I don't know him."

"Ha!" Mama pointed a finger at me. "Neither do I, so how about we give him the benefit of the doubt before accusing him of being anything but honest. Just like you did with Grant."

"Mama—" I groaned.

"Don't you Mama me. Two handsome men are waiting for dinner

in the kitchen, and I'm not going to keep them waiting. Now, I expect you three to be on your best behavior. Do you hear me?"

Annoyed and suspicious, we grumbled our affirmatives.

"Good. Go on and set the table, and when you've got your faces put right again, come back in there and pretend like you're having a good time."

She turned on her heel and marched out before we could respond, and we followed, sharing looks along the way.

On entering the kitchen, the two men were nearly nose to nose and speaking too low to hear, but whatever it was, it was a challenge. They looked like a couple of panthers ready to decide who the alpha was.

They broke apart, shifting into easy smiles and relaxed shoulders so fast, it left me wondering if I'd seen the exchange right after all.

Daisy went for the plates, and Poppy delegated the rest to Grant and me. We filed into the dining room with our assigned wares and began to circle the table to distribute them.

"What the fuck?" Poppy finally said.

The room exhaled, and my sisters and I were whisper-talking all at once. There were speculations and suspicions thrown around. Grant said nothing.

"Most of all," Poppy said, "why is he here?"

We turned to Grant.

With a sigh, he set a glass on the table "To check up on me."

Poppy's eyes narrowed. "Because you haven't signed us."

"It has nothing to do with you."

We were quiet watching him with such scrutiny, I thought he'd buckle. But he got taller, bigger. Smiled in a way that was almost self-deprecating.

"He does this. We've been playing a power game for a long, long time. And he won't just let me do what I came to do—he's got to have an opinion about every little thing."

"What's he want with Mama?" I asked, my arms folded.

"I don't know." He said it half to himself, his brows nocking together. "But I'll find out."

The promise hung in the air for a moment before floating away as more guesswork between three sisters took its place.

And I hoped beyond hope that he kept it.

***

Grant

I sat across from my father at the Blum's long farmhouse table, staring at a stranger.

He was shaped like my father, with the same cool eyes and dark hair, the same square shoulders and cut of his body. But I'd never met this happy, charming man.

And here I thought I'd dodged him.

Should have known better. Maybe I did and didn't want to admit it.

Conversation was as easy as his smile as he went on to Dottie about anything and everything.

And Dottie ate it up.

She had that sweet, doe-eyed look on her face, genuinely awed by him and frightfully aware of his attention on her. She was flushed and smiling, laughing and occasionally shy under his gaze.

She had no idea it was all bullshit.

Carefully, I kept my face in check, though Jo and her sisters were openly suspicious, assessing him with all the mistrust I was met with the first time I walked through the door. But through Jo, I'd won them over. Through Dottie, my father might be able to do the same.

The knowledge sent an echoing recoil through my guts. Not only because my father had no intention of carrying on any relationship with Dottie, but because I wasn't supposed to carry on with Jo either. Yet here I was, sitting by her side, watching my father do exactly what I'd done with revulsion in the back of my throat.

We weren't all that different, he and I. Everything I hated about him, I was, though whether it was by design or default, I wasn't sure.

This wasn't a new recognition. But it'd never hit me quite so painfully before.

Dottie laughed, touching my father's arm as he told some story I'd never heard about riding camels in Dubai, and the rest of us pushed our roasted chicken and mashed potatoes around with our forks, watching him.

I'd left for a few hours in the afternoon to go by the farms I had left to sign with a new offer that included a substantial increase in their payoff, and this time, they all asked me to leave the contract with them.

It was a good sign.

The truth was, most of the farms in this part of the country were struggling to stay afloat. Farming was already a poor man's racket, but when you factored in the climbing temperatures and water shortages, they were in fresh danger. It was why energy leasing had always been a boost to farm incomes. Though, rather than oil, was mostly wind farms and natural gas. The holdout farms were doing all right, which was why they'd been able to pass on the deal. But the county had just released another water restriction that would cut what was left of their crops by twenty-five percent.

And so, their pens hovered over the dotted line.

Now I just had to get Jo on board.

I hadn't said much through dinner, too busy worrying over what to do about my father. I knew my own intentions, and while they may have started out less than noble, I could say with some certainty that I didn't want to see any of these women hurt, nor did I want to manipulate them into signing. My plan had been to use honest tactics and persuade her as best I could. But by showing up tonight, my father had raised the stakes. I knew exactly what he was doing, and I couldn't stand by and watch him use Dottie, even if it was exactly what I'd been working toward just a few weeks ago.

Maybe that was why it rankled me so deeply. I didn't want to look in that mirror. Ever.

So my goals now came with risk that wasn't present before. Now I had to get them to sign as quickly as possible so my father would get out of Lindenbach and leave them alone. I didn't care if he was here to condescend or micromanage me. I didn't care that his presence indicated that he didn't think I could do my job, the job he groomed me for.

And maybe that was part of the problem. He took ownership over my career, which was interesting enough, considering he took no part in my life before I came to work for him.

Dottie laughed, her smile big and bright. I could see where the girls took after her, Daisy most of all. I only saw Jo in her in glimpses—she favored her father, judging by the multitude of photos of him in the house—but Dottie lived in Jo all the same.

I wondered if they thought I looked like my father and hated that they probably did.

"So how long did you say you were in town for?" Jo asked, her face pleasant but her tone glinting like the edge of a knife.

He didn't react, just smiled amicably. "Not too long, sadly. Lindenbach is some town. They don't make them like this on the East Coast."

"No," Jo said. "It's all proud and colonial where you're from, right? Cobblestone streets and brownstones and Paul Revere."

"I think I prefer this," he said wistfully as Dottie looked on, smiling. "There's something about a small town … quaint, quiet. People don't leave here—they have no desire to move. In big cities, people are transient, relocating when they get a new job or have a bad breakup. It's comforting to think there's a place where people stay just because they love it."

Poppy chimed in, "Glad we could provide you a little fantasy before you go back to your penthouse."

"Poppy June," Dottie chided, her face colored with disappointment. "I'm sorry, Merrick."

But he chuckled, leaning back in his seat, patting her hand. "Oh, it's all right, Dottie. I'm the enemy, right? A predator, a snake in the hen house. I'd hoped they wouldn't see me that way, but I don't blame them. But we all have our fantasies, don't we? Stories we make up about other people to protect us. They make it easier to deal with a truth we don't like. Like me showing up here with your mother."

The lack of challenge in his voice made his speech even worse than if he'd been an asshole.

"Truth is," he continued, "I understand. It's why Grant's never met a woman I've dated. His mother died when he was born, and I never brought anyone around, knowing it would confuse and upset him. I didn't want him to look at any of them like you're looking at me right now."

I swallowed hard at his lie—Was it a lie? Could it be true?—watching him with the weight of a lifetime's neglect in my gaze. A thousand words rose in my chest, smothered only by the knowledge that I would only fuck myself if I got into it.

"Did any of them want to steal from you?" Poppy snapped.

"Poppy," her mother warned.

"I'm sure they did," Merrick answered. "But that isn't what I want from you."

The three sisters laughed at the same time.

He looked on, his face seemingly honest, sincere. "Have I brought it up once at dinner? Dottie"—he turned to her—"have I mentioned the rights to you?"

"Not once," she said pointedly to her children. "In fact, when I found out who he was, the first thing I said was that I wasn't interested. He didn't even ask. And you three are being petulant and mannerless. Merrick is a guest in our home, and you have behaved abominably. I'm ashamed, and you should be too." She stood, throwing her napkin onto the table with a slap. "Now you three will clear this table and clean the kitchen while we go sit outside for a drink. I expect you out there with an apology before he leaves. Am I understood?"

The Blum women—grown women—glanced into their laps, muttering, Yes, ma'am.

"I'm so sorry, Merrick. Forgive them. They're suspicious by nature, but this is an all-new low." Her smiling face swiveled to her daughters, her eyes narrowing in disapproval. "I'll go make us drinks. Why don't y'all go on outside, and I'll be right behind you. Scotch?"

for love or honey

"That'd be lovely," Dad said, smiling that alien smile.

"And for you?"

It took a moment to realize she was talking to me. "Oh—I'll have the same. Thank you."

With a few parting words, Dottie left the dining room for the wet bar in the living room, and Dad stood, pushing in his chair before heading outside with a nod in the scowling girls' direction.

I picked up a few plates and followed them to the sink. Daisy took up a post there, Poppy went back for more dishes, and Jo got out glass containers for the leftovers. Once I'd unloaded my haul, I moved to her side as she scooped potatoes into the container with a splat.

"You okay?" I asked quietly, my hand resting in the small of her back.

"This is weird," she whispered. "I don't like it, and I don't believe his motivations are pure."

"You didn't think mine were either."

"Still on the fence about that one."

I frowned. "Ouch."

She met my eyes with a look on her face.

"Come on. Do you really believe that this—me and you—is about the contract?"

For a second, she considered, spooning violent loads of mashed potatoes into its container. "Only like...twenty percent."

I chuckled, leaning in to press a kiss to her hair. "Listen—I'm a great actor, but I'm not that good." Having earned a smile, I told her, "I'll find out what his angle is. Occupy your mom for a minute."

She sighed, clicking the top of the container on. "Easy. All I have to do is call her in here, and she'll be dressing us down for at least ten minutes."

"Look at you, taking one for the team," I said with a sideways smile.

"Yeah, well, you're going to be taking one for the team later when you have to spend an hour with your face between my legs to make up for it."

"I can't find the punishment in that sentence."

She chuckled, rolled her eyes, leaned into me for a second. Then nudged me. "Go on. Go figure out what the self-proclaimed snake wants in the hen house. Tell him his rooster costume sucks."

"Huh. I've always thought he was the biggest cock."

Another laugh, this one hearty, but she elbowed me. "Go."

"Yes, ma'am."

I headed in the direction my father had gone, figuring he'd wandered to the courtyard garden the house was built around. I hadn't seen a house quite like this, built in a big square around a large garden with seating in the middle. Two sides of the square were floor-to-ceiling windows that accordioned open to make a massive breezeway.

My father stood at the edge of the central patio with his hands in his pockets, looking into a patch of bird-of-paradise that stood taller than we were.

I stopped at his elbow, folded my arms. "So this was your plan?"

He shrugged. "Why not? It was yours too. Wonder which of us will close the deal first?"

for love or honey

A wave of disgust rolled through me. "Leave Dottie alone."

"Don't worry. I don't need to fuck her to get what I want. Unlike you."

"That isn't why I—"

"Don't be sanctimonious, Grant. You and I both know what's at stake here. And if you'd been on your game, it'd already be done. I don't want to be here. You, on the other hand, seem to have made yourself at home. Those pants are tragic. Did you get them at the feed store?"

Ignoring the jab, I continued quietly, feeding him the same old line that would keep him believing I was on his side. "I told you—I'm playing a long game, and you being here is fucking that game up. Go home. No one asked you to come."

He turned, laying that cruel, cold gaze on me, the one I'd inherited. "I'm not leaving. But don't worry. I won't do any more damage than you will."

His smile struck a chill that shivered down my spine. But before I could argue, Dottie came out, flushed and smiling and apologetic. But rather than sit with them where I'd have to endure my father's grand display, I excused myself to the kitchen where it was safe.

Except it wasn't safe, not really. Because Jo was there. My father's infiltration had driven a fierce streak of protection in me. I wouldn't let him hurt them.

But that meant I had to take control.

I won't do any more damage than you will.

There was a way to head him off if I could find it. If I could get them to sign, if I could convince them that their farm would be safe, I could head my father off and save Dottie from any heartache.

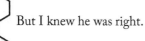

But I knew he was right.

I would leave a mark on this place whether I meant to or not.

And somehow I doubted it would be good.

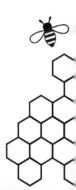

FRACK YOU

Jo

"Where are we going?" I asked as we took a slow and careful drive up a long dirt road in his Audi. "Isn't this the Kohler's farm?"

"It is."

"And what are we doing here?"

"Having a picnic."

I gave him a look, and when he glanced over at me, he laughed. And then I couldn't help but smile.

We'd waited the other night until my mother was out of Merrick's reach before heading to his place where he made good on his promise of the oral variety. While he was attending to his business that day and all day yesterday, my sisters and I had been busy working on a fundraiser dinner for the Lindenbach facelift. Poppy had the idea to have a big fancy black-tie dinner like they do in movies, sell tickets for a whole lot of money, ask for donations. Do a silent auction, that sort of thing. Thanks to the many weddings and such we'd hosted on the farm in the past, we had experience with events, which helped. Presley's boyfriend, who had all the connections, had called in some associates from the major metro cities, and he'd secured donors from Austin, San Antonio, Dallas, and Houston. Most folks in Lindenbach didn't have much to spare, never mind enough to restore Main Street to its former glory.

We'd thrown it together fast, but Jesse's sister was eager to show Lindenbach her stuff, so she agreed to cater at cost. My family would provide entertainment, and we'd lined up a few speeches, as well as some proposed plans for the strip.

And it felt good. To help. To contribute. I loved this town like it was a member of my family, and with every store we lost, it slipped away a little more. Lindenbach was too important not to save, or at least not to try.

Poppy was alight with plans for the city that just kept on getting bigger. Like a movement to propose sanctioning expansion of our broadband and cell phone coverage or another proposing small business curriculum additions to Lindenbach's tiny community college. She even had some grand designs to convince Old Mr. Creech to sell his farm to build a subdivision on so he could retire. Given the lack of affordable homes in the cities, she thought it just might bring some new industry to our town.

It was worth a shot, I figured. But before we could do much of anything, we needed to give our Main Street a face-lift, and that was going to take a whole lot of money—not just for the façades but to subsidize refurbishment inside the stores as well.

So Glow Up, Lindenbach was well underway.

Vainly, I was the most excited about the cocktail dress I'd gotten for the fundraiser dinner. That and the thought of Grant unwrapping me like a birthday present afterward.

Grant. A problem I kept telling myself wasn't a problem at all. It was just what I wanted—something casual, without strings or promises or expectations. He was gorgeous, smart, funny, and willing to take his lumps and dole them out. He was also a superstud in the bedroom, which was not a fact to be overlooked. Especially since it'd been a good long while since I'd been dicked down so thoroughly.

Two years, if anyone asked. I hoped no one did. I didn't like to lie, but I would.

But Grant's most impressive magic trick was that somehow, for some reason, I wasn't afraid of him. I didn't think he'd hurt me or lie to me, which was probably naive. But the temporary nature of our relationship had kicked down a wall we both seemed to have, a wall designed to keep people out. And as I smiled at him with a fluttering in my chest, I remembered why that wall existed.

Enjoy it while you can. He's leaving. It's fine.

It's fine. Everyone's favorite lie.

I searched out the window for a clue as to where we'd be stopping, but my curiosity went unsatisfied until he pulled off the road next to a copse of cedars and elms. We climbed out, and Grant got into the trunk, reemerging with picnic supplies. He reached for my hand with a smile, and I took it like a lamb, trusting to the end.

"This doesn't feel like the most impressive spot for a picnic," I noted.

"Way to rain on my parade, Jo. I even made a charcuterie, which was hard since Mariel's doesn't carry Havarti."

I laughed, trucking through the grass in my boots, reeds brushing my legs. I wore another sundress—accessibility had become the primary directive in choosing attire lately—and with my eyes down so I didn't trip, my field of vision was the bottoms of his jeans and boots, our hands connected, my boots, the hem of my dress.

The freeze-frame was too pretty, too perfect. One of those moments you know you'd remember when you were old and gray, looking off to the horizon from your rocking chair, thinking about all the days gone.

Inside the copse was a little patch of meadow, and in the middle of that, Grant set down the picnic basket and unfurled a blanket for us to sit on. I stretched out on my belly, rolling to my side so I could watch him unpack food and wine and plastic glasses.

"So this is where you wanted to bring me?"

He nodded. "Don't be mad."

"Why would I be mad? You even brought wine and frou-frou cheese to eat."

His hands paused, and he moved to the wine. "We should drink this first."

I frowned. "Okay, now you're starting to freak me out."

With a pop, the wine cork was loose. When it was glugged into a glass, he handed it to me. I looked at it skeptically.

"Drink it. Trust me."

"So I need wine to survive whatever you're about to do? You're not going to try any butt stuff, are you? If so, you're going to need to hand me that whole bottle."

His laughter was loud, surprised. "I mean, I will if you want me to, but that's not why I told you to drink up."

I took a sip and winced at the tartness.

"Not a wine girl?"

"Haven't had it much. We're more the beer and whiskey type of crowd around here. Most bars only carry two labels—red and white."

"Hope you're planning on a selection at the fundraiser dinner. You know how snobby those Dallas people are," he joked.

"I'll let Poppy know, but she's much more refined than I am. I'm sure she has it covered."

"Do you have a date?"

"A date?"

"To the fundraiser."

"I … well, I kind of assumed we'd go together."

He flashed a smile at me and lifted his glass. "Good."

"Will you still be here? Next week?"

Grant looked off and shrugged. "I think the Holseys are going to sign soon. They have the contract."

"Oh," I said in a tone that I hoped was neutral.

A small smile in my direction. "After that, I don't know. I'd like to see the fundraiser, though. Especially now that I have a date."

"We'll have to get you some dress Wranglers."

His face soured. "I'll wear a suit, thanks."

"Aw, come on. Texas black tie means your dressy shit kickers, pressed Wranglers, a sportscoat, and a bolo tie."

This time he didn't sour. He shuddered.

And I laughed. "Fine, wear your suit, city boy." In the silence, my mind turned back to him leaving. "Are you excited to be back at home? In your own bed, with your own pillow?" I asked, being a good sport and all.

For a second, he thought about it. "I've seen a lot of places in my life, sought corners of the world looking for something, I don't know what. But being here is …" He shook his head. "I've never been anywhere like this. I understand why you're protective of it, Jo. I really do."

"So we stack up to the Taj Mahal?" I joked, not knowing what else to say.

A chuckle. He took a sip of his drink. "This place isn't grand—"

"Gee, thanks."

His smile tilted. "It's superior in other ways. It doesn't have to try. It doesn't have to build a palace to be special, it just is. I mean, you should still fix Main Street, but—ow!"

I let go of the twist I had on the back of his arm, smiling so he wouldn't know how he'd moved me.

"I don't know what it is. But I've felt more at home in a shed watching you save bees than I ever have wearing a suit in a boardroom, which is where I thought I belonged."

"I've heard they're not particularly cozy rooms."

But he didn't laugh. "Do you ... do you get what I mean?"

So I didn't make a joke. "I do."

He hung his forearms on tented knees and looked off toward hills rolling off into the distance. "I feel different now than when I got here, and I can't figure out why, exactly. Probably something to do with the jeans and boots you made me wear."

"You like them."

A smile flickered on his lips. "I kinda do. Don't tell anybody."

"Well, Lindenbach looks good on you, Mr. Stone."

With an appreciative expression on his face, he said, "Thanks."

"So are you gonna tell me why I need wine to survive this picnic?

for love or honey

Butt stuff was my only guess."

He hauled himself up and offered his hand, pulling me to stand. Without letting go, he towed me through the grass toward the other side of the copse.

"Don't take anything I'm about to say wrong."

"Jesus, Grant—you're really building this up."

He stopped. Pulled me closer, our wine glasses extended so we wouldn't spill. "Do you trust me?"

"Against all laws of the universe, I do."

So he kissed me. "Good," he said. "Then let me say what I need to say before you yell at me."

I looked at him like he was crazy, since he was acting the part so brilliantly, but he pulled me through a break in the trees so I could see what was on the other side.

About a mile away, on the peak of a hill, stood a fracking well and the mass of equipment that came along with it.

My smile fell. I looked over the dig site in the distance, then kicked back the whole glass of wine, gagging when I'd gotten it down.

"I wanted to make sure you could see it with your own eyes. From here, can you feel anything in the ground? Can you hear anything? Smell anything?"

I checked my senses. Nothing from the ground. The only thing I smelled was dirt and grass baking in the sunlight. I did hear a distant truck motor, but otherwise, nothing.

"Not really," I answered.

"If you decided to sell, we wouldn't have any equipment on your land. In fact, the spot where we're drilling that could reach your shale deposit is right there. The damage is done whether you sell or not. See, we come at the shale sideways. Bill Nye said drilling straight down is like sticking a straw in a sandwich. You get the good stuff in the middle, but it's mostly bread. This way, coming at it from the side, all you get is the good stuff."

"Grant—"

"Ah-ah. Let me finish. Please."

Against all instinct, I shut up.

"Thank you. Here's the thing, Jo. This is happening in your town. It's been happening for a good while, and neither of us can stop it, not even me. I'm nobody. I make no decisions. So if it's not going anywhere, why not cash in on it? You could make enough money that you could almost singlehandedly save Main Street. Think of all the good you could do. And what's the risk?"

"Earthquakes—"

"Rare, and we've developed safeguards to stop them from happening."

"But the resources. The water it takes. The emissions—"

"It's already going to happen, and refusing to sign wouldn't change anything." A pause. A breath. "Don't answer me now. Just think about it. Talk to your family. I know how hard you're working to bring Main Street back to its glory, and this money could do everything you dream of. So just … just say you'll think about it."

I turned to look at him, searched his eyes, his face, and found no ruse, no lies. I found nothing but care and desire.

So I said, "I'll think about it."

He smiled. Took me in his arms, kissed me until I couldn't breathe.

And I had no idea how stupid that promise would prove to be.

JUST ASK BORIS

Jo

My sisters and I stood in a half circle around my mother with our arms folded, watching her put on makeup in her bathroom mirror.

"I don't see what the big deal is," she said with her mouth all weird as she did her mascara.

"You've spent the last two days with Merrick Stone, and you don't see what the big deal is?" Poppy asked.

"Jo spends all her time with Grant."

"And she catches hell for that too," Poppy noted.

"It's true," I said.

She capped her mascara and turned on us. "I am so disappointed in you three. Whenever do I date? Whenever do I pay any attention to men? Your daddy has been gone a long, long time, and I've never really dated anyone. Don't you think it's been long enough?"

"Of course we do, Mama," Daisy started. "We just don't think it should be him."

"Well, in that case, I guess you know best. Is that it?" She huffed, blowing past us for her closet. "I cannot even believe how you're acting."

"We cannot believe you're entertaining him," Poppy shot.

Mama whirled around. "You'd best watch your tone, Poppy June. Merrick is wonderful. He lost his wife just like I lost your daddy. We have a lot to talk about and a lot in common." We opened our mouths at the same time, but she stopped us with one pointing finger. "Don't even say it. We've had dinner and gone on a walk together. I hardly think that makes me a whore."

"Don't ask Marjorie what she thinks," Poppy warned.

"Well, Marjorie can just stick it."

"Have you kissed him?" Daisy asked.

She turned too fast for us to catch her expression. "That is none of your business."

"What about the contract?" I asked.

She didn't answer right away, pretending she was busy changing. "He made some good points."

Poppy and Daisy burst into objections. I kept my mouth shut. Because Grant had too.

Mama watched me for a second, and when my sisters saw where she was looking, they turned on me.

I put up my hands. "Don't start on me. She's the one kissing the devil."

"You used to say Grant was the devil," Poppy shot.

"And then I met his dad and learned better. Did you know that the equipment on the Kohler's farm is already up and functional, and they'd use that site to drill our land? The damage is done. But we could make money off it, money we could use to help Lindenbach."

"I cannot believe you just said that," Poppy breathed. "You two are a couple of Judases. The Stones tossed a bag of silver at you, and you're turning your back on what you know is right."

"Oh, stop it," I said. "I didn't say I wanted to do it, only that he made good points."

Mama nodded. "See?"

"Don't you go acting like I agree with you, Mama."

"Quit talking outta both sides of your mouth, Jo. It's not a pretty look."

I sighed. "It's not the same."

"Name me one way it's different," she challenged.

"I trust Grant," I said.

"I trust Merrick."

"How? You've known him for three days."

"And you think you know everything there is to know about Grant in that many weeks? It's a gut feeling. Don't tell me it's not." She turned back to her task. "Don't you three have getting ready to do? The boys will be here any minute."

"You can't sell to him, Mama," Poppy said.

But Mama's face darkened. "Don't you tell me what I can and can't do. I am a grown woman and your mother. I have no intentions of selling without talking to you first, but I'm perfectly capable of making my own decisions. Now, you go get the horses ready—"

The doorbell interrupted her, and she jolted in surprise.

"Shoot—I need a minute. I'll meet you in the stables." When we didn't immediately leave, she shooed us out.

We didn't speak on our way, the subject too big to open up on the way to answer the door. And on our front porch was the enemy. But for a second, I couldn't remember which man that was.

Grant's dour expression lit when he saw me, but we didn't move for each other, instead exchanging pleasantries before heading toward the stables.

For a moment, no one spoke in an awkward stretch of silence that Daisy eventually broke.

"So do y'all ride?"

"Not much," Merrick said. "But we do from time to time."

Conversation halted again. All I could think to talk about was how stupid Merrick looked in chinos. His shoes were at least workable.

"Well," Daisy said on a second go, "we have six horses in the stable, and I hate we don't ride more. But there always seems like something to do."

"How many stablehands do you have?" Merrick asked.

Daisy's cheeks flushed in embarrassment. "Oh, we have one farmhand who helps with the animals, but nothing like stable-hands really."

"Ah," was all he said.

Mercifully, we reached the stable and its familiar scent of wood and hay and animal. The horses nickered when they smelled us, and my sisters and I made our way around the animals, greeting them. We'd gotten them all brushed and saddled in advance of the men, and now I figured we'd done them a favor to not put them on the spot.

I cursed myself for not thinking to set Merrick up to look a fool in front of Mama. I didn't think he'd take well to a high-school-educated woman like Mama showing him how to do something a man was supposed to know how to do, despite his lack of experience. Like how the world expected them to work out, be tall, and only have emotions that end in angry.

We wouldn't have faulted him, but I got the sense he'd have faulted himself and taken it out on us somehow.

Poppy smiled like a liar, but Merrick wouldn't have known. She took him down the line and introduced each horse, saving Boris for last. And Daisy and I did our best to keep our faces straight.

Boris was so tall, Merrick couldn't see clearly over his shoulders, and so dark a brown that he was nearly black. On their approach, he stamped his hoof and chuffed, keeping his eye on Merrick.

What the unsuspecting interloper didn't know was that Boris was the meanest horse this side of the Comal River.

"Fine looking animal," he said.

"Glad you think so. I think he'd be perfect for your ride today," Poppy said.

Grant watched with curiosity blooming to understanding. I thought I might get in trouble when he figured it out, but instead, we shared a wicked look, and I counted myself among the lucky.

Unlike Merrick.

We took our horses' leads and led them out, Daisy with Mama's horse. Boris went willingly, and Poppy and I met gazes, wondering if we'd misjudged the beast. Maybe he was feeling amiable today, in which case Poppy's plans would be thwarted, and we'd be robbed of a chance to make a fool out of Merrick in front of Mama.

Until we were mounted.

Grant looked like a goddamn king on Tank, who was as big as Boris but with a regal temperament. He knew just when to listen and when not to.

Boris backed up, whinnying and stamping in protest. To his credit, Merrick did know how to control a horse, using the reins to show Boris who was boss and clicking his tongue.

"Here, let me help," Poppy said innocently, trotting her mare, Ginger, over to Boris, knowing full well that Boris hated Ginger with deep and unmatched passion. Probably because Ginger hated him back and pissed him off at every turn. Like right then, when she bit Boris straight in the ass.

Boris bucked and took off, but Merrick held on. Until the horse ran under a low-branched tree, scraping Merrick right off his rear end and flat on his back in the dirt with an oof.

We were off our horses, with Mama yelling from the porch as she caught up. She practically threw herself onto the ground over Merrick, checking him frantically as he wheezed and choked and floundered around in the dust. The rest of us shared a long look. Poppy shrugged with an expression on her face that said she didn't mean to, but he was probably fine, and also fuck him.

Mama shot us dead with her eyes. "Boris? You put him on Boris?"

"Somebody had to ride him," Poppy noted.

"And it shoulda been you. You're the only one who can ride him."

"We understand each other," she explained.

"Oh, don't even say it, Poppy June," Mama said as she struggled to help Merrick up. Grant found himself and moved to help. "You could have killed him."

"He's fine! Look, he's not even scratched."

Merrick gave her a look, but he couldn't speak, not yet having found the wind that'd been knocked out of him.

"I am so sorry," she said to him as they shuffled toward the house. "Come in and let me get you something to drink and we'll see if you're all right."

We made to follow, but Mama met us with a glare that stopped us dead. "You three better make yourselves scarce. I'll deal with you later."

"Does that mean we're not going to ride?" Poppy asked. When Mama's head looked like it was going to explode, she said, "Fine. We'll take care of the horses."

She swung up on my horse and turned to chase Boris down, and Daisy and I led the other horses back to the stable, but we left ours out, deciding to go for a ride anyway. Couldn't get more scarce than that. Within a few minutes, Poppy had Boris in tow and put his mean old ass back in his stall, praising him all the way.

And a couple of minutes after that, Mama came storming into the barn with hell on her heels and a thunderstorm at her back.

And so the three of us stood in the stable as Mama reprimanded us up, down, and sideways—inside out too, for good measure—like we were little girls again and not grown women. We were to apologize to Merrick, and if we ever pulled a stunt like that again, she swore she'd disinherit us, which wasn't true, but it wasn't a thing she threatened often. Only when she was very angry and very hurt.

When she'd whipped around to storm back to the house, she passed Grant, who she softened toward, touching his arm and nodding, apologizing if I had to guess. And then Grant headed to us, managing to both cringe and look amused.

"Is he okay?" Daisy asked.

"He'll be fine. Always said he was a hardass."

"Want to ride still?" I asked as he approached.

"I do. Plus, it'd be good to get out of shotgun range from the house. At least for Poppy's sake."

So we walked our horses out the other end of the stable and mounted up. And for a little while, we rode in silence.

As much as I hated Merrick, I loved Mama. And I understood what it was like to feel something for a man you shouldn't. The proof was in a saddle at my side.

"We've gotta leave her and Merrick alone," I finally said.

Poppy stopped so fast, Ginger sidestepped. "Why?"

"She likes him, Poppy."

"So?"

"So, she's right. She's a grown-ass woman, and she likes him. She doesn't want us to stop her any more than I want anyone to stop me from seeing Grant." I felt Grant watching from next to me, felt the weight on my heart. "If anything changes, if we find out he has ulterior motives, then we can talk to her about it. Like adults. Until then, we leave her alone. Deal?"

Daisy nodded. "Deal."

Poppy scowled.

"Poppy," I warned.

"How will we know if he's playing her?"

The three of us looked at Grant.

"You'll tell us, won't you?" I asked.

for love or honey

"Of course," he answered, and those two words were enough to make me feel better.

Because I had no idea they were a lie.

SNAKE IN THE WATERING HOLE

Grant

I might have been stretched out on a lounge chair next to the Vargas' pool a few days later, but I couldn't relax.

Jo laid by my side half asleep, her bikini blessedly small and her skin shining from sweat and sunscreen. Country music played from speakers somewhere around the sizable pool, which touted a massive rock feature with a slide and fountain. Presley sat at the edge of the pool with her feet in while her boyfriend, Sebastian, threw Priscilla around like a squealing rag doll that said again, again! every time she floated to the surface.

I watched them for a long time, long enough that I found an unbidden smile on my face, the simplicity of their joy infectious. The little girl was a pistol, as I'd learned firsthand, all smiles and laughter that had her parents laughing too, occasionally cracking jokes to each other or interrupting for a kiss, to which their child would wail ewwww before trying to tickle them apart. It was such an easy thing, it seemed … a family. They loved each other and enjoyed each other openly and honestly, the sight of it as alien as everything else in this town.

They made it look so easy.

for love or honey

Poppy and Daisy floated around on mesh loungers, hanging on to each other's rafts so they wouldn't be separated, and our elders had convened around a big table in the shade, including Sebastian's mom and grandmother, who was the Abuelita in Abuelita's restaurant.

And my father sat next to Dottie in boating attire and Wayfarers, laughing and smiling and looking like he belonged here.

My skin crawled at the invasion. The feeling should only have been a result of the affront—or maybe for my pride—at his lack of faith in my ability to do my job. I couldn't seem to draw a parallel between him and me even though we'd technically deployed the same tactic to get them to sign.

My arching hackles were territorial, and it had nothing to do with Flexion or oil or my job. It was strictly a reaction to a predator threatening the place and people I'd come to respect and appreciate so deeply.

"Quit staring your father down," Jo said with her face still turned up to the sun.

I frowned.

"And unclench your jaw."

With a sigh, I did, shifting my gaze back to the pool. "I don't like him here."

"Really? God, I thought you were organizing a parade," she deadpanned.

I hooked the hip of her bathing suit and snapped it.

"Ouch," she said, laughing.

"Did you try to talk to your mom?"

Now it was her turn to sigh, her smile falling. "We did, but she just got mad again. Told us we were being childish. That Daddy died too long ago for us to be jealous of a man she was interested in. Regaled the many wonderful attributes your father possesses like he was a goddamn apostle."

My jaw clamped shut again.

"They're going to dinner tonight," she continued. "He's taking her to San Antonio so they can walk along the Riverwalk. Which is far too romantic for my liking."

"Mine too."

"If she stays the night out there, I might lose my shit." She turned that over in her mind for a second. "I don't trust him."

"Has he been trying to get her to sign?"

She didn't answer right away. "Yes. And she's thinking about it."

My heart stopped. "What do your sisters have to say about that?"

"Well, they're not happy. But Mama's not the only one on the fence."

I didn't react, outwardly at least. I didn't even know what the knowledge made me feel. A little bit of everything, as far as I could tell.

"Wouldn't have figured I'd done any real convincing," I answered lightly.

"It's your number one trick. Somehow you convinced me to go home with you, and the Vegas odds on that were terrible."

I laughed, still stunned. Angry with my father. Hopeful at the prospect of getting him out of Lindenbach. Grateful I'd get my job done and the money that came along with it. Worried that it was the wrong decision for her.

"Anyway, I still think your dad's trouble, and you haven't once made me feel better about the feeling."

"His motives are above my pay grade," I lied again, because implicating him would implicate me too, if he had anything to do with it. "But he can't be trusted."

"What was he like when you were a boy?"

"I don't really know. He wasn't around, and when he was, he ignored me."

"That's just … that's just awful. I wonder what Mama would think of that."

I shot her a smirk. "Are you pumping me for ammunition to emotionally manipulate your mother?"

"Of course I am. Is he telling the truth about not ever bringing women around you?"

I nodded. "But remember, I barely saw him anyway. He … he loved my mother more than he'd ever admit to me, I think. Their photos are still all over the house … sometimes it's like living in a memorial of reminders of what he lost. And reminders that I was the one who took her from him."

"Surely he doesn't actually blame you."

"He does."

"How do you know that? He never talks to you."

"Because he likes to throw it at me when I disappoint him."

She fell silent.

"I don't know if he was always like this or if he used to be happy. With my mother," I said, my gaze wandering to his happy face on the other side of the pool. "Maybe that's the real version of him, and I only know the shadow. All I do know is that in this

situation, he isn't worthy of anyone's trust."

"Well, without some sort of proof, Mama will not be swayed. It's not every day that a handsome, rich, charming bachelor comes to town."

I made a show of stretching and said, "I know, lucky you."

"It really is lucky. Not gonna lie—I kinda wish your dad wasn't a supreme asshole. Mama deserves somebody to love who loves her like Daddy did."

"What about the curse?"

"Doesn't hurt to pay attention to it. You know, you're taking a grave risk fucking around with that kind of magic." Pleased when I laughed, she continued. "I do think there's something to it for Mama, but here's the real problem—she's known every man in this town for more than thirty years or since they were born. Every corner of this town carries a story of her and my father. Every person in this town knew him just as well as they know the rest of us. So not only is there zero fresh meat, but the meat that is here is somehow associated with my father. Doesn't exactly help with the whole starting over thing."

"What about dating apps? Hitting the bigger cities?"

She chuckled. "Dottie on dating apps? That should be its own reality show. No, we've tried. Made an account for her, convinced her to go on a couple of disastrous dates. I don't know if you know this, but men on dating apps only want to bone."

"You don't say."

"It shocked me too." Another sigh. "Mama might just be forever alone. If she is, that's all right. I'll be right there with her. Poppy and Daisy can go on and find someone—I'll hang back. We'll do puzzles. Get more chickens. Learn to knit. You know, spinster stuff."

"You'd rather make sure your mom was happy than go looking

for love?"

"It's easier that way, isn't it? I mean, aside from the fact that Mama has devoted her adult life to raising us, mostly alone. We're her whole world. Plus, if I stay unattached, that means I'm available for trysts with rich playboys who blow in and out of town with the wind."

"Playboy, huh?"

"Aren't you? You're famously unattached too, if I'm not mistaken."

"Okay, maybe I am a little bit. But it's not as glamorous as the name implies."

"No?"

With my eyes on Sebastian and his family, there was nothing to be but honest. "It's empty. Lonely. No one really knows you—people decide who you are because of what you are."

"But you have friends, right?" she asked quietly.

"Friends." I tested the word on my tongue, finding it didn't feel the same as it used to. "I know a lot of people. I hang out with a lot of people. But friends? If shit went to hell for me, if I lost all my money and moved away, I'd never hear from them again. Even now, the only people I've heard from are part of group texts or about fantasy football. I don't call them when I need something. I don't tell them … well, much of anything that's real."

"Who do you call?"

"No one."

She was quiet for a second. "You can call me."

I lolled my head so I could see her but didn't speak.

"When you leave, when you go home, if you need something—a friend, a shoulder, a date to a gala, a phone sex session—you can call me."

I couldn't even be clever with a response—I just laughed, reaching across the space between us to touch her smiling face.

"Thanks, Jo."

"I don't want you to be alone any more than I want Mama to. Difference is, Mama has us. And I hate—and I mean hate—that you don't have anybody. So I'll be your somebody."

"Never would have thought you'd make that offer when I was wiping warm egg off my face in front of television crews."

"The internet even made a gif out of you."

"Of course it did."

"Don't you want to see it?"

"Pass."

She pouted a little. "But it's so funny."

I swung my legs around and leaned in her direction. "I know. I was there." I kissed her nose and stood, heading toward the smoker where Sebastian stood, tending to what looked to be at least four different kinds of meat.

When I stopped next to him, I asked, "Got anything vegan in there?"

He gave me a suspicious look, his tongs poised to pick up a brat. When he saw I was kidding, he rolled the brat over. "That's a swear word around these parts."

"Need any help?"

"Sure. Grab the tongs on the tray and flip these brats and burgers so I can get these ribs off the fire."

So I did, taking care. "Jo said you work in charity. That you did a tour with the Peace Corps."

"I did. Almost did two."

"Almost?"

He shrugged. "I found something that meant more to me." He cast a loving look in the direction of Presley as she dried off their little girl. "You travel much?"

"The only time I feel at home is when I'm not at home."

"I know the feeling."

We were silent for a beat as I gathered my courage to ask, "What's it like?"

"Having a family?"

I nodded. "Ever feel shackled? Trapped?"

"I felt more trapped before I knew what I wanted. I think … I think I was looking for something, and I looked everywhere but here. I left Lindenbach, left my mom and abuela. Searched for meaning in the Corps, looked for answers in the faces of strangers, and while I found many, the answers about my future weren't among them. Then I found her, and I realized everything I wanted was right here after all. What's it like having a family? It's crazy and hectic and hard and beautiful. But I get to do it all with Presley. We share all that crazy—it's ours. And now those two are all I need." He laughed. "A little deep for flipping burgers. Sorry."

"Hey, I asked. You're happy. It's more than most people can say."

He jerked his chin at Jo, his hands busy with racks of ribs. "How much of this is about her?"

I shrugged, rolling another brat over. "I'm leaving soon."

"Yeah, so was I," he answered on a laugh. "This place has a way of grabbing you, and once it's got you, it's not likely to let you go."

Smiling, I rolled the last brat onto its other side and moved on to the burgers. "I don't think I'll be staying, but I can see how it'd be hard to go. I'm already putting it off."

"When are you heading back to DC?"

"Haven't decided. After the fundraiser for sure."

He made a noncommittal noise. "How about your dad?"

I felt my expression sour and tried to smooth it. "I don't know. Hopefully sooner than later."

"Pres said he's here to check up on you."

"It's what he does. But my work here is nearly done."

"All but the Blum farm."

"That one's not looking to be in the cards."

"If that family is one thing, it's stubborn, so it's probably best to cut your losses."

"Tell him that." I glanced at him, then back to my task. "I don't like him around Dottie."

"Yeah, none of us do. But Dottie seems happy, so there's not much we can say. It's been a long time since she's seen anybody. Don't know if you know what a big deal that is."

"I have an idea of the magnitude. As long as she doesn't trust him, she should be fine."

We looked over at her in unison, and on seeing her beaming at my father, we both knew she was likely not fine.

"Jo tried to talk to her," I explained, "but she blew the girls off for being overprotective. Told them to mind their own business."

"I'll talk to Birdie," he said, and my gaze shifted to Presley's mom as she adjusted the oxygen tube in her nose. "Maybe she can talk some sense into Dottie. Doubt she'll listen to the rest of us." A pause. "How dangerous are we talking?"

"Her heart isn't the only thing he'll ruin, if that's what you mean."

"Is he just cruel? Or is he after something?"

"He might just be trying to teach me a lesson," I hedged, not able to admit the truth. "Dottie won't sign his contract," was as close as I could get to it.

"No, she won't. None of them will, strictly on principle." Sebastian wrapped the ribs in foil to keep them warm and turned to me as I finished flipping burgers. "You care about Jo." It wasn't a question.

"I do."

He glanced at Presley again. "Sometimes, life comes out of nowhere and hits you hard enough to change everything. And all the things you thought you knew, everything you thought you wanted, were placeholders for the real thing. When you find it, you'll know. Your dreams change before you even realize it happened. So keep your ear to the ground. Maybe you'll hear the train coming better than I did."

"Daddyyyyy!" the little girl said, the Y bouncing with every footfall as she ran. "Frow me in the pool!"

He scooped her up, and without missing a beat, he took two steps, said, "Like this?" before chucking her, squealing, into the pool and diving in behind her.

I closed the lid to the smoker and headed back toward Jo, thinking about just how right he was. About how this town cast a spell that had woven its way around my heart.

But I knew the second I had the thought that it wasn't the town.

It was her.

She'd possessed me, claiming I was the snake charmer when it was her all along. The town, the people, the way I felt here … they were nothing without her.

For a moment, I let myself imagine what it would be like to stay. Most of my job was spent on the road, so I could do it from anywhere and fly back to DC when I needed to. I could find a place, a quiet place here in town. Go to dances every Saturday night and spin Jo around the dance floor. Spend my nights with her. Spend my days with her.

I could be happy here. I could make a home here.

Home. I'd been searching for that my whole life, building what I could from what I had at my disposal. Like a pigeon trying to make a nest out of take-out boxes and discarded straws. But here waited riches to build a life that meant something. That meant everything.

The feeling was so strong, I had to school myself so I didn't hurry back over to her, so I didn't say too much, so when I kissed her, it was brief and gentle, without the desire I wanted to claim her with.

Could I have this life? Would she want me here with her? Or was it easy to daydream and make promises, knowing I was leaving?

I didn't know. I didn't know if I wanted to find out. If it was just a fantasy, I could keep it in my heart in the dark. I could keep the daydream without the tarnish of rejection.

I'll be your somebody.

I hadn't realized I'd needed one until then.

for love or honey

And now I didn't know if I could do without one.

Without her.

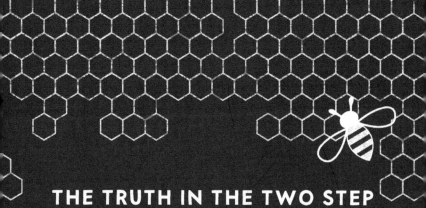

THE TRUTH IN THE TWO STEP

JO

Grant spun me around the dance floor so fast, I hung onto him for fear I'd fly away. But his arm around my waist, holding me flush against him, would never have let me go.

It was too beautiful tonight, too good. Too happy for words.

We'd sold out of tickets, thanks to Sebastian's connections. Half the crowd consisted of the top one percent of Lindenbach, and everyone had donated something over the price of their plates. The silent auction had been a wild success, earning us double what we'd thought.

But the real money had been in donations, and boy, had the donors shown up in a big way. At this stage of the night, we'd raised almost three million dollars. The two biggest were anonymous and totaled at a million each.

The thing about anonymous donations was that the person who accepted the donation knew, and if their names were on a check, even more knew.

Grant had given his check to Daisy and swore her to secrecy.

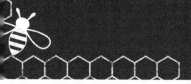

for love or honey

Merrick handed his to my mother directly.

My shock at the money was tempered by disbelief. It was an unfathomable amount, and each of those men wrote a check for it. Like, cash. I knew they were rich of course, but seeing an actual check for a million dollars was not something I believed I would ever see in my life. And certainly not from the man I was sleeping with.

I hated that his good and honest deed was made bitter by his father's check, which I couldn't believe was anything but a bunch of strings. Where Grant had gone to lengths to hide it from me—even now, he didn't know I knew—Merrick had given it straight to Mama. And judging by her reaction, I figured she was getting ready to say yes to the dress.

Nothing Merrick did sat right. But I wasn't turning my nose up at a cool mil from the devil. I just figured we'd better get down to the bank first thing and get that sucker cashed before he got wise.

Grant smiled down at me, dapper as all hell in a suit black as midnight. He smelled like the million bucks he'd given us, his smile so bright, so happy. Never would I have guessed that the man I'd met just a few short weeks ago could have transformed like he had. The man in this suit wasn't the man in the suit I'd ruined with egg yolk. He was something else entirely.

I'd spent the past few weeks pretending like the future wasn't a thing. That Grant leaving was nothing more than a bullet point on a calendar. That when he left, things would just go back to normal. I wouldn't miss him at all in that scenario.

No, I wouldn't miss the days spent with him tagging along on my workdays. Who even cared about those long nights we spent tangled up in each other or the sweet satisfaction he gave me in every little kiss, every little smile.

It didn't matter that it felt like I knew him in a way that defied time. In a way that had made him vital to me.

When he left, I'd be fine.

Especially if I didn't think of it now or ever.

Instead, I took in the night for a moment, soaking in the details. The fabric strung in elegant strips from a ring hung from a massive oak over the dance floor. The frame around the rectangular space provided a drape for the fabric and a place for the zillion lights strung up. Tables lit by candlelight were little glowing islands of happy faces and golden champagne around the wooden platform, at the end of which my family sang with all the joy I felt in my heart.

There were moments in life when you knew you were exactly where you're supposed to be. When everything made sense. When everything was right.

This was one of them.

I didn't want it to end.

The song ended, and a slow song started. Daisy sang, long and slow and lovely, about the perils of love. And Grant smiled on.

I smiled back.

"I'm still trying to figure out how you put this all together in such a short amount of time."

I shrugged my almost bare shoulders—only the tiniest spaghetti straps kept my dress up. "This space was already here, we just had to put up the fabric part and set up the tables, and we're the entertainment. The caterer was kismet, and the guest list was Sebastian. Daisy put together the presentation on development, and the speakers were easy enough. Everybody had something to say."

"Especially Mitchell."

My face soured. "God, I hate that he's even on my property. Can

211

you believe that motherfucker took credit for all of this?"

"Yes."

"Yeah, me too."

"Who gets credit for this dress?"

"What, this old thing?" I playfully glanced down at the pinky-gold sequined cocktail dress, its V deep and its hem short. The high waist banded around the most narrow spot on my torso, the skirt wrapped in the front, draping to make the slightest upside-down V, mercifully giving me a little bit of room to dance without fear of tearing anything. I smiled back up at him. "A friend of mine owns a dress shop in Austin and hooked me up."

"Send her my thanks."

"I will. And how about this suit? You didn't bring this with you, did you?"

"Also Austin, though no friend or hookup."

"Too bad. I bet my dress shop friend knows a guy. I'd introduce you if she wasn't hotter than me."

"Impossible. I've never seen a more beautiful woman in all my life."

His tone wasn't joking. It was hallowed, as were his eyes and his fingertips on my back.

So I laughed, my cheeks flushed and my heart aching. "You've gotta get out more."

"Don't do that, Jo."

I was quiet for a beat as we swayed under the golden lights. "I have to."

"Why?"

"Because … well, because."

"Because I'm leaving?" he guessed.

I met his eyes, searched them. "It's hard enough even when we're avoiding it."

"I know."

At the acknowledgment, we fell silent for a moment.

A silent war raged behind his eyes. "I didn't know when I came here that it would change me. You changed me. Somehow, you've managed to undo everything I thought I wanted and rewrite it. And now … I don't want to go."

My heart flung itself in his direction. I took a breath, soaking up those five words.

"I don't want you to go. But you have a job and a home and a life a thousand miles away. And I'm here. I'll always be here."

"All that's true about my life, my job, my home. I'm just trying to figure out if they matter enough to go back to."

My heart ceased its flinging in favor of climbing up my throat.

"I don't even know if I can leave anymore."

"But …" I shook my head. "Your job—"

"Is all over the country. I'm in DC maybe half the time, traveling the rest."

"Your home. Your friends."

"My home is just a place where my stuff is. And I only have one somebody, remember? You. I don't want to go." He held me tighter, searching for words. But all he did was echo, "I don't want to go," again, softly.

for love or honey

"Grant …"

He brought my hand, resting in his, to his lips. "I don't know what it means or what we'll do or how any of it will work. But say you want me to stay, and I'm here. I'm yours."

It was too much to feel, too much to answer for. To wrap myself around him, to tell him he could have me, to say it out loud was too scary, too big.

So I smiled my yes and asked, "What about that curse?"

"I'll take my chances."

"And you'll keep wearing those jeans?"

He leaned in a little and whispered, "I even got another pair."

My laugh was only for him. "How could I refuse?"

"Guess you can't."

Before I could be a smartass, he kissed me with tender care, a soft thing that weighed the same as his heart. And I was light as a feather in his arms as it dawned on me fully that he wanted me, wanted me so much that he was ready to leave his life behind for me. For this. For a smart-mouthed bee farmer in a nowhere town.

And I wanted him to stay. For the first time, being with someone, letting him in, felt like the greatest gift I could ever receive, not the burden I thought it would be. Having him for mine and being his was all I wanted, and I'd never known. Not until him.

Only with him.

The kiss broke. We swayed, beaming at each other.

Never had I been so blissfully terrified to feel happy.

Because I'd put my faith in him.

And I prayed he wouldn't break me.

THE DARK OF NIGHT

Grant

Hours later, I kissed Jo in the dark, slow and hot, backing her up the porch stairs and into my place without ever breaking the seam of our lips.

We'd left as soon as we could under the promise of Daisy and Poppy to make sure that their mother didn't go home with my father or vice versa. The party had ended, the night a success in so many ways, for so many reasons.

I hadn't known I was going to tell her how I felt. I hadn't even known I wanted to stay until I said it. I mean, I knew I wanted to stay, I just didn't think I could. Or that she'd want me to.

I'd never been so happy to be wrong.

There was no rush, no urgency in the kiss. Her hands slid between my shirt and jacket, sliding it over my shoulders and down my arms. Her fingertips patiently untied the knot of my tie with a whisper of black silk. Those fingers unfastened my buttons one by one, stopping under my ribs when I finally broke the kiss.

She was shadows and moonlight in the vastness of the night. That softest of light brushed the bridge of her nose, her cheekbones, reflected from her eyes and the space behind parted lips. Her bare shoulders down to the deep neckline of her dress beckoned, and I took the invitation to trace the moonlit planes I'd come to know so well.

In such a short time, just a moment of my life, my gravity had shifted. And in the middle of it all was her. She was what I saw when I closed my eyes. She was what I wished for when I woke.

Her lips quirked in a smile. "What?"

"Hmm?"

"You're smiling."

"I was just thinking maybe you're a witch after all."

Her laughter stirred my heart. "You're not feeling itchy, are you? I did this voodoo thing when you got to town that didn't take."

"It's the only explanation I can come up with for how I feel that makes sense."

"Not my charm and grace?"

A chuckle. "Let me have this, Jo."

Her face softened. She stepped closer. "That's the thing. You can have whatever you want."

"Anything I want?" I asked, cupping her jaw.

"Anything at all," she answered against my lips.

So I took them for mine.

If this was what it felt like to be happy, I hadn't known the feeling before. I'd felt accomplishment. I'd experienced the rush and awe that came with seeing the world. But never had I felt this. Elation, because she was mine. Satisfaction that she wanted me too, a deep sigh of rightness. Desire to show her what words couldn't say. But underneath it all was a desperation, a fear that I would lose the first person I'd ever needed.

In her lived a future I'd convinced myself was a dream, the kind of dream that movies and marketers used to sell us a life we could never have.

I never believed it was real until her.

My fingers slipped down her neck, to her shoulder, hooked the strap of her dress. Slid it over the curve as our lips opened and closed, our tongues seeking slowly. The thin fabric slid away, exposing her breast, and quietly I traced its shape, found the peak of her nipple but only grazed it, teasing us both. I freed the other breast—our lips parted. Her eyes closed, her head bowed, her forehead meeting my lips as I lowered the zipper, and her dress slid to the floor.

She was unclothed in the moonlight, but it was me who was naked, exposed, left disarmed and powerless.

She saw me, the me I'd buried beneath years of loneliness, years of schooling that self to hide, to protect himself. I'd turned into a version of my father, his manifesto the foundation of my life, my worth. No one could ever love me but me. Life was a one-man show. Power was as good as love, and vulnerability was equivalent to death.

Under the rubble of those lies, she'd pulled another man free. Dusted him off, helped him to stand. Even now, I saw that truth reflected in her eyes as she stepped into me until she was close enough that her heels rested between my shoes, that I could feel the shape of her soft body, feel the heat of her through my shirt. I peered down at her, my hands roaming the smooth curves of her ass. She gazed up at me, and her lips parted, a smile at the corners as she rose on her toes, angling for a kiss.

I granted her wish, though there was no tenderness. Only the fierce possession of a man on fire.

We twisted together, her shoulders high and hands on my jaw for a long moment. And then I picked her up around the waist, reveling in the weight of her in my arms, in the feel of her legs around me, in the sight of her face hovering just above mine, the ferocity with which she kissed me, the possession equally hers.

When I reached the bed, I laid her down, stretched her out where I could take my time with her body, where I could worship every curve and plane. But when my hips were fitted between hers, she shifted, signaling me to roll over. I pressed those hips into hers, grinding my length against her, and she softened, mewling in a moment of weakness. But then she shifted again, this time with more force, and I didn't fight.

While I'd taken her enough times to have seen her supine, Jo was not a woman to be told no. She surrendered because she chose to. She gave not as a weakness, but as a gift.

She broke the kiss to rise, straddling my waist, her eyes on her task as she unfastened my buttons to expose my torso. Her hands slid along the ridges and valleys up to my shoulders, so I rose, stealing a kiss as she pushed the shirt down my arms. My hands had barely found her when she laid a palm on my chest and pressed, so those hands took up post on her thighs as she worked to free the rest of me. All the while, I watched her, memorizing the sight of her naked and astride me, kissed by shadows and starlight.

And that was where I stayed, prone and without defense as she rid me of the rest of my clothes, sighing as she drank in the sight of me, stopping when she reached my cock. Her long, pale fingers trailed down the tender skin on either side of my length, then back up, her fingernails brushing my shaft, sending a shudder of anticipation through me.

She hinged, bringing her lips to my chest. My fingers slipped into her hair, thirsty to touch her as she made her way down my body, her nipples grazing my skin as she descended. Her hot breath against my crown. The wet swipe of her tongue in the cleft. Her lips closing over the tip, the gentle pull as she sucked.

My fist tightened in her hair.

Down she went, her hands taking what her mouth couldn't. And for a moment, I wanted nothing more than to lay there and live in the heat of her mouth. But my mind went restless with thoughts of her body. I wanted to taste her, wanted to hold her pleasure in my mouth, in my hands, and when there was no other thought left but her, I sat, reaching over her shoulders to grab her hips.

"Turn around," I commanded, and she did, following my lead as I guided her to straddle my chest.

Her back arched as she picked up where she'd left off, and with both hands, I grabbed her ass, spreading her open, my eyes on the flesh between her thighs. I thumbed the slick line, pressed the dip until the tip disappeared, circled the swollen peak. My gaze filled with only her, my nerves knowing only her hot mouth, her languid tongue. And the two senses combined were nearly more than I could bear.

I hooked my arms under her thighs and pulled—she released me with a yelp of surprise, then a cry of pleasure when my mouth found her, filled with her, traced every ripple, every peak. My arms curled tighter, bringing her so close I could barely breathe and didn't care. All I wanted was right here, on the tip of my tongue, between trembling thighs, my ears ringing with my heartbeat and the whimpering moans from her, the rumbling satisfaction from me.

She was close, her hips shifting in rhythm with my mouth, her hands on my thighs to brace herself. A pulse, and the long kiss deepened, hardened until she bore down, back arched, and came in shuddering waves against my tongue.

She hadn't recovered when I moved from beneath her, her senses slow, but when she found herself, she was already in my lap, the tip of me at the edge of her. Her palms on my chest, she sank onto me, her lids fluttering and mouth a soft O.

I buried my face in her neck—she lifted hers to the ceiling with a sigh, her arms draped over my shoulders. With a slow roll of her hips, she let me go only to devour me again with another sigh, a hum through sealed lips. Her heels grazed my thighs as she rolled her body, rising with the help of my hands on her ass, descending until I was fitted as deeply in her as I could get.

But I wanted more.

A growl and a twist, and she was pinned by my body, recumbent and lithe, her eyes still closed, her lips still parted. I slammed into her with a groan, and her neck snapped off the bed with a gasp and a cry. Again, a thrust that sent a moan of pleasure-pain from her lips, jostling her breasts. Her knees drew higher, her heels against my waist. And then her eyes opened slowly, finding mine. Her hand on my face, on my neck, pulling me into her until our lips could meet in a kiss that stopped all else. A long, hot kiss of promise and desire, of finding a thing you'd lost. Of relief and of that sweet desperation I knew I'd never escape, not when it came to her.

When I moved, it was slow and circling, deliberate and devouring, more than a meeting of bodies, more than a meeting of hearts. I felt release rise in her, and mine rose with it. She tightened, and I swelled. Her breath shallowed, color rising up her chest, climbing the column of her neck that extended, tightening with every long flex and release of my hips.

When she came, she pulled me deeper with every pulse of her body, so tight around me I was left breathless. The leash on my desire snapped. The world dimmed, electricity sparking, bursting behind my eyes, across my skin as I poured all that I had in me into her, body and soul.

She was mine.

I sagged over her, bracketing her face with my arms, my chest

for love or honey

heaving, too full to contain all I felt, all I wished for, all I wanted.

And through half-shut eyes, we found each other in the dark.

SAY IT

Grant

I'd been awake for a long while, since the shadows were still blue and purple and long, but I'd barely moved, content right here in the quiet room, wrapped up in Jo.

She slept soundly, her head in the curve of my shoulder and her legs twisted around one of mine. The slow rise and fall of her chest against my ribs matched mine, as did our heartbeats—I could feel hers steady, strong. And the thought that rose over and again was that I couldn't think of a single place I'd rather be, not in the whole world.

In the city, there was always noise, the gentle hum of people and life and living a constant companion. Here the only sound was a bird that lived in the pecan tree out back who liked to warble to greet the sun. It was usually annoying. But today, I wanted to run out there and throw that bird some seeds and thank it for being here to remind me of all the reasons I wanted to stay.

Jo was right—I wasn't the same man who drove into this town.

I didn't want to be him anymore.

for love or honey

I barely even knew who that man was. An empty shell, a purposeless husk. And now that I knew how it felt to be this man, there was no undoing it.

So my newfound goals were topped by the objective to get my father out of town, though I wasn't sure how. If they would sign, he would leave. I could get my bonus, get my father off my back, and keep my job intact. Today, I would talk to her for the first time in a while, the first real time. Maybe now that I was staying, she'd believe I had her best interest at heart. The money would do too much for her family and this town for me to let her to walk away from it.

I sighed heavy, stirring Jo. She stretched, exhaling long, her arm tightening across my chest.

I kissed her hair.

She kissed my pectoral.

"How'd you sleep?"

"Like I was dead," she said through a yawn.

"Wanna go for a run?"

"I do."

"Wanna fuck first?"

She laughed, shifting so she could see me. "Do you even have to ask?"

"Just being gentlemanly."

"It's a new look for you. I like it." She beamed at me like a ray of sunshine. "Are you really going to stay?"

"I really am. I was thinking … so, fair warning—I've been up for a while."

Her nose wrinkled. "Were you watching me sleep like a creepy vampire?"

"I fondled your boob a little, but mostly I stared at the ceiling and listened to that asshole bird."

"Unconscious boob fondling. Way less creepy."

"At least my intentions were clear. You never know what a vampire is thinking. Does he want to eat you? Nail you? Eat you while nailing you?"

"They're mysterious that way. Nobody knows what brand of sex offender they are until it's too late."

A chuckle. "So I think I'm going to cohabitate. Keep my place in Georgetown for when I need to be there, and the rest of the time, I'll be either traveling for work or here. Think Salma will let me stay?"

"I think she'd be downright offended if you stayed somewhere else. When will you head back?"

"Not until my father leaves."

"Yeah." One grim word. "What are we going to do about him?"

"Think your mom might listen to me?"

"It's possible."

"Let's get together with your sisters and see if we can't come up with a plan after we run."

"After we fuck," she said with a dirty smile.

I twisted, putting her on her back, angling for her lips. "Yes, after that."

The kiss was thick with intent that my hands knew all too well, skimming down her naked body, over her hip, and—

The sharp knock on the door parted us. Confused, we looked in the direction of the sound, then at each other. Jo snatched the sheets and pulled them up to her neck.

Because on the other side of the big window in the door, his shape muted by the curtain, was my father.

I rolled out of bed one way and Jo went the other, taking the sheets with her.

"Just a second," I said as I snagged a pair of jeans from the chair next to the bed and pulled them on.

When Jo had her clothes and had dragged her bedsheet train into the bathroom, I stalked to the door and opened it.

Everything about him was sharp, his eyes most of all.

"Come to tell me you're leaving?" I asked.

"We need to talk. Get the Blum girl out of here."

"I don't know how you haven't figured out yet that nobody tells Blum women what to do."

The bathroom door opened, and Jo walked out. Her hair was up in a bun on top of her head, which she held high even though the color on her cheeks belied her uncertainty. Her heels were hooked on her fingers.

She offered my father a cool smile. "I was just leaving," she said, picking up her clutch on the way to me. She stopped at my side, giving me a brief look of appreciation and support. "Get your running shorts on and meet me at the farm, okay?"

"Okay." I leaned in, kissed her tenderly, her hand in mine before it slipped away.

"'Scuse me," she said a little too politely so my father would get out of her way, which he did, though his expression didn't change.

When she was down the steps, I moved to let him in.

He let the screen door slap against the frame behind him.

"What do you want?" I asked with my back to him as I headed for the kitchen.

"So you gave the town a check?"

"I heard you did too. But I don't think our intentions are equal."

"The objective is the same. How close are you to getting them to sign?"

"I'm not." I took the coffee pot out of its cradle to fill it up with water.

"Your little Blum girls are trying to keep me away from Dottie."

"Since when is that new?"

"It's not new, just more successful."

"Thought you didn't have to fuck her to get what you wanted," I shot.

"Do you have any idea how serious this is? You want to fuck around here to no end when the only reason you came here is that farm. All you've managed to do is get that girl to sleep with you."

"You don't seem to be faring any better."

"I'll concede that it's harder than it looks, but I have a feeling I'm closer than you are."

"Go home. I'll close the deal. Alone." When the tank was full, I slid the pot home and opened the filter compartment.

for love or honey

"But now I'm having fun."

"I knew you were an asshole, but I didn't think you'd take advantage of a widow just to prove a point."

"Well, you don't know me all that well, do you?"

I released a slow breath, closed my eyes for a handful of heart-beats. I turned, dropping the vitriol in favor of virtue, if he had any. "You're not made of only evil. That I know for sure, no one is. So I'm asking you, man to man. Let's compromise. Leave this town and let me finish the job."

"Because you fell in love with your mark? That doesn't make me want to help you, do you realize that?" He stepped closer, his eyes hot with fury. "Why should you get to have it all? No, we won't be compromising. I'm going to close the deal. I'm going to get your bonus. And you're going to get back in line. Compromise." A short, joyless laugh. "No wonder you're losing."

"It's not a game for me. Not anymore."

"It is whether you're playing or not. You know," he started, daring to inch closer, "I don't have to sleep with her to get her to sign, but I will."

I took a breath, stretching myself taller. "You will not."

"Any means necessary." His face was dark. There was no smile, no amusement. No game. "I was wrong to ever think you could impress me. You had one job, and you failed. And now I have one job—do what you couldn't. To do what you never could."

"Leave them alone."

"When did you get so soft? You've been here too long, went too deep to get on the Blum girl's good side. You forgot where you came from, who you are. And now you're about to let a billion-dol-lar deal go. And for what? The hippie bee farmer you're fucking?"

In two strides, we were nearly nose to nose, my chin down, fists knotted at my sides. "Say another fucking thing about her, and I'll break your nose."

There—a smile.

"Why?" I asked. "Why do you enjoy this so much? If I'm not miserable, you're not happy."

Instantly, the smile was gone. "You know why."

"Say it."

"You're not in a position to make demands."

"Say it. Out loud. Tell me why you hate me."

Something in him changed. He grew, or I shrank as his chin lowered with his voice, emotionless. Steely eyes staked me to the ground. "I don't hate you. But every time I lay eyes on you reminds me that you're here, and she isn't. I hate what you stand for. I hate the way I feel when we share air. But I've always taken care of you, Grant. I've always provided. And I put my career on the line by taking you in. Your failure reflects directly on me. I've lost enough by your hand to lose respect in my position too, and all because you're too weak to do what needs to be done."

I held my ground, but hearing those words left me numb. There was no addressing them. There was no arguing.

"You care about her, but you're poison," he continued. "You think you're saving them. You think you're helping her. But the truth is that you've twisted her around, compromised her morals for the money. You don't care about her. You care about winning and money, so much so, you've tainted her for your own gain. It's what you do, Grant. It's what we do."

The truth of the accusation split me in two, renting my soul down the middle—who I was then, who I was now, and the wound that separated the two.

for love or honey

He was right. He might not have been inherently evil, but what evil he contained he'd used to possess me. The trace of it was left on every decision I made, everything I'd done.

But I could do one right. One final right.

"I won't play them, and you won't either."

He laughed, though the sound held no joy. "And how do you plan to stop me? Will you tattle on me? Because I'm sure they'd love to hear that your plans are no different than mine."

"Maybe once, but not anymore."

"Do you think that'll matter to them?"

The question struck me still.

Again with the cruel smile. "How will your little Blum girl feel when she finds out she was just part of a game? What will she say when she learns you used her? When she learns you lied to her? You knew my intentions all this time. And you never abandoned the game. You're playing it even now. When she finds out, what will she do?"

I'll lose her. Fear shredded what was left of me, leaving me ribbons and remnants.

I love her.

The light of that knowledge filled my heart, beamed through my ribs. But there was no hope in the feeling. It was watching a train leave the station, standing on the platform alone with nothing to do but watch her go, knowing it was the right thing for her even though it would be my ruin.

Nothing mattered but making it right. Because it wasn't about the money or my job. It wasn't about my father, who would never give me what I wanted, just keep me living on those scraps and crumbs. There was only one real thing in my life, and saving that was all that mattered now.

It was all that ever mattered.

"Guess we'll find out." I turned on my heel and headed to the dresser for a shirt, tugging it on to cover that ache in my chest that had just been so full. Nothing was left but shards, smashed by the sledgehammer of truth.

The truth they needed to know.

The truth I owed her, no matter what it cost me.

When he spoke, his voice held no levity. Only a warning. "If you tell them, I'll tell them what you did."

"Yeah, I got that." I stuffed my feet into my boots before storming to the table where my keys waited.

As I passed him, he gave his last ditch, the coup de grâce. "Do it, and you're fired."

I stopped, my hand on the screen door, my pulse loud in my ears.

"Then I guess I'm fired," I said, and walked out the door.

THE LAST TO KNOW

Jo

"I just don't understand what the big deal is," Mama huffed, pouring another cup of coffee. "How come Jo can spend the night over at Grant's, but I'm not allowed to see Merrick after midnight?"

"Because," I started, pulling my hair into a ponytail, "Merrick doesn't really care about you."

She gave me a look. "I know I'm old, but I'd like to think I still have my looks and a little personality to go with them."

"That's not what I mean, and you know it. All he wants is the shale under the farm."

"And how do you know that isn't what Grant wants?"

"It's different, Mama. He ... it's just different."

"How come?"

"Because he's staying," I blurted, my face flushed. "He's staying here. To be with me."

All three of them opened their mouths and eyeballs at the same time.

I kept going before they could speak, provided they had any words in their brains. "So I can't see how it's the same. I mean, Merrick looks like an apex predator who hasn't had a meal in a week."

"You realize Grant looks just like him, right?" Poppy noted.

"Except Grant proved himself. Look—I even got him in Wranglers and boots, for God's sake. You think you could get Merrick in jeans, Mama?"

She wrinkled her nose and eyed her coffee again. What she didn't do was answer.

Daisy frowned. "I don't understand how blue jeans are the deciding factor on trust here."

I sighed and rolled my eyes. "I don't have time to explain. Grant will be here any second for a run, so y'all better be quiet. We can talk about it later."

The rumble of Grant's car sounded, and instantly, I was smiling. But as I trotted to the back door, I saw another car behind his, sleek and black and expensive.

Instantly, my smile flipped upside down. "Who's that?"

"Oh, it's Merrick!" Mama said, hurrying to put her coffee down so she could fix her hair in the dim reflection on the microwave door.

I opened the back door, smiling but a little confused. When Grant's car door opened, I called, "Hey!"

And then he climbed out, dark and thunderous as a hurricane, and not in running attire.

He stalked toward me and up the steps, reaching for my hand as Merrick hurried behind.

for love or honey

"What's going on?" I asked before I was nudged out of the way to make room for Mama.

"What a nice surprise," she said. "You boys want some coffee?"

"No, thank you, Mrs. Blum," Grant answered. "Could we ... could we talk?"

"Sure," I said, "We can go—"

"No. All of you. Including you," he said to Mama.

Her smile had begun to fade as she took in Merrick, then Grant, then Merrick again. "Yes, of course," she answered absently. "Come on in."

Poppy and Daisy moved out of the way so we could enter, Mama and Merrick last. He'd done little more than cast her a tight smile, his focus entirely on Grant.

Grant held my hand so tight, my fingers pinched. "What's the matter?" I whispered.

But he only shook his head.

When Poppy and Daisy were sitting at the island and Mama fussed about a pot of coffee, Grant looked down at me with sorrow and regret written in every line of his face.

Merrick folded his arms across his chest and glared at Grant. "Go ahead."

When Grant let go of my hand, my pulse doubled. Something was wrong. Very wrong.

I backed toward the island with my eyes on him.

"I ..." His Adam's apple bobbed. But he still hadn't found the words—he raked his hand through his hair. I'd never seen him nervous or unafraid, not of anything.

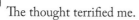

The thought terrified me.

"Dottie," he finally started, "I'm sorry. I'm sorry to do this to you, but I can't stand by and let him use you like he is. He doesn't want you, doesn't care for you or what's best for you—what he wants is your shale deposit. He came here with a plan to get it done because I didn't."

Mama had a strange smile on her face, her gaze bouncing between Grant and Merrick. "Wh … what?"

"He was courting you to get you to sign the contract. He wasn't here to manage me, or not entirely, at least. He had one goal—acquire this farm's rights. And you were collateral damage."

"That … that can't be right." Mama looked for confirmation from Merrick, but he was boring holes into Grant's skull with his eyes.

"I have no reason to lie, nothing to gain. But please, don't sign your rights over to him. Because every word out of his mouth has been a lie since he got here."

Everyone looked to Merrick for a response, an answer. Everyone but me.

I was looking at Grant.

"Did you know the whole time?" I asked. "Why … why he was here? What he was doing to my mother?"

The misery on his face hit me like a baseball bat. He gave a single nod.

Merrick finally sighed, watching Grant with disappointment and disgust. "I didn't think you'd actually do it."

"Why, because I've been such a pushover in the past?" Grant snapped, looming in the direction of his father.

for love or honey

"I just didn't think you were that stupid."

I expected him to keep talking to Grant, or apologize to Mama. I did not expect him to zero in on me.

"I promised Grant that if he ruined my deal, I'd ruin his. As self-righteous as he is about what I've done, he didn't tell you the whole story. Because he was using you long before I came for your mother."

"I already knew that," I said with my heart pounding.

"But did you know he was still using you? Did you know that everything he did was to get you to sign? Did you know I came to see him over a week before you ever saw my face?"

My face swiveled to Grant, praying for it to be a lie. But if he was misery before, now he was wretched, and I knew.

"He told me the day he got here that you were the key to getting your family to sign. That if he could get you to trust him, he could convince you to put pen to paper. And that you could convince the rest of them. When I got to town, he assured me you were a long game, a means to an end—this, minutes after you'd slept with him. He had no feelings for you then, and I doubt he ever will. He lied to you." He scanned our faces. "All of you. Think what you want—Grant is everything he hates about me. We're not that different."

"I'm nothing like you," Grant said through his teeth.

Merrick turned slowly, moving in Grant's direction until they were nearly nose to nose. "Everything I did, you did. Everything I am, you are. Except for the fact that you were willing to throw a deal out the window for a piece of ass—"

Whatever he was about to say was interrupted by the flash of Grant's arm as he cocked his fist and let it go almost too fast to see. Merrick wheeled back, hands to his nose.

The four of us were a mess of gasps, shrieks, and hands over our mouths. But none of us moved to help the traitors in our kitchen.

Merrick stood, his eyes narrowed and watering, his jaw firm, the bottom half of his face covered in gore.

"I told you not to say another fucking thing about her," Grant said so still, so quiet, the hairs stood up on the back of my neck.

"You need to leave," Mama said. I didn't realize she was crying until then.

They looked at her, then at each other, like they didn't know who she was speaking to.

"Both of you. Get the hell out of my kitchen. I don't want to see either of your faces again," Mama said, adding. "You can tell Flexion to fuck right off, because they won't be getting anything inside our property line. And neither will you."

I was too hurt, too raw to even appreciate my mother's casual use of the word fuck. My eyes, my heart, my whole soul were looking at a stranger.

"It was a lie," I said half to myself.

"It wasn't," Grant promised, taking a step in my direction.

I took one back. "I knew it was a game, but I thought ... I thought after ... after we—" I shook my head and swallowed, trying to master myself. "It quit being a game for me a long time ago, but how can I believe it was for you too? You lied about why he was here, even when he was here. You put my mother's heart on the line and strung mine along with it all for your deal. Were you going to stay just to keep me in your sights? Were you going to keep sleeping with me so you could get your daddy his money?" My cheeks were wet and cool—I was crying, when did I start crying?—my voice wobbling and as unsteady as my knees. "Get out."

for love or honey

"Jo, please—"

"Get out."

"Just let me explain—"

Mama stepped between us with the menace of a lioness in front of her cubs. "She said to get out. My shotgun isn't that far off. Don't make me get it. I don't wanna go to jail today, but I will—and gladly—if you don't get off my property right this minute."

Merrick gave my mother a cold look but said with a muffled nose, "It was just business."

"Maybe to you."

He watched her for a moment as if he had more to say, but decided he was best to leave, which was wise.

Mama wasn't kidding about the shotgun. And if she didn't get it, I was going to.

Grant's eyes were trained on the ground as he tried to master himself without luck. So he met my eyes, the pain between us a palpable, living thing.

"I never …" A hard swallow, and whatever he was about to say was gone. "I'm sorry. I'm so sorry."

His voice broke, and he turned slipping out of the house behind his father.

I pressed my hand to my mouth to keep the sob locked in my chest where it was. But when he was gone, my composure went with him.

And there was nothing left but regret.

BUSINESS END

Grant

That fucking bird outside my window chirped happily the next morning, rousing me from restless sleep.

Everything about the sound was wrong. There was no place for happy in the world, not after yesterday.

The sheets were damp with sweat, tangled around my legs and waist like I'd been fighting them all night. The faint scent of whiskey hung in the air, though whether it came from the sheets or me, I didn't know. My eyes stayed shut on behalf of the headache thumping behind them.

Yesterday's horror crept back in like noxious fog. A morning that had started off with hope and promise had gone dark the second my father walked through the door. He'd stood there in the Blum's kitchen like the grim reaper while I condemned myself along with him, and though I was certain he was just as satisfied that I'd lost the thing I'd wanted, nothing could top the feeling of his nose crunching against my knuckles.

I flexed that aching fist at the memory, wishing I'd hit him again before he got in his car and drove away with the parting words, I hope she was worth it.

Snide as he was, he wouldn't have believed that she was.

Jo wouldn't return my calls or my texts, and knowing she needed space, I gave it to her. I ran for hours, making it home soaked and spent without having outrun any of my pain. Showered, unable to wash the stink of regret off me. And then I dusted off one of the full bottles of bourbon in Salma's kitchen and drank until I was asleep.

But all I'd managed to do was kill time.

I sighed—the smell was definitely me—scrubbing a hand over my face. My father left town, that I was sure of. My job was lost, which I should have been upset about. My life as I knew it was gone. I could try to find another job, sure. But I didn't know if I wanted it.

I didn't want to be that man anymore. I wanted to be this man. I wanted to be Jo's man.

All these years I'd worked under my father were for him, I'd realized. Not for me. When I took his approval out of the equation, nothing was keeping me there.

The knowledge made me feel hollow, empty. Had I ever had purpose? Had I ever wanted anything so desperately, so passionately, that my future was written out for me? That there was only one path to take?

I couldn't even answer myself. It hurt too much.

A gentle knock on the door forced my eyes open, but only to slits. I rose to sit, swinging my legs off the bed. My head dropped to my hands, the heels of my palms in my eye sockets where they patiently pressed until the room quit spinning. With a deep breath, I stood, snagging a pair of sleep pants and pulling them on.

When I opened the front door, Salma was hinged over, setting a pie on the welcome mat. She looked up, surprised.

"Well, there you are. Just made two strawberry pies, and if I eat them both, I'll have indigestion until I'm dead."

I pushed open the screen door, holding it so she could enter. When she passed, she glanced up at me. "Bad night? You smell like Jack Daniel's business end."

A chuckle. Good to know I can still laugh. "I figured you'd have heard by now."

She shuffled her way into the kitchen and set the pie on the table. "About your daddy and Dottie? Or about you and Jo?" She gave me a look before making her way to the coffee pot. When I made to head her off, she waved her hand. "You're in no condition to do anything but sit in that chair and tell me what happened, if you want to talk about it."

Arguing wouldn't do me any good, so I sat while she made coffee, staring into the whipped cream peaks of the pie.

"I fucked up, Salma."

"I'll say," she teased gently.

"You … you have to understand, I've been groomed for this job, built for this purpose—for coming to towns just like these and convincing people to give me what I want. And this time, it was the Blum's shale over everything else. Jo was the only way in."

She flicked the button on the machine and opened the cabinet for a couple of plates and silverware. "And your plan backfired."

"It did."

"Because when you convinced her to trust you, you learned to trust her too."

for love or honey

A miserable nod.

"And when you learned to trust her, you fell in love with her."

My gaze slid to hers as she approached with a sad sort of smile on her face.

"Oh, don't look so surprised. In some circles, I'm considered to be wise—sage, even." She set down the plates and began cutting slices.

"Pie for breakfast?"

She nodded. "Sometimes, pie for breakfast is the only thing you can do." When she'd plated a piece, she handed it over with a fork.

I didn't argue.

Salma plated her own with knobby, speckled hands and sat next to me but didn't say anything, just waited.

Silently, I stared at the pie for a moment. "I'd convinced myself that I was doing the right thing. That Jo and her family would be happy with the money, never acknowledging that I was working to convince them to abandon their morals, their principles for my gain. I told myself I was saving them from heartache by letting my father play games with them, certain I'd get it done before him and no one would be the wiser. But I was just trying to save myself on that too. I didn't want to lose her."

"But then you did."

I shook my head. "She's not going to forgive me for this."

"Does that mean you're not going to try?"

I took a bite of pie while I thought over her question, and it melted in my mouth. I took another bite with a little too much enthusiasm, my stomach grinding now that food was in front of me.

"I have to try," I said once I'd swallowed. "I just don't think she's going to take me back. I don't blame her—I wish for it for my own gain again, not hers. What's best for her is if I just go. I'm no better than my father—I came here with the intent to use her. Doesn't matter that I … that I love her. Maybe …" I swallowed hard, though my mouth was a wasteland. "Maybe this is penance. Payment for every terrible thing I've done."

"Oh, now—I'm sure you haven't been so evil."

One of my brows rose in her direction.

She made a noncommittal sound, her mouth full of pie. When she swallowed, she said, "We've all done things we're ashamed of, but that doesn't mean we don't deserve to be happy. Think you'll still go on being evil?"

It was a joke, but I didn't laugh. "Not with Flexion."

"No?"

"My father made sure I understood that if I told Dottie what he was here for, I was fired. And that he'd make sure I left here with nothing."

"And you told Dottie anyway. Even though it meant you'd lose Jo."

"There was nothing else to do."

"Sure there was. You could have done any number of things, including keeping it all from them, sure. You could have helped your father. You didn't. You did what was right, even if it meant you were left with nothing."

"I can't feel proud of myself for that, Salma."

"I suppose not, not right now, at least. But Jo is a reasonable woman—"

I laid another look on her, and she bobbled her head.

for love or honey

"Well, she's eventually reasonable, once she blows off her steam. What are you gonna do?"

"She won't answer my messages. I was thinking about going over there, but I don't want to push her. I don't want to make it worse. But if she doesn't … if there's no hope, I can't stay here. It hurts too much, that slim chance."

"You're going to need to know sooner than later. If nothing else, you can get how you feel off your chest and let her unload on you."

"And let her run me out of town like she's been trying to do since I got here."

"Maybe she'll surprise you. She's been known to do that."

I nudged a strawberry with my fork. "Maybe."

She was quiet for a minute. "Ask her to listen. Start with that. Hope for that. And don't you say you don't deserve forgiveness again—I'm gonna go ahead and call that bullshit. Everybody deserves a second chance, son, and you're no exception. If you love her, go tell her. It's the only way you'll know for sure."

I nodded at my pie, wondering if it was possible. But the truth was that she was better off without me. So I decided to pack my things, even if there was a possibility she'd take me back.

I never did believe in miracles.

BURRITO GIRL

Jo

In the way of safe places in the world, burritoed in my comforter was easily my top choice.

I laid on my back, staring at the ceiling, grateful for the blackout curtains and central air. This morning when everyone got up to do chores, I stayed right here. Nobody even knocked. They probably figured I needed rest. Or that if they woke me, I might snap and gnaw one of their heads off at the shoulders.

Truth was, I needed a hug. Which was how I found myself rolled up in a down comforter with only my face showing.

I could tell by the slant of light behind the curtains that it was late and wished I'd been sleeping this whole time. But I'd spent yesterday in a sort of fugue state, once I'd gained my composure, at least. It was a long, quiet afternoon and evening as my sisters tried to distract Mama and me. Though Mama was in much better shape than me. At least she'd avoided sleeping with her interloper. And she'd kept her heart locked up better than I had too.

for love or honey

Instead of protecting it like I should have, I'd shoved my heart into a pasta maker and smushed it into spaghetti, left thin and brittle once the tears dried.

It was all a lie.

Every word he'd spoken to me. Every moment we shared.

Deep down, I knew that wasn't entirely true. But then I'd think about how he watched his father pursue my mother, never once trying to stop him, lying to me about Merrick's intentions when I asked. Or his father showing up after the first night we were together and Grant telling him I was just a part of his plan. Maybe Grant was lying to his father. Maybe he wasn't. But Grant and I had started off as a lie, and we'd ended with one.

There was no way to know what was real and what wasn't. What was true feelings and what was a manipulation. I shouldn't have blamed him. He told me he'd win, and I told him I'd win, and then I fell for him like an idiot. And now I was shocked that it turned out exactly like he said it would.

That was on me. All me.

Yesterday, I'd woken with my world filled with hope.

Today, I'd woken with that hope smashed to a thousand pieces.

The sick ache in my chest twisted and writhed at the thought of him, at the thought of the future I'd caught a glimpse of before it disappeared. Once, not so long ago, I'd believed that I was destined to be alone, and that I'd be better off that way. And the man who proved me wrong lied from the very start.

My nose burned, my eyes pricking with tears, and I pulled a flap of blanket over my face before they spilled down my temples and into my hairline, even though no one was here to see. Hiding here alone, I could cry as much as I needed to. The only shame here was my own.

Stupid, so stupid I'd been to trust him when I knew better.

I knew better.

And I'd still fallen like a fool for the worst sort of man—the man with an agenda.

The man who valued money and prestige over all.

But I'd seen another man too, a man I'd believed was so genuine, freshly hatched and experiencing the world for the first time. He'd spoken to me once about magic as if he'd only just discovered it. He'd held me in the moonlight and told me without words that he needed me. He'd said he wanted to stay.

If I'd signed his contract, would I have woken to an empty bed? When he told me he needed me, was it me he needed or the signature?

I was too hurt and confused, too bruised to know.

A soft rap on the door preceded a creak as it opened.

"Hey," Daisy whispered, "are you up?"

I didn't move in the hopes she'd leave.

"She's not up," Daisy whispered again.

"Oh, she's awake," Poppy said a little too loud.

The bed bounced as she climbed in and kept bouncing as she jumped on her knees, shaking my burrito like an earthquake.

I groaned.

"Open the curtains, Daisy." She shook me with more purpose. "Come out, come out, wherever you are."

"Leave me alone."

for love or honey

"We did that most of yesterday," Daisy said sweetly. She slipped into bed on the other side of me, and her hands rummaged gently in the area around my face, looking for entrance.

"I'll bite you. You know I will."

"You will not, Iris Jo," Daisy said without stopping.

"I will," I warned weakly. "I haven't eaten and am very hungry."

Having found a way in, Daisy pulled back the flap, exposing my face. Hers fell.

"Oh, Jo."

Tears sprang again. "Don't say, Oh, Jo like that, or I'll cry again."

Her chin buckled, but she nodded, somehow managing to cradle me in her arms.

Poppy's bouncing had slowed, then stopped. Next thing I knew, my sisters were spooning my hips.

We laid like that for a little while. Daisy had freed enough of my scalp to stroke my hair, and I cried even though I'd said I wouldn't.

Neither of them called me on it.

"I'm sorry," Poppy said.

"Me too," I answered.

"Can I set his car on fire?" she asked.

We laughed through muffled noses.

"Fine, can I put sugar in his gas tank? Slash his tires?"

"I think we can settle this without committing a misdemeanor," Daisy noted.

"Yeah, but it wouldn't be as satisfying," Poppy said.

"I knew better," I said aloud, which hurt so much more than it did when I'd said it to myself.

"We believed him too." Daisy petted my hair softly.

"I didn't," Poppy started. "I said from the beginning—ow!"

Daisy gave her a look over the top of my head, which must have been where her pinching hand had gone.

"How's Mama?" I asked.

Daisy sighed. "She's okay. I think she's more mad at Grant than she is at his dad."

"Ugh, fuck that guy," Poppy spat.

"Which one?" Daisy asked.

"Both of them, obviously. But that asshole Merrick coming to town to double up on us and use Mama for personal gain? No. Absolutely, a hundred percent no." She paused. "Do you think Grant was in on it? On his dad coming here?"

"No. He hates his dad." It was my turn to pause as my doubt rose. "Or at least I thought he did. He could have been lying about that too." That twist in my chest tightened, as did my throat. "God, this sucks."

"What are you gonna do?" Daisy asked gently.

"Live in my burrito until he's a million miles away."

"Well," Mama said from the doorway, "that might be a while, considering he's outside."

"What?" we said in unison, popping off the bed. My blanket slid off my head and shoulders.

for love or honey

"He's outside. Should I get rid of him?"

Poppy said yes when Daisy said no. They gave each other looks.

I hadn't said anything.

"Just hear him out," Daisy said. "Even if it's just for closure. Even if it's just to tell him what a stupid asshole he is."

"I'm all for the stupid asshole part," Poppy agreed, "but he doesn't deserve any more of your time and energy. And you don't owe him anything."

"It's not about owing him," Daisy said. "It's about her owing herself. She'll never forgive herself if she just ignores—"

"I can't even believe you'd tell her to entertain that son of a bitch after he straight up lied—"

"I'll see him," I answered quietly, unfurling my blanket slowly.

Mama watched me, worried. "Are you sure?"

"This is a bad idea," Poppy said.

"Oh, leave her be," Daisy chided.

I scooted off the bed, ignoring them. "I'm sure."

Mama nodded once. "I'll stall him. I think you might want to take a look in the mirror real quick before you head out. Maybe brush your teeth. I'm just sayin'."

On a cursory glance in the mirror in the corner, I made a face. I smoothed down my ratted hair and made for the bathroom.

"I'm gonna egg his car," Poppy said as they filed down the hallway.

"You will not," Mama answered. "Jo, honey—you might want to hurry. I don't know how long I can hold her off."

I couldn't even laugh. Or smile. I stuck my toothbrush in my mouth instead.

My chest was a painful flutter of nerves and emotion, too many to catch just one. Anger that he was here, that he'd come so soon to put me in a position to face him. There was the pain, the hurt I felt knowing he was here, right here, and I couldn't find comfort in him. Longing for times when he'd made me so happy, then humiliation in its wake when I remembered he'd played me. And fear—fear that I'd listen, that I'd trust him again when he'd broken my faith so completely.

Shame that I wanted to listen. That I wanted him back. That I wanted to believe him even now.

I spit into the sink and swiped fresh tears from my cheeks, brushed my hair and tried not to look at my reflection with too much scrutiny. At least my ass looked good in these sleep shorts.

I shamelessly hoped it hurt him desperately to know this ass was no longer his.

With a deep breath, I headed in the same direction my family had gone, toward the front door. They were whispering when I entered the living room but shot apart like shrapnel on my entrance.

"You didn't let him in?" I asked.

"Figured you might need an escape route," Mama said, cupping my arm when I approached. "You sure about this?"

I nodded.

The four of us seemed to take equal deep breaths before I turned for the door and stepped out.

And I immediately wished I'd had Mama send him off.

If it was hard not to miss him after he'd taken a baseball bat to my heart, I was doomed on the sight of him there in jeans and boots and a T-shirt, leaning against that stupid sports car with his hands in his pockets and his eyes on the ground.

I folded my arms and hugged my middle, stopping at the top of the porch stairs.

When he saw me in his periphery, he straightened up in surprise.

"Jo," he said, just one ragged word so full of pain, he somehow broke my heart again.

"What are you doing here?"

He didn't approach, just paused, his eyes flicking to the ground. They didn't rise any higher than the stairs.

"I … I just wanted to try to explain—"

"Mama told you not to come back. You're lucky she's in a forgiving mood."

He met my eyes. "Is she the only one?"

"She is."

A nod, his Adam's apple bobbing as he seemed to make some sort of decision. "I understand." Another pause as he collected himself. "I'm leaving town, so I just … just hear me out for a second. Please."

My brain had caught fire at the news of him leaving, screeching its shock and dissent. I couldn't speak, so I nodded like he had.

"When I came to town, I thought … I thought I knew what I was getting myself into. But I didn't. It started off as a game for me, just like it did for you. And then … you turned everything I thought I knew inside out. You showed me the world from a vantage I'd never seen. I was ready to stay here with you because there wasn't a choice to be made. There wasn't a question to answer. I just wanted you." His gaze swept the ground as he tried to master himself. "I won't ask your forgiveness, Jo—I don't deserve it. But you should know it wasn't all a lie. And that I'm sorry."

I swallowed, trying to force my heart, my tears back down without luck. "Everything we had was built on trust. The reason it worked was that we were being honest, honest about what we wanted and what we had to give, even when those things were part of a game. But while I was being honest, you were lying the whole time, if not about your feelings, then about your father, my mother, the safety of our rights."

"You're right. I didn't tell you about my father to protect myself, not you. I told you to sell, to turn your back on your convictions, because it benefited me. But how I feel about you has never been a lie. It's the most honest thing I've ever known."

I shook my head, my breath hitching. "But when did it stop being a lie and start being the truth? You can't name that moment any better than I could, I'd wager. So how … how am I supposed to believe anything you say to me when the cornerstone you and I were built on was faulty from the start?"

The misery on his face mirrored my heart. "You aren't. I won't ask you to. But I couldn't leave without saying so."

"Do you feel better?" I asked.

"Not at all."

"Yeah. Me neither." I backed toward the door. "You should go."

Another nod. He opened his car door, but didn't get in. He took that moment to look at me with all the weight, all the searing pain in his gaze. He stripped me bare again, his eyes tracing the shape of me, landing on my eyes once more, as if to memorize me.

"Goodbye, Jo," he said with a raw, rough voice before slipping into his car and driving away.

"Goodbye," I whispered at the dust and distance.

for love or honey

Because that was all that was left.

THE LONGEST ROAD

Grant

The highway rolled under me, the horizon stretched out in front of me, and everything I wanted was behind me.

I'd packed the rest of my bag carelessly, thrown it in my trunk. Blew through the house, tidying up as quickly as I could. Loaded the dishwasher and started it. Pulled the sheets off the bed and threw them in the wash. Sat down at the table with the stationery Salma had set up by the ancient telephone hanging on the wall in the kitchen and wrote two letters—one to Salma and one for Jo.

And then I got in my car and drove.

I'd gained hundreds of miles of distance, but I hadn't left it behind me. It was as if a piece of me had been pinned there, and the farther I traveled, the longer I stretched. My soul was thin and pale, taxed to its limits. It'd never be the same, no matter how many miles stood between us. Because part of me would always be hers.

Now I had to figure out who I was without her. My old life didn't fit anymore, like a shirt shrunk in the wash, buttons gaping and seams strained. I didn't know my new self well enough to have an instinct I could trust. But I was headed back to my old apartment at eighty miles an hour without hope I'd figure it out.

But going back was the only thing left to do.

Even if I'd left my heart behind me.

With her.

PIECES OF ME

Jo

Two long and empty days passed.

There hadn't been much left to say once he drove away, so I didn't say much at all. We got a call to move a hive that had formed in a playground structure, and I took the job as usual, enjoying the hours spent alone. I kept myself busy on the farm so I didn't have to see anyone, and when I had no choice, like at dinner, I pretended like everything was fine. Like I was fine.

But the best truthful adjective I could come up with was numb.

I didn't sleep much that night, too busy overthinking things to find peaceful rest. I wished I could have said I felt vindicated or justified, but there was no rightness in my heart. He was gone, and I felt his absence not as an emptiness, not as a space, but as a weight so oppressive, it crushed me slowly, breath by breath, inch by inch.

This morning, I'd woken not with purpose but with some amount of determination to adhere to a schedule. So just as the sun rose, I pulled on my running shoes, tightened my ponytail, put on the most ass-kicking playlist I had, and I ran like the devil was chasing me.

In a lot of ways, I supposed he was.

The sun was well risen by the time I made it home to find Uber Stan pulling into my driveway. We didn't actually have Uber in Lindenbach, just sweet old Stan, who everyone texted or called for a ride. He'd even made little signs for his windows that mimicked the Uber and Lyft logos.

Nobody had the heart to tell him that wasn't quite how it worked.

I jogged behind him, surprised when Salma slowly eased out of the back of his SUV. I hurried to help her out.

"Salma, what are you doin' here?" I asked, cupping her elbow.

She put all hundred pounds of her weight on me, her eyes on her feet so she didn't misstep. "Well, hey, honey."

"Hey. Come in for some tea?"

"Oh, that's all right. Can we just sit on the porch for a while?"

"Of course."

"Stan," she called into the SUV, "not gonna be too long. You wanna wait?"

Before he could answer, I said, "I'll take you back home."

"Oh, I don't want to trouble you."

"It's no trouble."

She checked my expression with rheumy eyes, but nodded her assent.

"Thanks, Stan," she said, and he flicked the brim of his feed store trucker hat.

"Anytime, Miss Salma. Y'all have a good day now. Don't forget—Ima runnin' a twofer special: get a ride from me, and I'll pick you up free."

"I'll spread the word," I said, securing Salma behind me before shutting the door with a thump.

Gravel crunched and popped under his tires as he backed up and drove away. And I offered Salma my arm and guided her toward the house.

"How are you, Salma?"

"Just glad I woke up this mornin', honey."

I chuckled. "How come the older people get, the more morbid the jokes?"

"Because when you get to be my age, no point in avoiding the truth. May as well make peace with it, and what better way than laughing? Anyway, it's true. Every morning I wake up surprised."

I led her to a rocking chair and sat in its twin by her side. "What can I do for you today, Miss Salma?"

"Well, first I wanna say I'm sorry for not coming by sooner. It's just that I didn't know Grant left until this morning. I figured he was just out here at the farm, but then Bettie told me he'd gone. Went by hoping she was wrong. And when I did, I found this."

Salma reached into an ancient purse from what had to be the sixties—it went perfectly with the hot-pink polyester cigarette pants she had on—and when her hand reappeared, it held an envelope with strong, hard writing on the front.

She extended it in my direction. I took it, rested my hands in my lap, fingertips heavy and aware on the paper between them. I didn't know what to do. Reading it would hurt. Not knowing what was inside would kill me.

for love or honey

I was holding a grenade with the pin out. And for a minute, all I could do was make sure it didn't detonate until I was prepared.

As if I'd ever be prepared.

Salma watched me for a moment, then turned her attention to the horizon. "He wrote me one too." A pause. "It's not my place to speak out of turn or pry, but one of the perks of being this old is that you can say whatever the hell you want, and nobody will tell you to hush." When I chuckled, she continued, smiling. "I know that Grant wasn't honest with you, honey. I know you're hurt at knowing his intentions were anything but pure. And that he kept his daddy's intentions from you too. He made mistakes. But that doesn't change the fact that the boy is in love with you."

Shock stopped my heart for a beat. It started up again, sending an electric flush across my skin. "He … he what?"

She shook her head a little, smiling softer. "He loves you. You love him too, if you hadn't figured it out."

"I … Salma, I don't …"

"Oh, yes you do. Whatever you were gonna say, you do." She sat back, looked off, waved a hand at me. "Plenty of this is in your letter, I'm sure, and here I am spoiling it. Read it, if you would. Go on inside where you can have some privacy if you want—I'm happy here on your porch. I've always loved this view. Used to sit with your granny out here and talk about our men, when they were still with us." Her thoughts drifted away with her words, and she sighed, rocking herself gently.

But I'd barely heard her, struck stupid by the observance of an old woman who knew more than I ever would.

Love him. I loved him.

And Salma knew before me.

A little laugh slid out of me even as my eyes filled with tears. I sat back in my chair too, setting my eyes on the same view as Salma for a moment. But there was no processing the news. My emotions were tangled up in a thick knot in my chest.

I slid my thumbnail into the flap and tore the envelope open before unfolding the letter with my heart in my throat.

Jo–

There are too many things I want to say, and no sufficient words to say them with. But before I leave, and for the last time, I needed you to know what you mean to me.

It's all I have left to give.

This town was supposed to be just like every other I'd come and gone from, a stop on a long train with no destination. And I was the same me I ever was, the only me I'd ever known. All my life, I've been searching without knowing what I was looking for. I had everything I could want, everything I needed. I had a life and ambitions, a future, the trajectory already set. I was happy, I thought.

And then you went and proved me wrong on every front.

I had no heart before you. Fitting that I should leave it here with you.

My father thinks me pathetic for finding myself—my truest self—in a little bee farm in Texas with a woman who wanted nothing I had to offer. But being with you shed light on that trajectory I was on, exposing its flaws, its wrongness. That path was taking me to my father's life, and it surprised me to find that was what I thought I wanted. Until I didn't anymore.

I wanted a life with you. Here.

I only wish I'd realized it sooner.

But I have you to thank for everything—I wouldn't have seen it if you hadn't shown me. And now that I know, I can rewrite the equation, put myself on a new path. I only wish it was with you.

for love or honey

I told you once I'd never been in love before, and at the time, that was true. But now I know what love is, what happiness means, how precious it is. And that's thanks to you too.

I'd beg if I thought I deserved to be forgiven. So instead I'll tell you that I've never regretted anything more than this. I'll say that I'm sorry even though the word will never be enough to describe how I feel.

I'll tell you that I love you because I want you to know that love changed me. I'll never be the same—I'll be more, forever better because for a moment, I saw myself through you and learned who I wanted to be. Who I'm supposed to be.

Part of me will always be here.

Part of me will be yours forever.

-Grant

I blinked away tears, reading and rereading, shaking my head and pressing my fingers to my lips to keep myself from sobbing. My hand lowered to my lap, the letter still unfurled.

Salma waited, still rocking in her chair as we stared off at the hills, patchy with sunshine between clouds.

When the clamp on my throat eased enough to speak, I finally did.

"He loves me."

"He does."

"But … he lied, Salma. He … he used me."

"I know."

"And now h-he's gone."

She nodded. "But gone back to what? He's all scrambled up. His daddy's not gonna forgive this. He's got no job and—"

"He what?"

Her eyes narrowed a little. "Which part?"

"His job."

Now she was frowning. "That wasn't in there? About his job?"

"No."

"Honey, his daddy didn't just threaten to tell y'all Grant's intentions—he fired the boy the second he left to come here. To come clean."

"He … Merrick fired him?"

"Well, yes. Grant blew Flexion's plan to get your rights and Merrick's plan to con your poor mama. He knew it meant his job, but he did it anyway."

I tried to speak, but I couldn't get past the stone in my esophagus.

Salma sighed. "He didn't even use that to try to get you back. That boy. I don't know whether to hug him or throttle him."

I leaned forward, abandoning the letter in my lap to drop my face to my hands. He loved me, loved me enough to sacrifice his job, the forever unfulfilled promise of a relationship with his father, everything he'd held dear.

Before me.

He loved me.

I loved him.

Is it enough?

for love or honey

"What do I do?" I said half to myself.

"Well, answer me this—do you think he'd ever hurt you on purpose?"

"No, never. Not on purpose."

"Do you think he'd lie to you now? After all this?"

I thought for a beat, playing out scenarios. "No."

"Do you believe him? Whatever he said in that letter?"

I glanced down at the letter and ran my fingertips across I love you. "I do," I said softly.

"Then I think the only question is, how are you gonna get him back?"

My breath hitched as a smile rose on my face. I reached for Salma's hand, my heart too big for my rib cage.

"I think I know just how."

COMPASS

Grant

I couldn't seem to find it in me to unpack.

My suitcase laid on my bedroom floor with clothes spilling out, except these clothes didn't fit here in this place. The boots, dusty and scuffed. The jeans, soft from wear. But the suits in the garment bag draped on the chair in my room didn't fit me. Not anymore.

I'd gotten here yesterday and hadn't worn anything but sleep pants and T-shirts since. They were the closest thing I had to the middle. The house was still and quiet and unrecognizable. Logically, I knew these were my things, but none of it felt like mine anymore. My life wasn't mine anymore, but the life I wanted wasn't on offer.

Two days driving and a day here alone had left me with too much time to think. My brain wanted a plan. What would I do for work? Because I never could sit still, especially not now. Where would I go, if not here? Should I stay? Go? It was all wrong.

None of those plans included her.

I ran my hand across my jaw, noting the feel of the beard I'd started, since shaving didn't feel like me either. My living room was too still and quiet, so I'd turned on music. Maybe I'd need to get a cat or something, anything to make this place feel like less of a tomb. Maybe I'd leave the country, go somewhere sunny and sandy to forget. To run away. But I knew better—if I wasn't able to leave my heartache in Lindenbach, my longitude didn't matter.

I didn't know how to make any decisions, my gut—which I relied on desperately and for all things—was broken. All I could think to do was sit here until I figured it out.

I was lost, my compass spinning wild.

I'd eaten takeout for every meal since I'd gotten back to my place—I couldn't even call it home anymore. Jo hadn't called, hadn't texted. As badly as I wanted to know if she'd gotten my letter, I didn't want to know at all. It was easier to think she'd thrown it in a fire than that she'd read it and decided not to call.

Rejection, I'd learned, came in too many forms. So many, I'd quit counting.

The doorbell rang—my dinner—and I heaved myself off the couch and to the door, not wanting to eat, but knowing I needed to. Maybe I'd go for a run, see if I couldn't chase some of my thoughts down. Or maybe I'd—

On opening the door, I froze, the doorknob still in my hand. Dinner was not on my porch.

Jo was.

God, she was beautiful, her hair shining in the waning sunlight. Surely I was dreaming. Surely I'd fallen asleep on the couch, and my traitor brain had decided its full-time job was torturing me.

Jo's cheeks flushed—I'd gone too long without speaking. "Hi," she said meekly.

"I ... Jo?"

The color on her cheeks deepened, and she rambled, "I ... I hope it's okay that I came, but texting just wasn't enough. Calling would have been weird. I mean, how do you just call somebody after everything we've been through and say I love you? The only thing—it's stupid now, I see that it's stupid—was to just get on a plane and come here and see if maybe—"

Whatever else she wanted to say was lost, her lips occupied with mine.

I breathed for the first time in days, the sweet scent of grass and flowers and wild summertime filling my senses. She fit in my arms so perfectly, so exactly—had I always known that, or did I only notice now?—and I wrapped her up, held her close to make sure she was real. She went soft against me, her mouth pliant and giving and relieved.

The kiss ended with our foreheads together.

"What are you doing here?" I whispered.

"Coming to get you back."

"Get me back? I was already yours."

"Even now? Even still?"

"Even more."

She breathed for a moment, our foreheads still together until her gaze rose to meet mine. "I got your letter."

"I figured."

"You love me," she said with a smile that was both shy and mischievous.

"I heard you love me too."

The smallest laugh.

"Jo …" My voice broke. I swallowed to smooth it. "I'm sorry. I'm so sorry I didn't tell you the truth about my father or the truth about me. Telling you would mean losing you. But I didn't have a choice in the end. I couldn't let him … I couldn't let myself …"

"I know." She held my jaw. "You said you didn't deserve forgiveness, but you do. What is true sorrow without sacrifice? You gave up everything to tell me the truth, even me. How could I do anything but forgive you? If I'd have known, I wouldn't have let you leave."

"Because I gave up my job?"

"Because you did the right thing, knowing you'd lose me. Your job too, and your father. You abandoned everything you loved to save us, to protect us. Grant, I don't let anyone in, and neither do you. But I saw you, not the man who stood on a podium talking about diesel in an Italian suit. Even if it started off as a game, what's between us is real. I knew it even then, I was just … it hurt. And it was easier to let you go than admit that despite it all, how you felt about me was as real as the earth or the sky or Salma's biscuits."

A chuckle made it past the clamp on my throat, and I held her face, lifting it so I could peer into her eyes.

"Come back to me, Grant. Because this … this isn't where you belong, not anymore. This isn't your home."

"No, it's not. I'm not even sure I know where home is."

"It's where I am."

I couldn't speak.

"I want to show you what that word means, home. I want to show you what it means to have a family, to have a place to belong. You told me once you wanted to take care of me."

"And you told me you could take care of yourself."

"But I was wrong. I thought I could be alone and happy, and maybe before you that was true. But not anymore. I need you. I want to take care of you like you want to take care of me. I want to love you and be loved by you. Will you come with me? Will you come home?"

"Lead the way," I said before kissing her to cover the ache deep in my ribcage, a blissful, disbelieving ache.

When the kiss ended, I smiled down at her.

"Think Salma's rented out my room?"

"I know she hasn't, but I've got a better idea."

"Oh?"

"How about you come stay at the farm?"

"I don't know if I can share a bathroom with your sisters."

Her laughter was a pair of wings on my heart. "We can stay in one of the cottages out back of the house."

I thumbed her cheek. "We?"

"Too soon?" she asked, her brows coming together in the slightest of shifts.

It was my turn to laugh. "Since when did you and I take anything slow?"

"Good," she said with a sigh and a smile that faded almost as soon as it had appeared. "What about your job?"

"I don't know if you realize this, but I don't actually have to work."

"Did I just land a sugar daddy?"

We were both laughing as she wrapped herself around me like a cartoon character. "You did."

"Except in blue jeans and boots? On a farm?" She pretended to try to climb me, and I helped her up until her legs were around my waist.

"Yup. But I'm keeping the car."

Smiling, she leaned in. "Wouldn't have you any other way."

And with something so simple as a kiss, I left my old world behind for the one I'd only dreamed about.

For her.

THE SCORE

Jo

I shifted the box in my arms, blowing a lock of hair out of my face.

"For someone who didn't feel like DC was home, you sure do have a lot of shit."

Grant laughed, taking the box from me when I reached the bedroom. "Would you judge me if I told you it's mostly suits?"

"You know I would."

"I don't even know why I brought them. I'm not even sure if they'll all fit in this closet." He eyed it skeptically, setting the box next to its buddies on the floor.

"You're renovating my closet in your head, aren't you."

"Maybe."

"You sure it's going to be enough for you, living here in a lowly little farm cottage?"

He strode to me, smiling. "It's more than enough. You're here.

for love or honey

Everything else is just details."

"Sweet talker," I said, threading my arms around his waist when he approached.

"Except it's true."

"How's that feel, being honest?" I teased.

"If I said I've never been happier, would you believe me?"

"Only because I feel the same."

Rather than answer, he took a moment to kiss me long and slow and easy.

The last week had been a whirl. I'd stayed in DC for a handful of days while we packed Grant up and waited for the movers to come. He'd shown me around the city, taken me to his favorite restaurants, even suffered through the touristy things like the Mall and museums. I'd met some of his friends at a bar one night, and I think it was weirder for Grant than it was for me. They didn't seem to understand why he was leaving or what he'd do with himself but were amused enough by me that it wasn't too awfully weird.

It was no wonder he had no ties here if those were his closest friends.

He put his place on the market, and we packed our things in one suitcase, throwing it into his trunk and leaving DC in the rearview.

When the kiss broke, I beamed up at him. Already he looked different, scruffy and smiling and relaxed. Free, maybe for the first time.

"I think you should pick your three favorite suits and we'll put the rest in storage," I suggested.

"Is storage the barn?"

"Maybe."

"That should keep them fresh."

I couldn't help but laugh. "We have an actual climate controlled storage building out near the cannery. They'll be fine. Plus, it'll leave room for something else."

"What's that?"

"Go look in the dresser."

His face quirked, but he did as I'd asked, pulling open the top drawer. A laugh busted out of him.

It was full of jeans. As was the one beneath it and the one under that.

"You bought me all these jeans?" he asked, fishing through them.

"The women of this town happily donated on the promise I'd parade you around downtown on a schedule." When he looked over his shoulder at me with concern, it was my turn to laugh. "Yes, I bought them all for you. The town biddies can thank me later."

"How much do I owe you?"

"Oh, don't start that."

"What?"

"Keeping score. What's mine is yours, darlin'."

He closed the drawer and stalked to me with a dangerous look on his face. "Everything that's yours?" When he reached me, he filled his palms with my ass and squeezed.

"Mmhm. Everything."

for love or honey

"Good. I'm keeping it."

"No returns, no exchanges."

"Final sale," he added.

"As-is."

At that, his face softened. "It's the only way I want you. Just like this. Just as you are."

I held his jaw, smiled the smile that was only his. "I love you. Do you know that?"

"You keep saying it, but I'm having a hard time believing."

"How can I convince you?"

Angling for my lips, he said, "Oh, I can think of a few ways."

And with a kiss, I did the best convincing I'd ever done.

So well, in fact, that he'd believe me for the rest of our lives.

THE END

Writing this book is the most fun I've had in a long, long time.

I don't know if it was just the characters or watching Grant as he was put through the ringer to teach him a lesson, a lesson Jo hadn't intended to teach him. Some of it was that this little bee farm means so much to me.

You see, my ancestors—five generations of them—were bee farmers in Boerne, Texas (say it like Bernie), my grandmother one of six children, all of who were born with an instrument in their hand. They did in fact go into town every weekend to sing at town hall dances, and during the depression, my grandmother's step-father really did make armadillo purses and take them into San Antonio to sell—my great-grandfather died of pneumonia when she was a little girl. And there's so much more to that story, but I'll write that one some other day.

So I brought a place and a family I've daydreamed about my whole life onto the page here, to share with you. So first, I'll thank you for reading this part of my heart.

As always, I'll thank my husband, Jeff, for always backing me up, always making space for my work, and for reading every word I've ever written. You're the real MVP, babe.

I'll also thank my K crew—Kandi Steiner, KA Linde, and Kerrigan Byrne. I'm so happy to be in a polygamist work wife scenario with you three. I couldn't get through these books without your advice, support, and occasional whipping.

To my alphas and betas—Amy Vox Libris, Sasha Erramouspe, Julia Heudorf, Melissa Brooks, Becky Barney, Sarah Sentz, and Dee LaGasse—THANK YOU! Your feedback was and always will be the most crucial part of my process. I'm so grateful for each of you.

for love or honey

To Dani Sanchez—thank you for meeting with me weekly to help me keep my shit straight and together, and for always being ready and willing to read and provide feedback, even when your world is chaos. I just love you to bits.

To Tina Lynne for keeping the motor running on everything Staci Hart! You're my hero, Teener!

To my bloggers—thank you for all the shares, all the excitement, all the love and support you've given me and this book. You make the book world go around, and I'm thankful for every single one of you.

To my readers—thank YOU most of all for letting me into your life for a few hours. I hope you enjoyed reading as much as I enjoyed writing it.

STACI HART

CONTEMPORARY STANDALONES

Small Town Romances
Bet The Farm
This lactose intolerant sunshiny city girl inherits a dairy farm with the grumpy farmhand, and neither is ready for the fireworks.

Friends With Benedicts
She's been in love with him since the first time she laid eyes on him. But they have one summer together, and they've got to keep it casual. Except their hearts don't get the memo.

For Love Or Honey
When the dark and devilish suit from the oil company comes into their small town looking to acquire the mineral rights to their bee farm, she's certain the only trouble she'll have is how fast to run him out of town. Too bad her heart has a mind of its own.

Bright Young Things
Champagne Problems
Everyone wants to know who's throwing the lavish parties, even the police commissioner, and no one knows it's her ... not even the reporter who's been sneaking in to the parties and her heart.

The Bennet Brothers:
A spin on Pride & Prejudice
Coming Up Roses
Everyone hates something about their job, and she hates Luke Bennet. Because if she doesn't, she'll fall in love with him.

for love or honey

Gilded Lily
This pristine wedding planner meets her match in an opposites attract, enemies to lovers comedy.

Mum's the Word
A Bower's not allowed to fall in love with a Bennet, but these forbidden lovers might not have a choice.

The Austens
Wasted Words (Inspired by Emma)
She's just an adorkable, matchmaking book nerd who could never have a shot with her gorgeous best friend and roommate.

A Thousand Letters (Inspired by Persuasion)
Fate brings them together after seven years for a second chance they never thought they'd have in this lyrical story about love, loss, and moving on.

Love, Hannah (a spinoff of A Thousand Letters)
A story of finding love when all seems lost and finding home when you're far away from everything you've known.

Love Notes (Inspired by *Sense & Sensibility*)
Annie wants to live while she can, as fully as she can, not knowing how deeply her heart could break.

Pride and Papercuts (Inspired by *Pride and Prejudice*)
She can be civil and still hate Liam Darcy, but if she finds there's more to him than his exterior shows, she might stumble over that line between love and hate and fall right into his arms.

The Red Lipstick Coalition

Piece of Work
Her cocky boss is out to ruin her internship, and maybe her heart, too.

Player
He's just a player, so who better to teach her how to date? All she has to do is not fall in love with him.

Work in Progress
She never thought her first kiss would be on her wedding day. Rule number one: Don't fall in love with her fake husband.

Well Suited
She's convinced love is nothing more than brain chemicals, and her baby daddy's determined to prove her wrong.

Bad Habits

With a Twist (Bad Habits 1)
A ballerina living out her fantasies about her high school crush realizes real love is right in front of her in this slow-burn friends-to-lovers romantic comedy.

Chaser (Bad Habits 2)
He'd trade his entire fortune for a real chance with his best friend's little sister.

Last Call (Bad Habits 3)
All he's ever wanted was a second chance, but she'll resist him at every turn, no matter how much she misses him.

for love or honey

ABOUT THE AUTHOR

Staci has been a lot of things up to this point in her life: a graphic designer, an entrepreneur, a seamstress, a clothing and handbag designer, a waitress. Can't forget that. She's also been a mom to three little girls who are sure to grow up to break a number of hearts. She's been a wife, even though she's certainly not the cleanest, or the best cook. She's also super, duper fun at a party, especially if she's been drinking whiskey, and her favorite word starts with f, ends with k.

From roots in Houston, to a seven year stint in Southern California, Staci and her family ended up settling somewhere in between and equally north in Denver. When she's not writing, she's reading, gaming, or designing graphics.

www.stacihartnovels.com

staci@stacihartnovels.com

Made in the USA
Monee, IL
18 October 2021